A DEAL TO DIE FOR

D0048214

A DEAL TO DIE FOR

A NOVEL

SUZIE SARKOZY

*To my brother, who didn't laugh when
I told him I was thinking of selling cars.*

*There would be no Birdie without his
advice, encouragement and commiseration.*

Truth is the most valuable thing we have.
Let us economize it.

MARK TWAIN

My dad, the car dealer, used to say: "The first guy that talks loses." Since I am the one here spilling my guts, I guess he meant me.

In a way, I could lay the blame for this entire debacle directly at the feet of my father and namesake, the great Albert Alton of Double Al's Auto Emporium in Midvale, Nebraska. Seriously, I mean the whole car selling thing including the hazing, lying, cheating, stolen sales and meager compensation—not to mention that little detail of a murder and gunshot wounds that almost killed me!

Just to be clear, I'm not saying my dad actually had any part in the decidedly screwed up mess. What I said was I blame him.

It certainly wasn't Dad's fault that they found my enemy's body in the service bay beneath my ex-boyfriend's truck, with my fingerprints the only ones on the murder weapon. I didn't kill the guy, but it might be hard to make anyone believe me. I didn't want to point a finger of blame at my only friend at the AutoMall or on my high school boyfriend.

How the heck had I transformed from a contented if not-too-happily married middle school librarian living a boring life in Midvale, Nebraska, to a car salesperson struggling to stay employed and out of jail?

It's a long, twisted story. Jump in and ride along with me. I promise to reveal the bumps in my rocky road while sharing the inside story of one car dealership in southeastern Arizona that harbored more than a few clunkers, both mechanical and human.

CHAPTER 1

Being the only saleswoman at the car dealership was like lying on a bed of nails. It doesn't kill you, but you are forced to deal with a lot of annoying little pricks.

From the start it was doubtful I'd survive my stint at the AutoMall in Copper Springs, Arizona. I didn't realize then that survival might be literal. It turns out that there had been a running staff pool to guess the exact hour and day the misplaced, thirty-seven-year-old, Nebraska librarian, Alberta "Birdie" Alton—that would be me—would throw in the chamois. As it happened, I was more resilient than any of us realized. Maybe I was simply more determined to prove I could succeed in this new career. Show who? My ex? My grandmother? My incredibly unsupportive coworkers? Or myself? Yeah, probably that last one. Definitely time for some successes in my life.

I arrived, running five states away from heartbreak and bad decisions, back to the town where I finished high school, discovering once again that my Grams would be the salvation I didn't deserve.

Six months of humiliation had passed since my husband and my middle school librarian job abandoned me, leaving both an empty heart and pocketbook in their wake. Neither was showing signs of refilling. When my wayward husband finally called his mother to say he was headed back to Midvale, I knew it was time for me to leave. My yellow Mini-Cooper, "Tweety," was stuffed with my summer sandals, five sleeveless shirts, my only two pairs of all-cotton jeans and three days' worth of chocolate chip Clif bars to fortify me until I arrived at my Gramma Lou's bungalow in Copper Springs, AZ. Of course, the snack bar inventory wasn't meant to tide me over the three days in New Mexico for a costly Mini Cooper repair. My treasured yellow "Tweety" bird was nine parts adorable but only one part reliable.

I pulled into my Gramma Luella's driveway stressed, from power-driving plus the New Mexico hiatus waiting for my Mini Cooper to be repaired, not to mention the implosion of my life in Nebraska. Grams, who was waiting at her wooden screen door, enveloped me in her warm embrace and I began to sob.

"Why did he have to leave me, Grams? We had been happy," I slobbered, my clogged nose making my miserable previous life reflections pour out as a nasal sounding whine. Grams handed me a Kleenex. I honked like a Canada goose as I blew. "I belonged to the right clubs—clubs his mother made me join. I played bridge and you know how much I hate bridge." Grams shook her head in agreement. "I had even agreed to get a boob job if Peter thought that would improve our life. But as you can plainly tell I didn't." I cupped my hands under the meager contents of my sports bra to illustrate my point. "Why didn't I see it coming? Why didn't anyone warn me?" But I knew. As I whimpered, the signs I'd missed scrolled down my frontal lobe—his sabbaticals, the friends covering for him on late evenings by calling to make sure I was at home and not out where I would see, the receipt for the kennel for the dogs when I was away even though he said he had been home—all were perfectly clear from a thousand miles away. "I could not be more humiliated and embarrassed. I couldn't," I told her and she did what she did better than anyone else in all the world. She listened.

"I was never going to get seniority in my school district unless two or three people died," I sniffled. Seeing her reaction, I added: "Don't worry, I'm not a killer." That statement seems quaintly ironic now with all that has gone down since. I kept trying to explain to her what happened. Was it her or me I was needing to convince?

"I was a great librarian. Did you know that my job wasn't about books at all? It was all about being a computer guru and Grams,

I'm a regular digital diva—I may never be that good at something again." And I didn't even want to try. I thought my head would clear and everything would look better once I set eyes on Copper Springs, but my profound sadness at being a complete loser was exacting a high toll and now I had to add major car repairs to that tally.

A few weeks of agony passed. I alternated crying jags and angry rants and managed to make Grams as miserable as me so she had an idea that I should get out of the house and stop my daily whimpering, but her idea was totally crazy.

"I think you should try selling cars," Grams said. "You know, you really remind me of your dad." Why? Was Dad a whiner, too, I thought? Just because my father, her son, was of course Albert Alton, the gregarious PT Barnum-style owner of Double Al's Auto Emporium in Midvale was brilliant at selling cars didn't mean I would be. The very idea that I could fill his shoes was ridiculous. But she didn't mean own a dealership, she just meant to try to be employed at one until I found something better.

Wouldn't almost anything be better?

We both loved my dad. I couldn't have loved him more. I'm so sorry now that one of the last things I told him was how much his advertising alter ego, the Cowboy 'Lonesome Al' of the Double Al Ranch embarrassed me in front of my high school classmates. Lonesome. It's funny to think of that word now. It might have been different if my parents had lived. Then again, maybe I would have tried my hand at his business a lot sooner. Her idea led to more discussion. One thing followed another and in a few weeks I had an interview and a precarious new job.

April Fool's Day, being my first, should have been a clue. One of the men loitering about the dealership sneered and said, "So, you're the woman 'Green Pea' Montello hired." Green Pea was the official industry term for a rookie salesman, a neophyte who knows absolutely nothing and will ask so many stupid questions that the rest of the crew will want to strangle him by the end of day one. He added the word "woman" to emphasize what an especially heinous choice the boss had made, then he looked me over.

"Say," he said while walking away, "has anyone told you that you look a little like Britney Spears, but a lot older?" Yes, a lot older than the twenty-year-old videos of the post-pubescent pop-princess he was thinking of. Anyway. I didn't resemble her in any way, except that I already seemed to be "Toxic" to everyone who worked there.

I received no orientation and no official welcome except for the personalized greeting from a salesman named Bingham. I easily remembered his name because he had a Bing-cherry colored nose and because his weathered, leathered face said he was the oldest and perhaps wisest among the group.

"I can't tell you how annoying that smiley, perky, bullshit of yours is going to be for me," Bingham said, welcoming me to the team. He considered himself the harbinger of news and advice no newbie could live without. He didn't stop there. Truth be told, he never stopped.

"The money they promised you'll make here is impossible—that's right, impossible—especially for a woman." Especially for a woman would become his favorite way to end a sentence when speaking to me. In less than a week, I would be finishing his sentences for him as committed couples tend to do. How many Green Peas had he dissuaded from coming back for their second day? Did our boss Mr. Montello send him out as a test or was Bingham a self-appointed naysayer? I doubted it was Montello, but then he wasn't exactly an optimist either. Those were in short supply at the Copper Springs AutoMall.

I met the AutoMall's General Manager, Mike Montello, the day before I arrived to work at the dealership. The guy looked more Italian than the Sopranos. He was sixtyish with slicked-back salt and pepper hair and he wafted the aroma of roasted garlic. What surprised me most was that he came to work at a grubby car lot dressed to the nines, or, more correctly the 1980s. Every stitch of Montello's attire came straight out of Ronald Reagan's closet. He talked exclusively about himself.

"I was an assistant manager in a haberdashery in New Jersey before I started managing car dealerships," he said. He'd dredged up a word that had been in a basement cedar chest packed in mothballs for at least half a century. He told me that he was from a brilliant well-educated eastern family of writers and artists but, unlike them, he didn't have to go to college.

"Why would I go to college when I could make so much money selling cars?" Why indeed? I thought. A lot of good my six years of Library Science were doing me. While he listed his accomplishments, I got a better look at the guy. He was dressed from head to leather-clad foot in expensive, but out-of-style clothes no doubt left from his haberdashery stint. His jacket collar was too big, his silk tie too narrow, and his pinstriped pants creased with wide cuffs that men no longer favored. He wore beautiful Italian leather loafers buffed to a mirror finish. Despite being completely out of date, his wardrobe had attitude, and I could immediately discern that Mr. Montello thought he was the cock of the walk.

"Women excel at this sort of thing," Mike continued. He made me wonder, if all that was true, and if I was hired, then why was I the only woman on the sales floor?

As I listened to him, I looked out at the all-glass showroom. It resembled a gigantic fish tank where salesmen of different stripes swam in and around the aquarium in front of plastic ficus and philodendrons. If only I'd realized at the time how many of those fish would turn out to be bottom feeders.

Mr. Montello gave me the distinct impression that he was not stuck with me. No sir! I could be gone at any time. He thought that scared me, but he didn't know that the last guy, my husband, had dispatched me after fourteen years on a whim with a text he sent from Spain where he was on a month-long sabbatical with his grad student.

Sorry Babe, I'm finishing the summer in Barcelona

Drury & Hazeltine will send you the paperwork

I didn't mean to end it like this.

And they say people over the age of thirty-five are no good with social media. "How can it only be six months? It already seemed like an eternity. No, no, no, "Call me Mike" Montello wouldn't be the first to oust me. I tightened my jaw. He might think I wouldn't last but I would. Oh, yes. Did Mike even know what a text was? He seemed to me more the FAX machine and mimeograph type of guy.

———

As I stood on the cinders in the front lot the next day, with the plastic car lot pennants flapping and snapping above my head, alone for the first time, I thought about my interview. What a joke. The General Manager had asked only one question. Not, "Do you have experience selling cars?" or "Have you ever sold anything?" "What do you know about cars?" or "What are you doing in this little God-forsaken town?" or even "Where is the husband that goes with that ring?" Nope. None of the above. His only question was, "Can you golf?"

"Can I golf? Yes," I fibbed, counting my ill-fated stint on the Copper Kings first high school golf team a hundred years ago. If that was going to be his solitary question, shouldn't it at least have been "How well do you golf?" I figured he would have forgotten my answer by the end of the interview when I'd have had time to trot out the much bigger fibs, but no, that was the interview. One question, one fib, and he said, "You start tomorrow." And that was that. I couldn't believe he asked me *that* question. Who played golf in Arizona in the summer? I figured nobody. Was golf even a viable sport anymore? And even if it were, what could that possibly have to do with selling cars?

So, there I was on car lot blacktop that radiated heat in the manner of well-lit Kingsford charcoal in a steel BBQ. The soles of my sandals stuck to the pavement and my naturally straw-colored, shoulder length hair was now spun into the real barnyard-style straw after only a few short weeks in Arizona. I didn't own sunglasses or sensible outdoor shoes. My size 12 skinny jeans were khaki colored, even though they had started out the morning white. I would never have worn a hat—I didn't want to be a dork. I mean, I didn't want to look like one, but I'm a librarian, being one was going to be unavoidable.

As ridiculous as that occupational sidestep, or more correctly, fall from the upward trajectory of my librarian career was, at least I wasn't in Midvale, Nebraska, facing all of my so-called friends—turns out Peter got custody of those. Why not? I realize now they always belonged to him.

As I stood alone in the Arizona wind, broke and demoralized, I remembered the day we turned down the house on campus that went with Peter's professorship so we could live out of town on the Sander's family farm and plow my inheritance into the complete remodel of the old original Victorian home on the estate. Every penny gone and now their attorney was claiming it was a worthless vacant outbuilding. It was funny, I now hated Peter's mother and her lawyer more than I hated Peter.

Grams wasn't alone in encouraging this little car sales escapade. She'd double-teamed me with my Uncle Patrick, her youngest son, recently retired from a sales position at a gigantic Toyota dealership in Omaha.

"Working at a dealership is in your DNA, kitten," Uncle Pat said. "It's the family business, after all," he added exhibiting the pride of a Mafia Don inducting a favorite nephew into the Mob. I guess it was my mother's DNA that was telling me to sprint for the hills as fast as my long spider legs would take me. Instead, there I stood amongst a misfit menagerie of used Chevys, Fords, Hyundais, VWs and every other brand you can imagine because my Uncle Pat had said, "Spend your time on the used lot, Kid, that's where the money is." Did I say used? Of course, I meant Pre-owned.

I thought about what Grams had said. "Aren't you desperate for income, sweetheart?" she innocently asked. I must have been. But as soon as I arrived at the sprawling AutoMall, I was terrified. Scared to death that someone would drive up to have me show them a vehicle. And yet, I stood stoically in a sea of sheet metal, waiting for Carmageddon. *Run, Birdie, Run!*

A red-headed salesman I recognized from the morning's meeting walked up and eye-balled the sporty blue Chevy Malibu parked between us. He wore a white shirt and a loud purple tie. I could hear it from across the lot.

"You're Richard. Correct?" No answer. Maybe he wasn't Rich? There was Clay, Rich, Eenie, Meanie, Miney, and Moe, and that was just the sales staff.

"Is it always this windy?" I hollered. In case he had a hearing issue. Again, he didn't answer. He got in the Malibu, closed the door, gunned the engine and drove off, pelting me with gravel and leaving a sedan-sized hole in the lineup, not to mention the dust settling on my legs and coating the toes peeking out from my strappy sandals.

"I guess that was Meanie," I said.

The Malibu exited onto the highway toward town just as a battered miniature Nissan pickup with mismatched hubcaps and missing side trim bounced up over the curb. It veered toward me and skidded to a shaky stop—frightfully close. I glanced down to check that I had all my toes. My pounding heart and whatever logic my brain had left debated whether to flee toward the tall grasses and cactuses that framed the side of the property, trailing the long-eared jackrabbit who bounced away a few moments before.

Wasn't anybody going to come out and help me? Hello. Green Pea out here, alone. I popped in a Tums, grinding it using molars as mortar and pestle. Fight or flight?

Too late for option two.

In car sales vernacular, I was about to get my first 'Up' as in first up at bat. I should've known. I play softball worse than I golf.

A compact brunette, almost as wide as she was tall, hopped out of her dilapidated pickup. Her blue chambray work-shirt was firmly tucked into permanently creased belted tan trousers. Not a great look for her, but I was hard-pressed to think what a good look might be. The bad attitude she wore was accessorized with a scowl, like a 'before' image looking for a makeover program.

"I need a truck, whadaya got? Has to be a crew cab," she sputtered. Her much taller, burly, teenaged son slid out of the passenger seat wearing jeans so low-slung that if he put another nickel in his pocket they would fall off entirely. His black T-shirt read, "Meet my friends: Smith and Wesson." I was ambushed from both sides.

Ms. Attitude rocketed down the rows of vehicles with me stumbling along behind, my head snapping back and forth in hopes of finding her a small light-weight truck with a crew cab, whatever that was.

"Here's one," I said, relieved to see the back of a truck bed. I didn't care what it was attached to.

"That's not a crew cab; it's a quad. The back seat isn't big enough for my kids." She gestured toward Smith and Wesson boy. With a sort of skip-step, she had already advanced two vehicles over. "What's the price?" she asked.

I maneuvered my way to the windshield where I studied the yellow sticker affixed to the front window. It had the stock numbers and prices simply encrypted, numerals printed in reverse order with some extra letters added. Deciphering the thing should be so simple that a caveman could do it, but my inability to do so was glaring.

My impatient new friend stepped right in front of me and almost crushed my toes for a second time with her lace-up steel-toed work boots. She glanced at the tag.

"It's $9,995," she said.

I slumped, deflated. She was probably right. I didn't even bother to recheck her work. I had only been in an actual sales encounter for ten minutes, and I had already given up the secret code. At this rate, I would never be authorized to get the secret handshake.

"I used to work in Detail," she informed me. Whew. I hadn't divulged corporate secrets. While Mom looked the truck over, her son thought I'd like to know that his sixteen-year-old brother had just moved out.

"He wanted to leave the hell hole," he said. He kept chatting on like a kindergartener. Attitude told me she had $4,000 and not a dime more to buy a 4x4 truck. I took her at her word.

A viewing party was beginning to form at the floor to ceiling showroom windows. They resembled pari-mutuel betters lining up at the rail to view a horse race. *I have a customer and you don't; take that, you mute jerks.* Day one, hour three and I'd already become combative with my fellow workers.

Two trucks and a dozen questions that I couldn't answer later, Attitude liked a black four-door, Ford. The yellow tag on the windshield told both of us that we were asking $8,995.

Here's where I made my first big mistake as a car salesman. I assumed two things: one, she couldn't afford this truck, and two, that we certainly would never sell it to her for the four grand she said she had. A few moments later, she had finished looking it over then gave me her number and her first name only—Loretta.

"If you know my last name you'll know which lousy no-good family I come from."

"I don't know anyone here," I assured her. But I admit it made me curious to know who the folks were who were so bad the woman living in the "hell hole" didn't want to be associated with them.

As if reading my mind, her son whispered to me. "I have an uncle who's a drug dealer. He killed someone once, but that was before I was born." I gave Loretta a hand-written card with "Birdie" on it. Of course, they don't waste money printing real cards for any Green Pea until they know if you are a keeper. I think most at the dealership thought I was looking more like the catch and quickly release variety.

As I watched my first official 'Up' drive off down the road, I was on cloud nine. My first and it went well. A girl never forgets her first.

A lanky, tall fellow, that everybody called Stretch, looked like he was approaching on stilts. He perpetually had one cigarette tucked above his over-sized ear. Was he bumming all of them? Was it the same one he never smoked?

"Hey, Mike wants to see you." I felt smug. Would I actually get the hang of this? I had a showing, and I had a phone number. What more did I need? Right? Well, of course, a sale would be nice but that was just a short matter of time. Right?

In the main office with the GM was Wade Winchell, the pock-marked nephew of the dealership owner. He was a rotund man with a skimpy handlebar mustache. I hadn't officially met Wade, so I assumed this would be that introduction. I stood tall and proud in the doorway awaiting my accolades but I never got inside.

"Where is she?" Wade barked, sounding as though he was interrogating a kidnapper. When I looked at him all I saw was his wiggly mustache under a rubbery looking nose and lazy half-hooded eyes that made him look like some species of scaly catfish. Introductions were going to be a forgotten formality.

"She left," I said. "She only had four thousand dollars and the truck we found that she liked was $8,995. She couldn't afford it and I'm sure we wouldn't discount it by half." My words were sparks lighting a fuse that burned toward a makeshift bomb. It took two, maybe three, endless seconds to explode, sending shock-waves all the way to the service bays. I had unwittingly broken inviolate Car Lot Rule #1: Don't let a prospect walk. Ever. The first blast was followed by the two men taking turns lobbing more incendiaries at me.

"You let her leave and didn't turn her over to someone? Never do that! You don't know that we wouldn't sell her that truck for

$4,000 dollars. You don't know that she couldn't get more money together to get it. Maybe she has a rich uncle. *Or a drug-dealing brother.* "What? You didn't have her drive the truck? These people never come back when you let them go. We don't invest tens of thousands of dollars in advertising money to get traffic on the lot just to have you broom them off of it."

The shrapnel of their tirade shredded my self-esteem while the rest of the troops watched with pleasure from the safety of their bunkers, like naughty kids, giddy that it was their sibling in the crosshairs. Stretch seemed particularly pleased for luring me into their trap. I apologized to both men then slunk back onto the showroom floor where I ran into the dour and ever-discouraging Bingham.

"I don't know how in the hell you're supposed to know what to do when they don't even tell you any of the proper procedures," he said. This mistakenly made me think I could have been wrong about Bing, the Red-nosed Cherry. Then he added, "Women don't last in the car business—I've worked with many, and if you last a month, you'll be doing good." He told me he'd seen hundreds of salesmen come and most were gone very quickly. Didn't I know that this job causes depression? And so, on he went. I was disinclined to listen, but Bingham's was the name at the top of the white leaderboard where my name had been added over many obvious erasures of the legions of salespeople preceding me. Birdie Alton was just an eraser swipe away from total, inevitable failure here. I believed that was how Bingham would have put it.

As bad as the dressing-down by the managers was, it was oddly the dust-off by this old crusty salesman, who I already knew to be a complete blowhard, which stopped me from walking out in giant cheek-staining tears right then and there. Instead, I decided to double down on the idea that I could do better than this bunch of numb-nuts. Anyway, I couldn't quit after my first try. I'm a stick-it-out girl, my fourteen-year marriage being a prime example.

Bingham's banter was amusing until he dropped the bombshell that totally destroyed my first day.

"You know, they only hired you because you can golf." Finally, Bingham, the world-class killjoy, had struck on something to rivet my attention.

"What?"

"Old Wally hasn't won the town golf tourney once in his three years as owner, even with his semi-pro ringers from Phoenix. This year they made a rule that the team had to be made up of staff only, but don't worry, they will for sure let you go after the Fourth of July tournament—unless, of course, you win it for him."

"So, you really think I can last 'til the Fourth of July? Wow, what a vote of confidence." The truth was I didn't remember the first thing about playing golf. I wasn't sure I could tell a nine iron from a Big Bertha and for the first time, I understood the only actual question of my interview. "Can you golf?" Remembering my embarrassing performance on the high school golf team, I simply told an innocent little white golfing lie. Did I really have until the tournament to try to make myself indispensable? How the heck could I last that long? I didn't know then that it wouldn't be the golf that did me in—that would have been the easy way out.

CHAPTER 2

After my encounter with Ms. Attitude, I hit the tarmac to commune with the one hundred and thirty pickups lined up like tin soldiers—by tin, of course, I mean aluminum in the case of Fords. I looked for the four-door configurations and found they were indeed the most popular. The Crew Cabs had almost the same room in back as the front seat. The Quads had less leg room, and the Mega Cab had a back seat so large you could set a table for six and have room to pull out captain's chairs. I had never noticed pickup door sizes before my first customer pointed them out.

My brain throbbed with the anxiety of the sheer quantity of statistics and data I needed to assimilate to keep a sales position at the AutoMall, even until July Fourth. Information I had not once in thirty-seven years sought out and I had no mechanical framework on which to hang the bits and bytes of knowledge I was collecting in the recesses of my brain. Uncle Patrick had assured me that Internet-educated buyers are so knowledgeable, a salesman no longer needed to know a thing about the vehicle that is the apple of their customer's eye. I was sure that was hyperbole, but I hoped it had a kernel of truth in it.

"You just have to write the sale up," he said, "You librarians are Internet experts aren't you? You'll be great."

"That doesn't stop potential buyers from asking a million questions I can't answer," I'd said. Unknown to me was that even filling out the forms to make a sale would make me look stupid— something I sorely hated. The Internet was not going to improve my ability to do that. But his words did have the wisdom of forty years of experience with a real dealership, one that was on the up and up. So, I listened.

"Always remember that just because you're asked a question doesn't mean you have to answer it," he told me. I didn't know it then, but that pearl of wisdom turned out to be the best advice I ever received.

As I drifted back into the showroom, a snazzy looking young man in tasseled loafers was depositing a gigantic pink and white striped box emblazoned with the name Bernadette's on the office counter. It contained four, maybe even five dozen plump fresh donuts from the Bakery and Restaurant by the same name on Third Street in downtown Copper Springs. It's a bakery so, of course, I had already located it. He placed the gift square in front of Maggie, the cute little receptionist with the big green sparkly eyes, and eyelashes so thick that if she batted them any faster she could catch that stray fly that had been pestering the rest of us. She flashed donut-boy her toothy almost silly smile then stepped to a 1970's style built-in intercom and with a voice deep as a baritone, announced the delivery. Conrad and the Service Department grease monkeys were called first. They dropped everything and made a Pavlovian dash through their swinging doors where they swarmed the countertop to grab a lion's share of the bounty. The sales staff, meanwhile, stood back like trained Labradors waiting for Maggie's nod, their signal, then the parts guys followed suit in their turn.

It all played out like a YouTube dog training video, making it evident that Maggie thought the men in the Service Department were the alpha males. At the end of the exercise, only one badly disfigured donut remained, half its pink frosting crushed into a greasy smudge on the bottom of the box—over-dried coconut stuck out everywhere. I lifted it to my skeptical mouth and took a bite. *My God, it's delicious.* Coconut was my favorite.

As we ladies watched, dapper donut delivery boy headed empty-handed for the Annex building.

"He's snappily dressed," I said.

"He can afford it," Jeannie, the office manager huffed in her grumpy, frumpy manner from her desk in front of the back window of the building. "He's the TV rep from Phoenix. His station rakes in a ton of money off of Wallace and the dealership." At the water cooler a few moments later, the fellow that pelted me with gravel out on the lot sidled up beside me.

"That TV guy's a leech," Rich said. He sucks up to Wallace and gushes about what a great actor he is and all. What does he think? If he brings donuts, we'll all encourage Wally to spend more time as a Javelina?" Something told me that Rich knew a world-class brown-noser when he saw one, but he was my instant hero just for speaking to me. Rich was actually paler than me and his mop of curly Irish red hair fell down into his eyes when he took a drink from the fountain, then he wiped his mouth with his plum-colored tie. Clearly not on top of the leaderboard, he wasn't even earning enough for a haircut.

"He gives Wallace season tickets to all the U of A games, too," Rich continued. "There's not a football or basketball game all season where old Wally isn't on the tube inviting folks to Copper Springs." Of course, I'd seen the ads, even with the little time I'd spent in this town.

"So, what you're saying is, you don't think Wallace, dressed up like a giant talking Javelina named Harold, snorting 'Short Drive-Mega Savings!' is the pinnacle of effective marketing?" I thought I was being cute, but Rich took a step back and stared like he wanted to take one long last look before I was scorched from the Earth.

"No! That is not what I said."

What? No one here could take this stuff seriously. Could they? Apparently, our AutoMall ads, however ridiculous, were sacred ground I had just trampled on, and Rich would have not had one whit of remorse quoting my comments whenever it served him.

"Well hey, I think they're great. Don't you?" I quickly added. The truth was that Harold the Javelina made me very lonesome for my dad, the cowpoke Lonesome Al. I hadn't yet met Wallace.

Grams told me that Harold the Javelina started out as Jose, the politically incorrect Javelina and was quickly rechristened. I didn't think much more about the big boss because I had more pressing worries, and Montello told me that Wally only came in to open his mail and get a break from his wife. *Open his mail and explore his thespian side.*

CHAPTER 3

Rich followed donut guy to the other building and then came back with a Jack Russell Terrier on a University of Arizona printed leash. He made a show of prancing the wiry-haired pooch around so it could pee on the minute patch of real grass out front, presumably grown for that purpose only. It had no redeeming landscape value.

"Does Rich bring a dog to work?" I asked Clay, the jovial-looking sales guy whom I deemed the most approachable of the crew, probably the worst superlative he could be saddled with.

"That's Orbit, Wallace's dog. They're filming the dealership TV ads and Rich is willing to do almost anything to suck up to Wallace." Almost anything? Taking the dog out didn't seem like it was too far up the ominous "almost anything" spectrum to me.

Clay was the only one of the four salesmen I had met so far who would deign to visit with the latest Green Pea. He was amiable and cute in a big, stuffed teddy bear sort of way. When I asked how long he had been at the dealership he answered, "Since Molly, my seven-year-old was three." Like many good dads, he recounted his life history in terms of his children's timeline. As we talked, a Ford King Ranch pickup truck, being driven by the dapper donut-man, swerved off the lot with one of his two passenger's little cold nose and flapping ears sticking out of the passenger-side window as they rolled away.

I wouldn't be meeting Wallace today.

With Clay and I standing at the back of the vehicle, the six-ty-year-old Bingham squired the wife of the local dentist into the supple leather seat of the banana-yellow convertible on the show-room floor, after she made the mistake of asking the price. He was coaxing her to start the engine right there in the building which she was coyly refusing while giggling like a teenager with a mad crush. They were sitting so close that you couldn't squeeze a tube of toothpaste between them. It seemed like a tawdry little show that would come to nothing but an embarrassment for the old guy when Bingham called over and asked if we'd hold the big doors open. Then the two of them sped through the opening to fetch her 'hubby' for a drive. The last thing we heard was "Born to Be Wild" as Bingham told his A-1 prospect in the driver's seat, "The only thing that sounds better than the engine is this radio!" As a salesman, Bingham was a heck of a lot smoother than his scruffy appearance and advanced age would suggest.

The exhaust from the dentist's wife's new ride hung in the show-room until the smell of burritos overpowered it. Yes, burritos. Had I taken a job in a short order restaurant instead of a car dealership?

A thirty-something Hispanic woman deftly pushed through the service door with a flat tin-covered box in front of her, hanging with the help of a strap around her shoulders. I wondered if she moonlighted as a hot dog vendor at the ballpark, or maybe this was her moonlight job. For some reason, she bypassed the office altogether then strode directly toward me with the air of someone spoiling for a fight. I instinctively took a step back thinking she would pass by me. Instead, she came up face to face pressing the metal box between us.

"You want a burrito for lunch?" she said to me in perfect English that surprised me. *Was that a racist thought?* "I have bean'n cheese today and muskmelon plus chocolate chip cookies." I looked down in the box at a sanitary looking, professionally organized assort-ment of foil bundles s that smelled incredible despite the fact that I had downed a coconut donut not that many minutes before.

"You make these?" I asked. She nodded. Before anyone sat down to eat, the Mexican goddess exited, throwing a peeved look back at

Conrad, the service manager, who stared at her and shoved his wire-rimmed glasses up to his bushy eyebrows with a one-finger gesture. If that was meant for the Burrito lady she was already gone. I was ravenous once I smelled the burrito; fresh cilantro, jalapenos in the refried beans and the gigantic handmade flour tortilla still crisp on the edges. I hadn't had restaurant food with that much flavor in eons.

"Do we get these every day?" I asked to the salesmen gathered as if they were cowpokes at the chow wagon.

"No. She comes in to keep an eye on Conrad," Rich volunteered.

"Why on Conrad? I asked, "Does he owe her money for burritos?" I thought it was a distinct possibility since I didn't see him pay and he had a shifty scowl like a guy who would take advantage of a burrito lady.

"He's her husband," Clay said, and then he took the last chair and left me standing alone like the kid nobody wants to choose in a dodgeball game. I finally found a ledge near the office and parked my rear there to devour my lunch.

Maggie was once again at the service desk next to Conrad. She seemed to spend a lot of time in his office space. I observed the cluster of men laughing and eating together and once again felt like the unwanted interloper. *What am I doing here?* I huddled in my misery, chewing on the scrumptious burrito until someone from the doorway behind yelled out for me. The usually accurate car lot adage, "Customers who leave the lot never come back," was about to be dispelled.

Ms. Attitude became the exception to the rule. She was back on the lot refusing to get out of her truck. Next, she called the showroom from her vehicle and demanded to see me and no one else. It was a hostage situation. "Send out the blonde chick with the skinny legs—alone," she probably demanded. *This is Arizona, isn't it? Of course, she'd have a gun.* I met her outside, and we went on a short drive.

The real trouble began when we got back to the dealership. I had no earthly idea where to start filling out the paperwork and management seemed perfectly content to let me muddle through, collecting routine info to fill in the required fields. I forgot to note the exact vehicle mileage so I trudged back out to the Ford, now parked near the service entrance where a heated argument behind me was loud and getting louder. Conrad, the burrito-stealing service manager, was hollering across the hood of a one-ton truck with the Logo of Lone Pine Ranch on the door. A ranch I'd never heard of even though my grandpa had every brand in the valley on his walls at the old Rexall store. A large man with his back to me, wearing a well-worn straw cowboy hat and what looked like a Woolrich plaid shirt, was hollering back.

"You're nothing but a two-bit thief," the customer said. His wide shoulders shook with his arm gestures. The back of his head and the back of his Wranglers looked vaguely familiar. The fellow was obviously infuriated about his bill or about the condition of his truck or maybe Conrad had purloined his burrito as well.

"Go to hell!" Conrad shouted. I cringed hoping my customer hadn't noticed. Across the way, I noticed a little sprite of a woman I had seen pop-up here and there several times since my odyssey at the AutoMall began. She wore skin tight jeans, a cut-up, frayed gray sweatshirt and had a long, dark braid down her back, almost to her rear. I threw her a 'did you get a load of this?' look. She nodded then she flitted off again. *She is sort of like Tinkerbelle.*

Mike invited Ms. Attitude into his office, took my sheaf of badly-filled-in papers and dispatched me to fetch a bogus service list of the work that had been done on the red truck we'd just driven.

Clay strolled up to me, trying to look like he hadn't been eves dropping, which any fool could tell he had.

"Absolutely nothing has been done to that truck and Mike knows it." Clay said, once we were out of earshot of the customer. At the service counter, I was told Conrad had already left for the day. The guy kept banker's hours. By the time I got back to tell Montello that I couldn't get the list until tomorrow, Ms. Attitude was already outside climbing into her old truck.

I sprinted to his office door. "What happened?" I said.

"She can't afford the truck, and we certainly won't reduce the price of a popular vehicle to four-grand." Mike Montello saw no irony in telling me this in almost the exact same words I had used earlier that set him and Wade off on their massive tantrum. I watched helplessly as Attitude left the premises. Did he just throw away my sales opportunity? Doesn't he know we spend tens of thousands on ads to get these people in?

"Will I get some instruction on how to do this?" I innocently asked my manager, meaning filling in the paperwork.

"Nope," he said. "You'll learn by doing."

"Who do I see to get issued a computer to keep track of these customers?'"

"We don't use computers here," he said, as he sat in front of his own computer screen. "Wallace doesn't want the boys playing games on them all day. Ask the office for some 3x5 cards." *3x5 cards! Are you kidding me?* I remembered rectangular cards from the Jurassic or maybe the Paleozoic period of Library Science. Either way, they were ancient history. He had to be joking.

Later, I asked Clay if I'd be assigned a desk."

"Oh, no, you don't have one," he said. "There are five desks and seven or eight salesmen depending on who has just been fired. They keep it that way so we all stay a little agitated. *A little agitated?* I was beginning to understand, this would be the company tenet, agitation to all and to all a bad night. There was no Santa Claus in the offices of Copper Springs AutoMall.

I looked over at what appeared to be Bingham's personalized, not shared, desk with at least one hundred ratty 3x5 cards in the semblance of a stack. "Oh lord. Don't let me be a career man like Bingham," I prayed. Not much chance of me being here thirty days, much less thirty years.

CHAPTER 4

When the tire-sized wall clock said 5:30, the office and sales staff fled the premises and the place locked down like a cell in the local jail. Only one vehicle had been sold. The building hadn't seen a viable customer since noon. As I made my way to the side door, Montello mumbled something about my having had a fine day but it was no great shakes of a compliment. Even at that, it was more praise than I had earned. I wanted to call Uncle Pat to tell him about my first day but what was I going to say? That I didn't have a snowball's chance in the Arizona heat that this sales experiment would work? I got out my cell and called him anyway.

"Uncle Pat, believe it or not, we use 3x5 cards here instead of computers. It's like the old-time days in the library, not at all what I thought it would be."

"Those folks must be kind of unorthodox down there. Why wouldn't they want you to have a computer to keep track of customers?"

"How long did it take you to get started? I mean to start selling?"

"That's a long way back, but now-a-days they sort of give each of the Green Peas a few sales to get started and of course, they train with a pro for several months. You're doing that, aren't you?"

"Not exactly," I said. I had dozens of questions for him. For example, what in God's name made you and Grams think I could sell cars and then encourage me to answer Montello's desperate-sounding ad in the Copper Springs Gazette? Those were not for tonight. "Uncle Pat, I sure wish you had taught me more about how to play golf."

"Well Kitten, you have a lot of years yet to learn to play golf."
I didn't have the heart to tell him that I had only until the Fourth
of July. I ended the call. How did it get to this? How did I screw
up so badly? I felt like someone had pulled on the parking brake
in a speeding Maserati and sent me crashing through the broken
glass windshield of my so-called life. How did I ever think I could
drive a ¾ ton pickup truck let alone sell one? The more I needed
this job, the more panic was setting in. My bills were piling up in
a basket on my dresser at Gram's, the way fear was stacking itself
up on me. Why did I buy the $2400 E-bike that had no hope
of fitting in Mini Cooper? So, I could join the Biking Club with
girlfriends that haven't called or even texted since I left? I knew all
too well that a golden parachute financial escape wasn't coming out
of Nebraska. I hadn't heard one word from my bad bargain of a
divorce lawyer either.

When I got to the bungalow, I stumbled in like a drunk coming home at 2 a.m. I kissed my darling Gramma Lou on the cheek,
said a few words about my day then headed right for my little
bedroom. She placed a plate of warm Snickerdoodles in my free
hand I passed by.

There are a few rooms in the living spaces of our lives that
transcend all others and become a womb of comfort and safety.
My bedroom at Gramma Luella's was such a place. Its pristine condition belied the fact that it had been exactly the same for twenty
years as if under glass awaiting my return. It was still decorated in
little girl lace and eyelet—décor too juvenile for the broken and
wounded sixteen-year-old that had so abruptly shown up on the
doorstep twenty years previously—and far too childlike for the
broken and wounded thirty-seven-year old that has turned up here
for the second time. Here I am, Grams, returning like a bad penny
once again in need of change.

Over the top of the bird's-eye maple dresser, the scene out the
window onto Arrowhead Park behind the house caught my eye.

There was the dilapidated merry-go-round of my youth. A piece of playground equipment banned most places and yet there it was in our park, just where I left it. A silly thought came to me. I got my first kiss on that merry-go-round when I was visiting my grandparents at age eleven. A neighbor kid named Jack Stein—Yeah, little Jack Stein—kissed me, and he had to stand on his tiptoes to do it. I don't think I ever saw him again. Wasn't that just like all the men in my life? I lay down on the fluffy bed that enveloped me and rested. How long would I be able to stay? And who would I need to rescue me next? Were my thoughts when Grams called me to dinner.

"Does old man Stein still live two doors down?" I asked, serving myself mashed potatoes and gravy.

"Yes," she said, "Why do you ask?" Was it my imagination or was she a bit defensive about her neighbor? I persisted, as I took a scrumptious looking pan-fried pork chop on my plate.

"Does he still own the hardware store?"

"Yes," Again a clipped answer. Her prickly attitude was very uncharacteristic of the little lady who had so gently tended so many of my life's wounds. Maybe she didn't get along with her neighbor and wanted me to drop him as a subject.

"Who'd you sell a vehicle to today?" I noticed the quick change of subject.

"I didn't sell one Gram, but I drove a lady named Loretta. She wouldn't tell us her last name because she didn't want to be associated with her questionable family."

"I bet she's Jesse Moore's kid. The Moores are always scrapping about something. I think they had something like fourteen kids, but a couple of them died. Their oldest was a real rascal; I hear he went to jail several times. I don't think Loretta has done any hard time though, but I'm not sure. She has kids of her own now."

"How do you know them again Gram?" Gram's knowledge of a family that lived in the "hell hole" worried me. Loretta didn't strike me as the sort of woman that Gramma would play bridge with. Poker maybe, but not bridge.

"Loretta's kids all hate each other. Half the time there's a police call for guns going off at their place."

"Whoa. Wait. How do you know guns are going off?" I wasn't surprised about the guns at Loretta's, but I didn't want my Grams to know the details.

"I have a police scanner," she said as if it was as natural as the summer monsoons. "For safety, I have it for safety"

"Where is it?" I demanded.

"Here, in the cupboard." She jumped up and proudly flung open a door to reveal a device that looked like my old VCR.

"I don't always have it on," she said. I was pretty sure it had never been on since I arrived.

"So, when did you start playing Law & Order?"

"When that guy broke into Nelson's Grocery store then hid in the neighborhood last year."

"You didn't tell me about that. Do we need to get a security system set up?" Was he hiding under that merry-go-round? I knew it should have been removed.

"We've all got scanners now. I may as well have my reality entertainment a little closer to home. Anyway, it lets me know who to stay clear of too, like the little gal in the office at the AutoMall"

"Who? A trouble causer at my workplace?" I surprised myself by calling it my workplace. This whole conversation had gone off the rails.

"I think her name is Margaret?"

"Do you mean Maggie? She was mentioned on your scanner?"

"Uh, huh, last week. It was a domestic." My gramma talking like Danny Reagan from Blue Bloods had begun to unnerve me.

"Gram, I don't think Maggie is even married. Who was she domestic with?"

"No, the fight was with another woman at Maggie's house," Gram said. "The woman threatened Maggie, and they both got arrested. You know my friend Geneva?"

"Geneva got arrested?" I hadn't met Gram's best friend Geneva, but I was certainly going to have to put my foot down if Grams was running with this wild of a crowd. I'd arrived just in the nick of time!

"No, no, no, Geneva wasn't arrested, but her daughter, Dana, works at the police station. You'd like her," she interjected. "She's the one that helped me pick out the right police scanner. She said your boss came and picked that girl Maggie up."

Was this actually confusing or was I too tired to follow along? "You mean the owner, Wallace?"

"No honey, your boss. Mr. Montello, the one with the fancy clothes."

"Good grief, Gramma. You're quite the source of info tonight." I sat back to contemplate. What else went on there at the dealership that I was completely unaware of? Ironic that I was so stupid when I first arrived. "Maggie sells Watkins products, Gram. She can't be too dangerous. She's armed with black pepper and a bottle of vanilla"

"I didn't say she was dangerous. Say, can you ask Maggie tomorrow for a large can of cinnamon? I used all of mine on the apple crisp tonight, and my last Watkins lady died." My Gramma could segue to a new subject as smoothly as a souped-up Mustang passes a semi on the I-10. "And I'll take a bottle of double vanilla too."

She finally brought out the pan of apple crisp. A half-hour earlier, I would have been thinking how safe I felt living back here under my Gram's roof, but now I wasn't quite so sure. Might that cute little button of an office girl Maggie pose a legitimate threat? I doubted it.

But little did I know that in a very short time, Maggie would be in the thick of big trouble and I'd be right there with her.

CHAPTER 5

Every morning since leaving Nebraska I sat cross-legged on my bed for a half-hour with my laptop, scrolling through Jobs.com and ZipRecruiter.com with the fervent hope that a librarian position might open up, and I could right the ship of my life by once again employing my Master's Degree in Library Science. My flimsy fourteen years' experience couldn't protect me from my school district's reduction in force at the end of the last term. There is a little-known fact that librarians with tenure often die in their positions. Several in Cather County, Nebraska, were dead already, but nobody recognized it. I found not a single opening in the Springs, in Tucson, Tombstone, or Tempe. Nothing on this planet, it seemed. Maybe one on Jupiter but the commute would kill me. This car sales thing didn't have a snowball's chance in Phoenix, but it did pay me $1000 a month for showing up and trying. My credit cards were now a month overdue. Until they kicked me out, I would search every morning and cry on Uncle Patrick's shoulder with a call on the way home at night.

Several days went by without any action for me at the dealership. Clay was giving Bingham a run for his money on the leaderboard. Stretch had closed three of the leads that Catfish Wade had gifted to him and red-headed Rich with the garish purple ties had Ups aplenty but closed only one. Clay and I watched Stretch get an assist from Wade to close another sale.

"Don't think you will ever get any of the Internet leads. All those go to one person and one person only."

"Let me guess, tall, dark, with nicotine behind the ears?" I began to notice that as far as loyalties went, the sales staff lined up as either Wade's guys—Rich and Stretch, or they were Montello's guys—Clay and Bingham. Even though I may never meet him, I was Wallace's golf guy, and that wasn't good in a whole raft of ways, but especially bad because the way to get a sales lead was to get it spoon-fed to you by the GM or the Used Car Sales/Internet Manager.

"Everywhere else I've worked, the leads are divvied up equal like," Bingham informed me. "All around, to everybody, here, all the leads and phone calls go through the office, and whoever is best at kissing ass gets them."

"Best ass kisser? That would be Rich then, right?" I said. It was too early in our relationship for it, but Bingham cracked a little smile.

While we chatted, a clanky, rattletrap, two-ton tow truck with no apparent muffler pulled up at the side door. It finally bounced to a stop and a burly man, with a Duck Dynasty beard and his head covered by an Aspen, Colorado ski cap, lumbered down from the rig. He was probably in his forties but stoved-up like a geriatric. He was followed close behind by a black and white doggie, as ratty as the truck, with one torn black ear and part of its tail, or at least the fur, missing. The poor little thing walked with a hind leg limp, occasionally holding the leg up altogether.

"That's just Mater," Clay said.

"Mater must be a pretty decent guy if he adopted a rescue dog."

"Don't get all sweet on him." Clay huffed and stomped off like a jealous beau. The tow truck guy was just another of the wacky character actors that constituted our little production.

"He'll be loading some cars to take to Monday's Phoenix Auto Auction," Bingham told me. "He's Conrad's buddy. I guess they worked together a long time ago in Colorado or Wyoming or someplace, but watch out for Mr. Mater. He likes to charm the girls," he said, another reference to this guy's appeal. Maybe it was the dog; it was kind of cute in a sympathetic sort of way. Mater wore a pair of overalls over a wife-beater T-shirt. Underneath his bare arm, a pistol was strapped much like an undercover detective on NCIS might conceal one under his jacket. Concealed, it wasn't! He had nowhere to conceal it even if a permit were required.

The phone on the desk rang and startled all of us. The office was closed on Saturday so five hands grabbed for the handset on each desk. Stretch, with his inordinately long arms, was quickest.

"Just some woman calling for ConMan," he reported after he hung up, making sure we didn't think he'd gotten a lead off that call. So, ConMan, or Conrad, was popular with the ladies too. This place was a regular lady-pleasing Chippendale's—bare arms and all. I giggled, imagining the tow truck guy in a black bow tie like Chris Farley on SNL.

"That was his wife calling," Clay said. "She's always looking for him."

"You mean the burrito lady? Does this mean we have to find our own lunch today?" I asked.

"Yes, the burrito lady. Her name is Juanita, and she doesn't deliver on Saturday. She just comes by here to keep an eye on the ConMan. He's known to have a bit of a roving eye."

"Think she can stop that with burritos?" I said.

"But you have to admit they're very good burritos."

Mater fiddled with the lock on the door to the service counter like it was the first time he had handled a key.

"The tow guy seems like an odd duck," I said to Clay later, but I meant sort of creepy.

"He's probably more used to opening a door with a Slim Jim or a screwdriver, if you know what I mean," said Clay. "You know we call him that because of the tow truck from the cartoon, right?"

"Clay, are you implying that a middle school librarian wouldn't get a kid's cartoon reference? But please don't tell me that Conrad is Lightning McQueen in this scenario." Just then, Clay skittered out the side door and Rich scampered out the front. When I turned around, I realized why.

"Where's Mike? I need him to sign for these junk cars," the tow man said. With his workaday appearance, I expected him to smell bad, but he didn't, or at least he covered it up with a dousing of Old Spice that actually smelled great.

"He's out puffing with his troops." I gestured to the flock outside smoking. The funny little doggie came right to me and let me scratch his good ear.

"Don't you smoke?" Mater asked.

"No, but I'm thinking about starting." And I sort of meant it. It was hard to watch them all outside laughing. Whenever I did join them, I broke that group up too.

"Pretty girl like you should stay away from the fags as long as you can," he said. I could see something of a twinkle in his eye, and I was taken aback. This was the nicest thing that had been said to me since I set foot in the AutoMall.

"Are you a friend of Conrad's?" I asked. I didn't know how to chat up a tow truck guy.

"Who said that?"

"I just heard he got you this job, that's all." I was a salesman now and was supposed to be able to converse with anyone and everyone, yet I was at a loss.

"I get my own jobs," he said, and then added, a few seconds later, "Conrad and I knew each other in Denver." He had doubled back to my first question. This conversation was like a game of Red Rover. Red Rover, Red Rover please send an answer over.

"Denver?" Well then, you're a Broncos fan." I was making worthless guy-style conversation.

"I was an Elway fan."

"That's old news, Mater."

"Actually, I lied. I was more of a Bronco's cheerleader fan. You were probably a cheerleader too, right? Miss?"

"I'm Birdie. No, I was never a cheerleader. Or a Bronco fan. And for the record, there is only one real football team of any stripe in the U. S. of A."

"Really, who?" he asked, as though he was almost interested.

"Big Red! Nebraska Cornhuskers. There is no other team. I once went to a game with my dad and met Coach Tom Osborne." I said, not meaning to make it sound like bragging.

"Now who's talking old news?" he said, dissing my bragging rights. As I was about to pledge my undying Big Red loyalty, the telephone rang, but before I answered, I asked Mater what he called his dog. I guessed Lucky.

"JuiceBox," he said.

Did he name his doggie JuiceBox? How cute is that?

"He's sort of accident prone, I take it," I said.

Mater turned back. "You know, you look a little bit like Britney Spears?"

"But a lot older?" I added. When I had told the caller the service area was closed, I googled the famous pop star. We were the same age—exactly. Until I came to the AutoMall, my life had a lot less trouble than Britney's and of course, I had a lot less money to show for it.

The Marlboro men outside circled around Montello, hanging on his every word, laughing at his jokes and trying to top each other with clever put-downs of anyone out of earshot. Stretch had finally lit up the cigarette that had been an ear adornment all morning. I could hear most of it through the window. Montello was a true leader. He led his puffer boys in derision and name calling. There were laughs all around for ten or twelve minutes until he took the last draw on his unfiltered Pall Mall and stamped out the butt with his European leather loafer. This happened six or eight times a day. If the AutoMall guys didn't have a serious smoking habit before they started, matching Montello stick for stick would certainly give them one.

Rich was now inside with me because he was too lazy to get up and go out and I was inside because, well, just because, I guess. Not being in the circle contributed to what was already seen as my aloofness—another comment on the evaluation from my last employer. I was consistent. I hated BS.

Some salesman I was, with no BS in my arsenal.

CHAPTER 6

When I left work, I was not in a barhopping mood, but my dear grandmother had a regular date with some of her friends and insisted that the Dback Bar was where she was cooking my dinner.

Tweety, my old yellow Mini-cooper with the black top and white racing stripes, fit just about anywhere in a parking lot, even golf cart spots in a pinch, but in the canyons between all the half ton and ¾ ton trucks, those spots were hard to see. One thing was clear, nearly everyone in town drove a truck. Note to self—spend more time on the truck lot. I parked up near the front door next to the Lone Pine Ranch truck that had been at the center of the fracas in the Service Department. Was the angry cowboy inside?

The Dback was an old-school honkytonk-style watering hole, named J Bar T when I was a girl. Back then, no one respectable would dare go near it, but social lines in Copper Springs had blurred. The little country club had gone broke and was taken over by the city for a community golf course and folks of all incomes and persuasions got at least one meal a week at the local bars. Unlike yesteryear, the parking lots were paved now, and the music playing at dinner hour was a very low decibel, Dan Fogelberg. Whoever thought America wasn't dumbing down had never spent a Saturday night in Copper Springs.

When my eyes finally adjusted, I spied Grams and made my way to the booth with the wooden plank table where she was already deep in conversation with a fellow I had not met. Her soft, slightly lavender hair was done up in a sixties style French twist. She looked like a tasty cotton candy.

"Did you sell a car today?" she asked. I gave her a peck on the cheek and wished she had started our evening with any other query. It was becoming more embarrassing every day that I was not a "producer" like Bingham.

"This is David, a friend of mine," she said. *Where was her ladies' group?*

David's left leg bounced up and down under the table so frequently I could feel the wooden floor vibrating. His knee seemed to hit the crosspiece underneath and he grimaced. Thankfully his gyrations stopped. But this was the exact moment I realized my sweet little Grams was trying to set me up with this guy.

"Grams, what are you up to?" I whispered in her ear as I slipped into the wide red leather booth beside her.

"Birdie dear, you and David have a lot in common. He's a mechanic. He works on my car, and he's a farmer just like you used to be."

That statement was particularly irksome to me because she knew I had resented but now hated the Sanders Family Farm, whose lawyers were stating that I, in fact, had no claim to anything including the value of the home that they now called an "outbuilding".

The farmer thing was David's cue. He reached around to retrieve a container from the flat spot above the booth and he opened it slowly as one might show off the treasure of the Sierra Madre or a diamond necklace in a hinged Tiffany box.

It was in a hinged box, all right. It was a carton of eggs. The gift he held out to me was a full carton of eggs.

"I brought you these—just gathered them before I came out to have a burger with Luella here."

I took the offering and stared at the contents. Most of the eggs were similar sizes of creamy white, but one, much bigger than the rest, was deep chocolaty beige with chicken shit and straw still stuck to it.

"I know. You're right. It's huge! It has three yolks," he said. Never was a statement made with more pride than David must have felt for that dinosaur egg perched in the crate that my palms were cradling. He couldn't have been more puffed up if he'd laid it himself. I stifled a giggle, then another, but by holding back it made me sound like I was coughing up a hairball.

"Won't that just make a wonderful omelet," Gramma said as she gave me the elbow then sped on to her next segue.

"You two are both in the car business."

"Well, I'm just barely in the business and not likely staying there," I said. Grams was getting a bit huffy and David's knee began knocking again.

"How about a round of drinks?" David said as he bounded off toward the bar like a retriever after a duck I'd just shot.

"Farmer? Really, Gram? I lived on a corporate behemoth of a food producer. You do know that I never actually planted any carrots or peas, don't you?"

"I just thought it was high time you started to get out some. Can you give me one reason why maybe going out with David wouldn't be kind of a nice change of pace for you?"

I gazed at David's gift sitting before me on the table.

"Gram, I can give you a dozen good reasons."

David returned with the drinks and proceeded to regale us with horrible tales of the AutoMall's abominable service department.

"Everybody hates that Conrad guy. It's almost like he doesn't think he is there to do the service department business."

"I'm getting that already, and I just started," I told him.

"Just between us, I hope he stays there a good long time because I get to work on a heck of a lot more cars in my little shop now that he works for Wallace."

I was getting clearer on the inadequacies of the AutoMall with every new person I met and Conrad seemed to be at the center of many of the complaints. Little did either of us know how much upheaval would be wreaked on Copper Springs AutoMall in the very near future that would change all our lives.

CHAPTER 7

The country band was setting up for their first set so Gramma and I said our goodbyes to David, who moved up to the bar where he was probably hoping for better luck. We made our way to the exit. Grams had the doggie bags, and I had both the egg carton and marvelous new dirt on my co-workers. I was delighted. Gossip, I realized, was going to be the coin of the realm at Copper Springs AutoMall.

Someone held the door for us when we stepped outside. I murmured thanks when the man asked, "Al, is that you?" I turned sharply to get a better look but hadn't completely cleared the space. The door handle hooked the cuff of my jacket sleeve and yanked my elbow as it shut, dislodging my cargo. I grabbed for the strap of my purse, but the egg carton intertwined with it made a slow upward arc like a teacher drawing a rainbow on a whiteboard then headed for disaster below. We three stood motionless as most of a dozen eggs scrambled on the sidewalk between us. I dropped down to try to clean up the mess. Was this who I thought it was? I was afraid to look back up at him.

"Why, Burke Buchanan. I never see you anymore," Grams said. Oh my God, it was him. "How are things out at the ranch? How's your Mama?" Keep your head down, Birdie, keep your cool. Above me, the two of them were hugging. Could this night get any worse? I fell forward from my crouch and began to collect the sticky shells, oblivious to the fact that both my knees were now mired in yellow goo. David was right, that egg did have three yolks.

Burke Buchanan hovered over me and then he crouched down and whispered. "Alberta, you haven't aged a bit in twenty years. What are you doing here?"

The eggs and I were trying to melt into the cement as if we were in a frying pan that could transform us into an exotic frittata that even Rachel Ray couldn't recognize.

"Most people call me Birdie now," I mumbled.

"No, I mean it. What are you doing here in the Springs besides having an egg toss?" He smiled, gently taking the carton from me and throwing it in the garbage can by the front door.

"Don't you live back up in Nebraska somewhere?" He stammered it out as he did after our high school graduation, the night he told me he loved me, his high school sweetheart.

"Well, I live here now," I said, as if that explained everything. Burke grabbed a shop rag from the back of his truck and handed it to me.

"You have some egg on your face," he said. No words were ever truer.

"She got a divorce and moved back here to live with me," Grams said, clearly happy that the evening had presented itself with an opportunity to perhaps get me a date after all.

"This is your truck? Is the Lone Pine what your ranch is called now?" I asked.

"It is," he said. "How'd you know that?"

"I saw you with that truck at the Copper Springs AutoMall. I didn't realize it was you." I was using the shop rag he'd handed me to mop my knees, keeping my head lowered so he wouldn't notice my burning crimson face and my mortification as I encountered the last person I'd care to see.

"The ranch got split up," he said. "My family got half and Uncle Ken and his family kept the original part when my dad passed away about ten years now. We still run it together. We just re-named our half.

"You broke up the ranch?" Could Burke and his beloved Kenny be on the outs? Not possible. Kenny was a mentor and best friend to Burke since he was just a babe in John Deere brand rompers. Ken was one of the finest men God ever created. Why would they break from one another?

"Has it been that long, Burke?" Gramma interjected, but he couldn't take his eyes off of me and I had enough time to take in his full 6'2" frame. The gangly boy I remembered had muscled out and tanned. I was instantly an eighteen-year-old again with my old boyfriend. It reminded me of the last time I saw him when he was leaving Copper Springs for Ag school in Colorado and as it turned out, I was leaving Copper Springs for good. I had forgotten how devastatingly handsome the man was. Or maybe becoming a man made him that way.

The tap, tap, tap of my pulse thumping inside my ears began interfering with my hearing but I distinctly heard Grams say, "How's your boy?" Burke turned to her and missed seeing my crestfallen look. Of course, he was married with at least one child, maybe six. My dear darling Grams had followed my explicit direction to never mention him to me, and now I didn't know the first thing about this man.

"Wonderful," Burke said. "He's trying his hand at Pro rodeo. He's a bareback rider.

"I better get you home, Grams," I said, anxious to get out of Burke's view and gather my thoughts. I always meant to contact him. I did. I meant to answer his letters, and now, he was not only married but had a grown son.

"She's headed for the left-over apple crisp in the fridge," Grams said. "Do you want to stop by and have some?" My God, she was not inviting Burke Buchanan to our house tonight, was she? How could things get any more awkward?

"Grams, I'm sure Burke is busy." I ushered her around to her side of the car.

"Are you at the Public Library or the high school?" he asked innocently. He had clearly kept up with me enough to know I was a librarian. I was flattered, but it meant I had to tell someone whose respect I used to value greatly that I had become a used car salesman. I would have to wear my humiliation for all the failures that brought me to this place tonight.

"She works for the AutoMall," Gramma said as I stuffed her into the Mini Cooper to try to keep her quiet. I dropped her bulging leather bag in her lap, gave her a serious scowl, then slammed her in.

"You have all that education, and you're working in the office of that place?" *Wrong again Burke. Not the office.* I couldn't bear to correct him.

"Good to see you, Burke," I said. In order to open the car door, I stepped closer to him, and he didn't step back. He smelled sweet like new-mown hay. The cowboy removed his western hat and nodded his goodbye then did a classic head scratch like he was Gary Cooper in an old western movie.

"I thought you'd never come back, Al," he said. His voice was low, way too intimate for a married man.

"I'm full of surprises." As I took the driver's seat, I could feel the overwhelming slump of shame. It was shame for ignoring Burke's attempts to reach me, shame for taking ten years longer than I should have to end a bad marriage with Peter, and shame to have finally succumbed to the family business. Then, for some ungodly reason just before I shut the car door I said, "You look good, too." We pulled out of our parking spot, leaving him standing behind his truck as we drove away.

"It was a shame about his wife," Gramma said.

"His wife? What about his wife?" I said.

"His wife was killed in a car accident on the way to Phoenix, not long before his dad died. I'm sure I told you about it," she said.

"I think I would have remembered that." In my shock, I spoke more sharply than I intended. Grams was just following my instructions to not tell me any details of Burke's life.

"Gosh, you were flirting with him big time tonight, so I thought you knew."

"I was not. That's it for you, Miss Matchmaker. No more evenings out, and anyway, I don't think he would be much interested in someone who knows more about his diesel engine than about a chocolate cream pie." I may have mortally embarrassed myself tonight, but at least I knew what truck he drove so I could hide when I saw it.

"He was crazy about you, Alberta. Surely that information didn't pass you by."

"No, it didn't, Grams. But I wasn't very nice to him at the time, nor have I been since.

"When you're as crazy about someone as that boy was crazy about you, you don't forget it," she said. No, you don't, but you can try. I had almost put the embarrassment of the night behind me when I reached in my bag to get the house keys and pulled out a solitary unbroken egg.

Ever the optimist, Grams said, "I guess we can have that omelet after all."

CHAPTER 8

More than a week had passed since I darkened the threshold of Copper Springs AutoMall as the token female (or token golfer, if Bingham was correct,) and I had yet to sell a vehicle. I might be the only Green Pea in history that couldn't even make it out of the pod.

Before our morning meeting, I wandered out to the Detail bays, and for the first time, I met the little lady in the jeans and sweatshirt with the long braid down her back that I could now see some gray hair in—she wasn't as young as she looked, but still she reminded me of Tinkerbell.

"I know you saw that son of a bitch ConMan get in a fight with another fucking customer the other day," she said. Not the Disney variety of Tinkerbelle–she was more the HBO kind. As she talked, she was pestering an orange soda stain out of the passenger seat of an SUV, not giving up until it cried uncle and disappeared. She was a genius.

"I did," I answered. "And, it turns out, I know the guy he was arguing with. I used to live here when I was in high school." I decided to leave the discussion of her boss to later.

"And you couldn't find someplace better than Copper Springs to come back to? You weren't looking very damn hard."

"I'm Birdie," I said. Then she surprised me. She thrust out her hand and gave mine a solid shake.

"I'm Angel," she answered. *Strong for a little thing.* I surveyed Angel's lair, full of dripping fifty-five-gallon barrels, dirt-caked car parts, seats ripped out of trucks being worked over, and enough bottles of acrid products to stock the cleaning aisle at an Ace hardware store.

In the back of the dealership, the used vehicles had the muddled stench of a thousand pet messes, preschooler calamities or college road trips gone wrong. These were collective odors that were the exact opposite of the sacred sweet new car smell that was prized by the customers out on the showroom floor. Before we could get acquainted, the loudspeaker summoned the sales crew to the conference room.

Montello began the meeting by introducing a tall, clean-cut, Richie Cunningham-looking kid sitting at the back of the room, as the new salesman. In less than a week's time I was no longer the newest guy. I hoped he didn't think he was getting a desk. The NewKid looked like a high school sophomore, but we were told that he had just finished his first year of college and was back for the summer. Montello added, "Of course, you all remember him from the years he was our lot boy." I sized him up. No doubt I could sell more cars than this lot boy, but he did have an endearing smile that the old folks would probably fall for.

As the meeting came to a close, Wade announced, "The used car lot needs a rodeo today." Everybody around me groaned. I was just relieved that I had survived another meeting, and still seemed to have a job, even with little income.

Rodeo, it turns out, was the term the crew used for rearranging and straightening up the car lot. The task was necessary much more often than an outsider would think. The used lot looked like the aftermath of a Texas flood with random vehicles hunched together at one end, all akimbo and almost on top of one another. I made myself conspicuous as one of the first to spring through the broken front doors and hit the tarmac. See how teamy I am? "All for one and one for all." I could be a Musketeer if I had to. The rest spilled out behind me with dumb looks like they'd just been pushed through curtains onto an unfamiliar stage and didn't know their lines. It's a rodeo, time to send in the clowns.

"Let's get this over with, "Clay said.

The first vehicle we tried to open was locked with the keys inside. Stretch hiked to his heap parked toward the back of the building, produced a metal strip called a Slim Jim, the professional version of the wire coat hanger the rest of us use and he approached the driver's side door. He slipped the device down below the window and in less than fifteen seconds, he had the set of keys in his hand. I wasn't surprised at Stretch's prowess but still, I was impressed. Skill and speed.

Several vehicles were out of gas so I gallantly offered to drive down the road to the Shell station to take myself out of the lot design equation. When I returned twenty minutes later with the heavy five-gallon can, I asked Austin, the current lot boy, to unload it for me. Not realizing we needed it, he took it back to the Detail Department.

"Where's the can?" Rich asked.

"Where's my head?" I thought. I was about to confirm two of the reasons I was despised here. 1. I couldn't keep my head in the game; and 2. I was too sissy to carry my weight, at least the weight of the five-gallon gas can.

"Let me get it," the tousled blond NewKid said. Bless his heart. I liked him instantly.

In my absence, the problem of who was in charge had not been resolved. Rich eventually grabbed the lead, but within moments he was unsure of how he wanted to proceed. Then Clay stepped in, with everyone offering suggestions. We had six surprisingly different views on how to accomplish this task. My art minor at Northwestern told me that this was a simple geometric my eleven-year-old middle schoolers could have drawn. How hard could it be? Stretch quietly lit up the Pall Mall plucked from behind his ear while we waited for the hubbub to settle. It seemed so painfully easy to see exactly where the lines of cars should be, but as the greenest of Green Peas, I actually followed Stretch's lead. I kept my mouth shut. After all, this was my first Rodeo.

Painful yes, but not easy. Rich retook the helm and we began to move cars as he motioned us into place but none of us could decipher his hand signals. Did a held-up palm mean all ahead full or stop in place? He was slurring his gestures and unwittingly spelling out obscenities. He augmented this by actually yelling obscenities.

"No, not there! Back up, goddamn it! No, no, no! Come back forward for Christ's sake. That was goddamned terrible! Okay, stop. Too close." And that was just the first vehicle.

We jumped in and out of cars like Keystone Kops in a silent movie on fast forward while Rich continued his hand motions. When we finished, I came up front to look. The line was as crooked as a Washington politician with scoliosis. Fifteen cars were parked and not one lined up with the rest. Was it possible we had gone through this aggravating exercise just to leave the lot in worse shape than we found it? Angel drove out a new lease return, lined it up perfectly on one try with the first vehicle in the line with no direction from Rich and shook her head at the ineptitude as she walked back in.

Rich grumbled. "We'll need to do this all again," he said as if it was anyone's fault but his own for being so 'goddamned terrible' as a lineup guy. Across the car lot, Conrad was all by himself watching our charade. He leaned against the tire air machine about to fall asleep as if he had pulled an all-nighter and he lit a cigarette. As bad tempered as he was, it was a good thing he was a loner.

After we had screwed around long enough, Bingham stepped in to take over, causing Rich to storm into the building, both front doors crashing behind him. In less than forty minutes with the remaining five of us parking, the lot looked like a "goddamned geometric art piece" according to Clay. We had created oblique chevrons of subcompacts, pencil-straight lines of sedans and a half circle of ¾ ton trucks. When we all entered the building in triumph, we saw that Rich had snagged the only decent Up, and he alone was well on his way to a lucrative sale.

"Lesson learned," said Clay. I thought there was no way Rich was smart enough to see that advantage, but we all filed his stomping off technique in our minds for the next reviled rodeo.

CHAPTER 9

In late morning, a haggard-looking woman, who was probably in her early forties but looked to be fifty, drove up in an '05 Ford Sport Trac, the pickup version of the Ford Explorer or as the guys called it, the Ford "Exploder." Even as a Green Pea, I knew a small sized, 4x4 pickup was a great trade for us to acquire so I approached her before anyone else knew she existed. She explained that she had purchased this pickup with her husband and now she wanted something new—in both a vehicle and a husband. She was recently divorced. Although I was not yet fully divorced, I felt her pain.

"I'm not picky," she said when I asked what car she was looking for. My heart lilted. Women seemed to enjoy working with me, and this woman was ready to pick out a new vehicle, new to her anyway, and get the deal done.

In no time, she chose a modestly priced sedan as she filled me in on the intimate details of her split from the "sleazy jerk" she was married to and didn't at all care if she ever set eyes on again, then she said that she was rather new to a job cooking at Maria's Mexican. Great, she has a job. Just what a used car salesman wants to hear.

Karen was her name (the sleazy jerk of a husband's name was Ernie). The sordid story of her personal life spilled out as we left the driveway and slipped onto the highway. Ernie, the bastard, had cheated on her three different times, took her paycheck, forged her name and then lost the cash at the casino. It worried me that after driving only one vehicle, she moved too quickly to saying yes to the deal. People with good credit ask questions; they hesitate. She rushed to the signing table like she was Dale Earnhardt Jr. in the final turn at Phoenix International Raceway. It had taken a mere thirty minutes to bring her to the showroom where she shared that this was the only dealership that had treated her well. Terrific. How long would it take me to begin brushing off customers like Karen as I raced away for the more profitable Ups with the rest of the real salesmen?

This deal had so little hope now that even I had trouble going through the motions of collecting VIN (Vehicle Information Number) numbers, odometer readings, and financial info on how much she owed on the trade. I turned it in. Mr. Wiggly Mustache didn't even bother to come out to talk to her himself. He sent Stretch.

"Could you get a co-signer?" Stretch asked. I looked at her face to see if she knew that it meant she would need to get someone, presumably with better credit than hers, to agree to pay if she couldn't. It was something no one I've ever known would do for any reason except for their kid's first vehicle.

"I'll call my sister," Karen said and dialed from our desk phone. No answer. "I'll call the other one." The second sister answered, and the woman seemed amenable to lending her name to this deal. I already knew that people with no credit didn't seem to mind lending something that didn't exist. However, we could all hear the sister's husband yelling at the top of his voice and then she hung up.

"Not that one either," she said. Rich and Bingham were circling around us like turkey vultures. Then, without any drama, Stretch stood, hovered over us and asked Karen an unthinkable question. I couldn't believe what I heard. What did he think he was doing? I should have stepped in and stopped him but I was too shocked to talk.

"Could you ask your ex-husband to co-sign for you?" The awkwardness froze the very air around us. He didn't know about her terrible divorce. Of course, they were all terrible, weren't they?

There was stark quiet in the room for what seemed like an eternity. Of course, she couldn't ask him, it took everything in her being to ditch the lousy loser and…

"I'll call him," she said.

She calmly reached across in front of me for the landline receiver and dialed a number. I watched her like a voyeur at a car crash. I could see the carnage inside wriggling around right before a semi-truck slammed into the wreck and finished the whole thing off.

"He's on his way," she said. What? If I did this job a hundred years, God forbid, I would never have thought to ask that question but that's what successful car salesmen do—they ask. Can you not pay another bill this month so you have a down payment? Can your mother watch the kids for a few weeks so you can give us the childcare money? They might say something like this: "You told us you can only afford a payment of $225. $350 is not too much more. You can manage that, can't you?" They nod their heads in agreement.

In no time, the no-good bastard Ernie, whom I felt I knew, came through the side door and sat beside Karen at the desk. As soon as I met Ernie, I had to agree, she was not too picky. As Karen chatted with her "SOB, good for nothing, divorce was the best decision of my life" ex-husband. Stretch leaned in and dropped the next bomb.

"Rich thinks this is half his deal."

"What? Rich has been at the next desk watching us all afternoon. She hasn't even said hello to him," I protested, although I knew Stretch was not the decider on the subject.

"Apparently, she called and left a message for him this morning," he said.

What did that mean? Where did he know her from?" Is this another prank?

"All I know is that Rich said he's on half this deal." Stretch exited to have a smoke while I dealt with the signatures and got the paperwork ready to give back to Wade.

Rich walked back and forth at the other end of the building like a caged cat, his mop of red curly hair bouncing up and down while he kept tugging on his purple tie. The lazy twerp thought there was no deal so he let me do it. He was probably right. Finally, Wade sent Stretch out to tell Karen and Ernie that they could go on to work and that we'd call her later. We made our friendly goodbyes almost a hug but not quite and the two exes left in their different vehicles. I felt bitterly disappointed but at the same time, I had written up my first real sale.

Before we left for the evening, I asked Clay, "What will happen next?"

"That deal has zero chance or we would have never let them walk. She's a 'roach' and everybody knows that. Now you do too."

"What's a roach?"

"No credit," he answered.

"How can Rich claim half the deal?" I asked.

"That's how this business works," Clay said. "All that has to happen for anyone to get half a deal is for a customer to ask for you."

It's that easy? I was elated. That was a game I could win. Even if the customer couldn't remember my name, I was the only woman here. "Ask for Birdie" would become my new mantra. I didn't get a sale today, but I got a customer to third base, and I was confident that my next one would be a home run.

The bones in my feet felt like they had fused as the day came to a close. I limped along to our parked cars where I kicked off my shoes and drove home barefoot. I kissed Gram, skipped dinner and fell into bed like a rock. I went to sleep happy because it hadn't yet occurred to me that just because a customer said my name that didn't mean any of the SOBs I worked with would actually admit I was even there. That lesson would come later.

CHAPTER 10

Just a touch of "almost success" revived my attitude and amped my energy levels. Today I would make a sale, a complete, commissioned sale.

Wade looked out from what was called the tower, an area where his desk sat that was eight inches higher than the rest of the floor, presumably so he could have a better view of his underlings. Seeing no one but me, he hollered over. "Hey." I doubted he knew my name. "Drive the follow vehicle for a delivery in Sierra Vista. Go out and see Angel. You'll be going with her."

Inhabitants of the dealership did multiple duties, like utility infielders for the Diamondbacks. But I was being sent completely out of bounds to wherever Sierra Vista was. Balking at the assignment wasn't an option. Even if I tried, I was too green to have earned a choice. But why didn't the seller of the vehicle deliver it? Maybe it was Wade's house deal and I could get on his good side, assuming one existed.

I followed Angel with the shop car to make the drop-off in Sierra Vista. What a vista it turned out to be. From the top of the pass leading in to town, I could see all the way to Tucson. Wildflowers were everywhere—incredible beauty as far as the eye could see. Where was this Arizona when I lived here before?

Angel was delightful. On the hour-long ride back, we each filled in some, but not all, of our life stories. I mentioned that I had come to live with my grandparents who owned the local drugstore when I was a sophomore in high school.

"Which drugstore?" she asked. "The one with the advertising at the corner of annoying and aggravating?"

She made me smile.

"No, it was the old Rexall drug on Main Street. It's an exercise place now. What about you?" I asked, launching her into histrionic tales of her three issue-laden teenagers, how her Granny Amelia found her American husband in the barn on her family's Italian villa during World War II, and how every Sunday found her whole family chowing down on meatballs and baked ziti.

Angel, who had to be ninety-eight pounds soaking wet, was a serious pasta lover. She was coarse like a street kid, but she was not a kid. I had watched her outwork every guy in the back. She amused herself while I drove by removing grime from around the colorful stones of her golden ring with a toothpick she'd found in the shop car. Angel was obsessed with dirt, both the kind you can scrub away and the kind she had on everybody. She was a one-woman National Enquirer. We played a game of free association where I named a name, and she would tell me a tidbit. It took some effort to move her along because she could rattle on better than a sixth grader.

My first question was, "Who sold the car you just delivered?"

"Stretch, but he was going to be late today. You became the sucker when you came in early." Which of course removed all incentives for promptness.

"Wade," I said.

"He's a sadistic bastard. He ran over his kid's babysitter's dog and blamed it on the FedEx driver." Naah, that can't be true I thought. She nodded as if to overcome my doubt.

"Really, I think the kids are the ones who turned him in."

"Wade has kids?" I pondered that then asked. "Bingham?"

"His wife has been fighting breast cancer all year, supposed to be in remission now," she said. That surprised me, where Wade being a sadist didn't. Bing had said nothing about it. It might explain his constant crankiness. Maybe I should cut him some slack.

"Stretch?" I asked.

"We got Stretch with Wade, sort of a two for one, very Black Friday deal if you know what I mean. Those two are tighter than ticks. Don't get between them." I didn't really want to be anywhere near them let alone between them. "I don't trust Stretch," she said. I considered myself warned.

"Conrad," I said, knowing it would elicit a big reaction.

"Oh, he's a case." Angel became more animated and wiggled in her seat. "I'm not sure how he got himself hired. He can hardly see, you know, God help him if he ever loses those wire-rimmed glasses of his. He doesn't know a carburetor from my granny's cannoli, and he's got some sort of scam going. I haven't figured it out yet but I will. A lot of sleazy looking characters hang around since that low life started here. It wouldn't hurt my feelings one bit if he were to drop dead tomorrow—the jackass."

I grinned. "So, he's your favorite co-worker then?" She shook her head. Conrad was her immediate boss, but Angel seemed to be the queen of all the activity from the oil change wall back.

"Seriously. Something's been off at the dealership since he arrived. He's never there a moment past five. Even if a customer is talking to him, he just walks off. He says it's in his contract, but he comes back in and works nights after everyone is gone. Doesn't that seem suspicious?"

"So, he scoots out when the boss is watching and then works when no one sees it? Yeah, that is odd," I agreed. "Most guys are more like Rich. I doubt he'd so much as pick up a gum wrapper if he didn't think someone was watching."

"See, I knew you were smart."

"Montello," I said, keeping our game going.

"That one's complicated." She hesitated before she answered, her gaze focused outside the window. "On the one hand, he's a dedicated family man. He'd do anything for his wife and his daughter, and he has grandkids. On the other, he'd take the last dollar out of an orphan's bank account if he made the house a better deal.

The whole negotiating thing is a game for him, just a game, but sometimes that game gets in the way of his humanity." The drive time was going by quickly and my insider knowledge was growing.

"Now I've got one for you," Angel said just as we closed in on the dealership.

I put on my apprehensive teacher hat. I preferred asking the questions. I nodded.

"Are you still married? I heard rumors."

I grinned and said, "That depends on who wants to know." The words, "I've been traded in for a new model" I wasn't anxious for anyone to hear, including myself. I dodged the question, but Angel was on to me. It wouldn't be the last time she asked. The explanation would have to include details like how I sank the last of my inheritance into the glorious restoration of a hundred-year-old Victorian house on a family farm that I thought I would live in forever with my handsome college professor of a husband. Meanwhile, Professor Plum had squired his European History grad student around Iberia where he obviously checked out more than some dusty old books.

I gently removed the ring and pocketed it when I was sure Angel wouldn't notice.

CHAPTER 11

had been back at the dealership from my sojourn with Angel for almost two hours when I casually questioned Stretch.

"Did anything happen with the deal from yesterday?" I wasn't expecting an affirmative answer; I was just asking. "I gave Rich the paperwork file so he could follow up. That seemed fair—fifty-fifty, correct?"

"Rich is off today," he said, continuing to look at a comic book one of the customers left behind.

"So, nothing happened then?"

"Well, we completed the deal, if that's what you mean." He gestured toward Karen's bright yellow trade-in truck sitting just outside the window. I was shocked that I hadn't noticed it just six feet from the chair I'd just occupied. "Rich is off today," he repeated.

"That's great," I said. I practically skipped to the portly Wade's office. He didn't look up even though he knew I was standing there. His disdain for me knew no bounds.

"So, I guess I need a celebration for my first sale," I proclaimed. He still didn't look up, and he didn't answer immediately. He stroked the ends of his wimpy handlebar trying to get them to curl at the ends. In the few dealings I'd had with him, I already thought of him as a spoiled rich kid with a capacity for rudeness that far outpaced his actual skills and now, I knew Snidely Whiplash was a dog killer too.

"Wade. You're not really going to give Rich half of that money are you?" I said. "He didn't even say hello to Karen. She doesn't even know him."

"Well, it's worse than that," he whispered to the newspaper in front of him. "You're in the middle of the deal, and since it can only be split two ways, Stretch will get the second half. You were the middleman, so you're out."

I wasn't believing my ears.

"Are you telling me that none of this deal is mine? After I did all the work and spent the whole day on it?" My voice box tightened as I spoke until a kind of laryngitis was all that was left. "What kind of B. S. is that?" I squeaked out, sounding like I was mocking his whisper. This was my first deal!

"No B.S. It's just the way this business works. Get used to it." He said this with no inflection or apology. He had yet to look at me. He was so calm that it almost felt like he had said the words in slow motion, like the corporal at an execution calmly giving the privates with the guns the signal to shoot.

"You weren't here when your customer came in this morning. Someone else had to handle it," he said. What he seemed to imply was, "Take your capital punishment for goofing off with Angel and shut up."

"I wasn't here because you sent me out on an errand to deliver Stretch's sale! All the way to Sierra flipping Vista!" Heads in the office were turning, and the sales guys drew closer to get the details of my meltdown. I was dumbfounded. "Is there any proof that she even really asked for Rich?" I asked.

"Bingham took the message."

"How do we know it was even the same lady?" I pleaded.

"He said it was." I was utterly unconvinced. "Stretch finished the deal and did the delivery while you were gone, so he gets the other half. Sorry, you're in the middle of the deal, and that guy gets nothing."

"There was no delivery." I tried to yell with no voice. "She bought a used car. We had already discussed every inch of it thoroughly. All he did was hand her the keys and put on the forty-day sticker." I called on all my years of crisis training at the school to say this as calmly as my frantically beating heart and knot in my stomach would allow.

"Well, it's unfortunate then, isn't it?" Wade said with world-class insincerity.

"Is this a joke?" I croaked out.

He finally looked at me with a menacing glare. "No. It's no joke. You have a lot to learn about the car business." He waved me out of the office and calmly went back to his paper.

I was at a loss to understand what had happened, but, for some unexplained reason, the whole episode intrigued me as much as infuriated me. What just happened here? Was I being played? Was I set up so I'd miss the delivery of my first sale, so he could give it to his buddy? Was it a test or a ritual hazing for the Green Pea?

Let's face it. I was troubled almost as much by the fact that I didn't recognize that bright yellow bomb with the net tailgate and ripped black leather seats sitting outside the window next to me as I was that they didn't give me the commission. This was how that ornery Billy Francisco smuggled the Cigarillo Cigars into my school, distributed them and then with his two buddies crouched behind the last oak shelf in the back of the library and smoked them half gone before Principal Jackson came running in to ask me if anyone had reported smoke in my area. I looked across the showroom floor to the trade-in. *Please, Dear Lord, tell me that if this yellow truck had been burning, I would have at least noticed that.* I plunked myself down, de-starched, in the desk at the foot of Wade's Tower—Stretch's usual spot. The rest of the staff looked at me with the lack of pity reserved for a pathetic loser. I felt like I might slide off the chair when my gaze landed on the corner of the commission check sticking out of Stretch's spiral notebook. I pulled it out very slowly. $830.00. Half of the commission on this deal was over $800 damn dollars! Suddenly, the loss of commission was the most important thing. The anger rose up in my chest and flushed my face. Did they steal this $1,600 deal from me because of how much it was worth? What now? File a complaint with

Montello on my very first sale? Hell no. Then I'd be like the kid in the principal's office with the high-powered dad who swooped in to save him. Nobody liked that kid. My thoughts careened. No doubt these guys would turn back these checks that they knew perfectly well didn't belong to them, I reassured myself. I needed that $1600 bucks. As every day went by, I needed it more.

"Tough Day?" a voice above me said. Guilty of trespassing, I almost jumped out of my skin. "Oh sorry, I didn't mean to scare you."

"Why, if it isn't Burke Buchanan," I sputtered at the man who once again showed up at an inopportune moment.

"Hey, it's only noon, the day is bound to get better, and I don't see eggs anywhere near here." He flashed the 1,000-watt smile I remembered so well from our high school days. Even in his Carhartts and work boots, he could be mistaken for a model who'd just walked off Ralph Loren's Colorado Ranch.

"Wanna go to lunch?" It took me a moment to answer. I started to regurgitate some platitude like 'successful car salesmen don't leave at lunchtime' and then I reconsidered.

"I need a knight in shining armor right now. Is that going to be you?" What? Did I just say that out loud? It was the anger talking.

"You got it, Double Al, let's go." He offered his elbow for me to take his arm. Before I took my jacket off the chair and made a show of leaving, I thought about tearing up the check in my hand that was mistakenly made out to Stretch instead of me. Instead, I dropped it in his filthy garbage can and then accidentally knocked his half-drunk Big Gulp 44 oz. soda on top of it. Wade glared at both of us as Burke once again held a door for me. There was a better than equal chance I wasn't coming back. Middleman, my ass!

CHAPTER 12

———

"**S**omeone's out here anxious to see you," Burke said. In an instant, I was wrapped up in the biggest bear hug I'd had in twenty years.

"How the hell are you, darlin'? You're a sight for sore eyes."

"Uncle Kenny!" It had probably taken this delightful man as long to forgive my skipping out on Copper Springs as it did Burke. But the joy I felt in seeing him was genuine and his seemed to be as well.

"My God, you look terrific, girl. A few years up in sandhill country didn't hurt you any. Burke told me you were here, but I had to see for myself. You can't trust the story from a guy like Burke who doesn't know which end of a heifer to pull the calf from."

There was nothing wrong with the relationship of these two. It was silly of me to think there might be; they were still best friends. Kenny gave me another kiss on the cheek and made me promise to come to the ranch for dinner soon, then he drove off in the ¾ ton truck they were picking up from the service department. Their ranch seemed to have a lot of truck problems.

"You look to be in a much better mood today than the last time you came to the dealership," I said to Burke.

"Well, better than you." He grinned again. "I actually came in to see you. If I'd come in to talk to that SOB in the Service Department, I wouldn't be so friendly. I let Kenny talk to Conrad today and I stayed out of the way.

"So, what? You're in sales? Not that you wouldn't be great at it but it just surprises me that you'd want to hang out with these guys." He chose his words as if they were dodging verbal landmines.

"I'm in sales, but it seems they don't want to credit me with selling anything." I changed the subject. "It was great to see Kenny." Did that imply that I wasn't as excited to see Burke? I hoped he didn't read it that way. Perhaps another subject change was due.

"What's been happening with your truck?"

"Montello's Service Department man is proving to be ethically challenged," he said as he pulled onto the highway toward town. "Twice he has charged us for work that was covered by the warranties and then denied it. I'm pretty sure he pockets the difference. I can't seem to catch up to Wally to tell him he's hired a common thief."

"You're a personal friend of Wallace then?" I was curious about Burke but also curious about the dealership owner I had yet to meet.

"My dad was a good friend of his, back when the dealership was on the up and up. Kenny is a friend of his still, but you know Kenny, there isn't anyone he doesn't call a friend. From what I hear, Wally is on the golf course or out of town most of the time, and he has turned more and more over to his no-good nephew. Do you work with him?"

"His no-good nephew?" Yep, he is one of my no-good bosses who just screwed me out of $1,600, I almost said. "It's hard to know who's the real boss," I added. "I bet you never thought you'd see me selling cars, did you?"

Burke pulled his truck out of traffic, stopped, then looked directly my way. "I never thought I'd ever see you again period." With such unbridled honesty, I almost melted. He looked at me like he did the day we said goodbye a hundred years ago. Then he got to the questions he had wanted to ask for twenty years. "Why didn't you stay in touch? Why didn't you answer my letters?"

"I meant to." How could I have been so taken with Peter and lost my way back here? We took our conversation to the local drive-in, BurgerTown, the very one we knew as kids. He remembered and ordered my favorite sandwich.

"It took me a long, long time to move on," he said between sips of his shake as though I had asked the question. "I just wanted to hear from you. But your grandma was good about telling me what you were doing, and I have to admit I lost interest after a while when she told me you were never coming back."

"Well, I guess that turned out not to be true," I said to him in mock insincerity. It was time to confess. "I should have been kinder to you, Burke. It took a lot of time for me to grow up. I think I may have just done it recently. I felt so ashamed that I made Grams swear not to tell me news about you and I think it was the first time she has actually done what I asked. I feel even worse now that I didn't know about your wife or your father. I didn't even send you a card."

"To be perfectly honest, I've never read any of the cards people did send. You should've just told me that you sent one. The cards are all in a paper grocery bag in the back floor of my closet. I may never read them."

For a long while, we didn't speak. Instead, we just sat in his front seat and dipped fries in paper baskets of catsup. It seemed as though the years we'd spent away from one another were floating over us, indistinguishable, one from another like a fog.

"I never forgot you, Al," he finally said. "I can't tell you how glad I am to have you back in town." He was wearing his heart right out there on his Carhartt sleeve. This was the reason for all my years of guilt—he was a wonderful, kind man. It felt so good to be sitting in the pickup with Burke that I forgot about the dealership until a ring of my cell jolted me back to reality.

"I'll have to check to see if we still have it," I said, knowing full well that the Jeep Rubicon the caller was inquiring about was having warranty work done. I felt my heart quicken. Here was another "be-back" and a good one. "Can you come by at 3:15 this afternoon, if the SUV is still available?" I had already learned that trick of asking for the appointment and setting a specific time. A salesman always moves to offense when the customer shows his weakness by calling back. With the spell broken, it was back to the showroom instead of riding off into the sunset with Burke.

"Sorry," I told Burke. "I guess I am still on duty."

"Do you like the job?" he asked. His simple question threw me.

Did I like the job? Of course not. The bosses and salesmen were total dweebs. Who would like walking out on a dusty lot and stepping in front of moving vehicles to prevent customers from driving by? Who would like to have a job thought to be sleazier than a...? Well, there was nothing sleazier, but his question did make me think.

"Unfortunately, I need a job, and I've exhausted every option in a hundred mile range for something in my career field. But if you think about it, everyone who lives in the west needs a vehicle of some kind, don't they? We aren't overrun with mass transit like they are back East. People here need their cars to earn money, to transport their children, to take someone to the hospital. I see myself as filling that need for people. I try to make the best fit between the need and the ability to pay for the ride, or the need for security and convenience or style and speed. Everyone has a need, I guess. Like you needing enough horsepower to pull your stock trailer."

"Wow, when you put it that way it sounds very—respectable."

"I just wish my dad, or Uncle Pat would've warned me about the shenanigans behind the scenes. So, do I like it? The jury's still out on that one, but thank you for asking." I'll need to keep asking myself that on a daily basis.

"This may be kind of forward," Burke sputtered. "But do you want to come out to the ranch and have a sunset dinner with me on Saturday night?" I looked at him, startled. Did he just ask me to ride off into the sunset with him? "Oh, it's nothing really," he continued. "We sometimes grab some fried chicken and head up to the ridge and watch the sunset from Logan's Point. But you're right. It might be kind of early. I don't mean early for us, I mean early in the year. We can talk about it next time." He was actually blushing and speeding out of the parking lot.

"I'd love to do that sometime." We sat quietly until he pulled up at the front windows of the dealership. Burke jumped out to come around and open my door. I let him.

"Watch your step," he said and helped me down from the one-ton truck by holding my arm at the elbow.

"It's great to see you again Burke." Was I gushing?

"Yes, mighty fine to have you back in the territory." He was adorable.

I took my leave and strolled in the side door. I didn't look back at Burke because I had already moved into combat mode. It took every ounce of my concentration to remember the different steps to a deal. If they wouldn't give me yesterday's car deal they sure as hell would l give me the one I would snag today. I went out to Service and wove my way around the work pits to talk to K.C., the mechanic working on the Rubicon, to ask if it would be done in time to show it at 3:15. Affirmative. Of course, I told K.C. that I needed it at 2:45. That was how we did business in "Don't Trust Anyone to Get the Job Done on Time or Done Correctly" world, and I was quickly mastering the nuances of the native tongue.

CHAPTER 13

I took the shortcut to the showroom through the service writer's area, still brimming with delight at my first lunch with Burke in twenty years and anticipating my serious sales prospect. I glided along unaware of what was coming next.

Something pinched my elbow, so tight it might have been a hay hook. I nearly toppled. I reacted on pure instinct, remembering the women's safety programs I'd attended. With speed and reflexes I didn't know I possessed, I yanked my knee up. It connected solidly with the aggressor's wide-open groin. The attacker's knees buckled and I looked down to see the top of the Service Manager's head. The rest of him was doubled over below. Just like that, we'd gotten better acquainted.

Angel had entered the small space behind me in time to see the grab, but she didn't have the angle to see the knee. She grinned and gave me a vigorous thumbs-up when she realized ConMan was groaning, then backed herself around the corner toward the restroom. Conrad couldn't see her, but she could watch from there to make sure this went no further. Was she worried about him or me? When the monster finally came up for air, he was mad as Godzilla.

"I didn't mean to hurt y—" I started to say, but he interrupted and spat half-breath words in my face.

"You stay away from my mechanics, you, hear."

"Don't ever grab me like that again, you, hear." He liked my comment even less than the knee. He leaned closer.

"Don't mock me, sweetie. You stay out of my work area, and if you need vehicle information, you come to me."

"You were at lunch," I growled, using the lowest register in my voice. I winked at Angel as I backed away and she scurried out the other side of the hall. I had no idea if he was at lunch or not, but it wasn't a risky guess.

"Then it can wait," he said. He slumped in his chair, put his glasses on the desk in front of him and continued to rub himself in the groin. He certainly didn't need to know that I was showing the Jeep at 3:15. I strolled to the showroom where my buddy Angel had already told the tale. Clay and NewKid were standing like athletes listening to The Star-Spangled Banner before a game with their hands crossed firmly in front, covering their private parts.

"Here, sit at this desk. Would you like us to get you coffee? Is this chair okay? We could switch it with that desk over there?"

"All right, you guys have made your point," I said.

"Not as decidedly as you made yours," NewKid said. They moved on outside to the smoking parlor. As they left, Clay looked my way but spoke to NewKid.

"And I heard all that old ConMan did was tell her he couldn't get her Mini Cooper in for an oil change today." They were being cute, but I was not happy to have had such an uncomfortable exchange in my first real meeting with our esteemed Service Department Manager. Riding off into any sunset, especially Burke's, was sounding better and better. The job was just too hard, the people too rough. Then I asked myself the most important question: If I left today, what would I do tomorrow?

I gave Mr. Montello the heads up that I had a be-back coming in. The story of the incident disseminated in less than ten minutes. Angel joined the smokers for a moment or two, so at least they heard the news from the eyewitness. My anxious customer arrived at 3 p.m. When he spotted me, he waved like we were old friends and practically bounced across the glossy vinyl floor.

In car lot parlance, Jeffrey was "one-legged," which meant he was alone without his other buying half so the onlookers assumed there was no deal. A "one-legged" Up was typically worthless because those folks were information gatherers. Sure, one day they would buy, but would it even be from this dealership? I can already hear the ladies screaming. I'm single. I make good money. I buy my own car. For every single woman who actually buys her car alone, on the spot, there are one hundred more accompanied by a father, brother, or friend assisting and advising. And of the married women, only one in 500 would buy without their hubby. The funny thing is only the women got offended by this observation, yet very few of the men who come in one-legged buy. Jeffrey Rubicon was the exception; he already had his wife's permission. I was well on my way to making my first deal that no one else could claim—ever. *So, Birdie, don't screw this up.*

I'm not great at poker, but in Jeffrey, I saw "tells" everywhere. He had the nervous energy of a newborn pot-bellied pig rooting around for his first meal. Earlier in the week when he had come in with his wife, his cheeks looked like someone had sandpapered them. Today, his entire face was crimson; even his oversized ears seemed on fire. He had a well-used checkbook pad without a cover sticking out of his shirt pocket. No doubt his wife handed it to him as he left after lunch when she removed the fancy keychain off the set of keys that proclaimed them to be Steelers fans. The keys were now on a simple ring ready for the trade. "Tell, tell, tell!" Sorry, Jeffrey, I win this round. You aren't leaving here without a Sporty Red Jeep today.

"Montello would like someone to drive your trade before we make the final deal," I told my customer. This was standard procedure. He handed over the keys but like all traders, he couldn't help but add a few comments that he should have kept to himself.

"The clutch is sticking a little, and remember, it had a new odometer put in a few years back. The paperwork's in the glove box." He was blabbering as I was putting the keys on Montello's desk. I didn't relay the clutch concern to Mike—why would I? Whatever was wrong with Jeffrey's car was not my problem. I attempted to chat him up.

"Have you seen the paper today? How about those Pirates? Would you like a soda?" My luck was nothing if not bad—Mike had asked ConMan to be the evaluation driver. Angel told me that he knew nothing about cars, that he'd never even been a mechanic, but for him to evaluate this car on this day? Maybe his sore crotch might disqualify him.

I looked toward Montello's office, but he was already out smoking again. Was it possible his smoking habit had stepped up since I came on board? Of course, ConMan would screw the deal if he could by slicing and dicing Jeffrey's trade. I wondered, did Montello ask him on purpose to see how I'd react? Now I was as nervous as Jeffrey. I spent the waiting time trying to control my own tells. If I didn't get this, I told myself, this was my last day in this purgatory. I felt a sense of relief at making that decision. I guess I didn't like the job after all. Okay, Bingham, you win. I almost picked up the house phone and announced it over the loudspeaker. Who has today's calendar date for the "guess how long this worthless rookie lasts" pool? My pity party was interrupted by the manager summoning me.

"Conrad found a serious knock in the back," the boss said. "He thinks the trade needs a new rear end."

"Of course, he did," I bellowed, then I launched into why I was sure ConMan would love to scuttle this deal today or any day but Montello stopped me.

"I heard about your trying to rearrange some of his manhood, so I asked K.C. and he said it might need a clutch. Other than that, solid and he had worked on this rig last month—just minor stuff and Conrad knew it. Send your customer in and let's get it done."

And just like that, it's easy-peasy when the powers that be, want it to be. Jeffrey became the owner of a newer SUV, but not before he had to call the wife to bring down the title of the trade that he had forgotten and the snow tires he had promised to have in the back.

Within the hour I was set to perform the ritual of attaching the temporary license plate to the back of the sold vehicle for the first time in front of the windows where everyone could watch. Fifteen minutes later Mr. M. handed me my very first commission check. $1,015.45! Whoa! *I'll give this Godforsaken place one more day.*

I practically skipped out to the parking lot because I was so anxious to head home and tell Grams that I'd collected my first commission check. A big one. As I drove through town, my mind wandered back to lunch with Burke. Do I trust myself not to break his heart again? Or would he break mine this time?

For some strange reason, all I wanted for dinner was fried chicken.

CHAPTER 14

To avoid the ConMan the next morning, I walked around the back of the building and entered through the Detail bays, hoping no one saw me.

"You're in early today aren't you, Austin?" The darling Hispanic lot boy was oil changing. There was no sign of Angel.

"I'm helping out doing inventory at my granddad's hardware store tonight."

"Which hardware store?" I asked.

"Stein's Hardware," he said, "the old one downtown."

"Austin, are you my Gramma Luella's neighbor?"

"Sure. Me and my dad, we both live with my Grampa Mario."

"Who's your dad?" It sounded like an interrogation.

"Jack Stein, but everybody calls him Cuervo." Austin continued to work so he didn't see the surprised look on my face. Jack Stein? My first kiss Jack Stein?

"Your dad is Jack Stein? I thought he lived in California." This time he stopped working, stood tall and looked at me with what appeared to be annoyance.

"We did, but we live here now. My mom and dad are divorced."

"So you know my Gramma Lou then?" I asked.

"I told you I did. She used to have us over to dinner all the time before you came back. We just live two houses away from you."

"Does your dad work at the hardware store?"

"Oh, no. He's a parole officer. He works with border patrol agents too. He drives around the county mostly, but he has a lot of time off."

"Nice," I said, feeling conspicuous because K.C., the jeep mechanic, had stepped over to make sure his charge was working. God forbid ConMan thought I was short-changing his department again.

"Good talking to you. I'm sorry Grams doesn't invite you over now" I added. Awkward. It was yet another reminder of how much I'd disrupted Gram's life.

I tried to ignore the Service Department, but I saw the guy that Angel called ConMan's cousin having words with our service manager. Our showroom wasn't a bastion of fine fashion. There was a joke in the industry. What would you say to a car salesman wearing a suit? Will the defendant please rise? With this crew, I doubted they would wear anything other than jeans to their own funeral, fancy dresser Montello excepted. Even so, ConMan's cousin stuck out as especially grubby in his "Gun Control is How Quickly You Acquire Your Target" T-shirt, flip flops, and khaki shorts. When he left, I noticed his truck had Montana plates, and I saw that he also stopped to visit with Mater.

CHAPTER 15

It's no secret that the car sales industry is dominated by a fraternity of miscreants, opportunists, and scallywags. Three perfect specimens were idly lined up at the windows of the dealership waiting for the next sucker to drive in. I was with them. Was I the miscreant or the opportunist? It was muggy and overcast, strange weather for April. Everyone knew that bad weather meant no business, the whole day a complete waste of time.

The moisture reconstituted a bitch session from a couple of days earlier about how the number of prospects at the dealership was dwindling and how there were too many salesmen on the floor. It was a regular beef. They didn't even bother to mention saleswomen because they didn't think of me as a threat—I'd soon be gone. They didn't think of me as anything, and that had begun to be insulting.

"You know what I noticed recently?" Bingham dangled his question like we were all going to chomp on it. Nobody bit, but he continued. "There aren't any teenagers dragging their dads in to look at cars anymore."

"Come to think about it," Rich said, "at graduation time, we used to have kids all over that used lot."

"Well, of course, there is a significant cultural upheaval in play," I chimed in. They gawked at me like they didn't even realize I had the capacity to speak. "Really, it's true," I continued. "Teens in the '50s, '60s and '70s had to have wheels to meet up with their friends. They needed locomotion for socialization. Youngsters today have their smartphones to connect them. Friendship is no longer based on geography, haven't you noticed? Kids aren't even getting their licenses anymore. If they want to physically go somewhere now they just use Uber." My male cohorts continued to stare at me like I was from outer space. "No, really," I said, "it's a complete paradigm shift."

"What the hell is she talking about?" Rich huffed. "You can't feel up a girl in the back seat if you don't have a car and all you have in your hand is a cell phone." They all snickered and started to head off. Oops, I did it again—I broke up the party. Some things I'm better at than others.

"You can if you have the virtual reality headset," NewKid added, then he winked at me. NewKid could actually visualize what he was talking about, so he won the smart remark contest, at least in my book. As he left he whispered, "These guys all think Uber is a character in a Disney movie. You're not dealing with Raytheon scientists here, Ms. Alton. I thought you had tumbled to that a while back."

NewKid was smarter than anyone else in the building unless Wallace's dog Orbit came in, but I didn't let myself get attached. He'd be back at school soon and I desperately hoped I'd be back at a school, any school, somewhere soon as well.

An hour later the clouds produced an Ark-floating deluge and through that a muffler-challenged, rattletrap vehicle put-putted by the front window. What appeared to be a late twenty-something woman with dark black hair was at the wheel. Even through the downpour, we could see that the girl had numerous tattoos, multiple face piercings and was carrying more than a few excess pounds. Bingham and Clay turned away and pretended not to see her. The others ran to the far reaches of the building like rambunctious puppies let off leashes. Thirty seconds passed and the conversations in the showroom started up again as though she wasn't even there.

In the musty key room, I uncovered a stained yellow Marlboro Man rain slicker that was hanging on a nail under an old sales banner. By the look of it, it had belonged to the actual Marlboro Man who had left it behind when he galloped off to Madison

Avenue in the '60s. I hung it on my shoulders then trudged out into the driving rain which I expected to be cold. Instead, it was oddly warm, like a shower. Good thing because the slicker leaked.

I found the young woman and her passenger in the front seat of a fire-engine-red sports coupe with a five-inch wide air spoiler on the back. It was inexpensive car but dolled up with a few doodads to interest the twenty-something market. Good value or not, I knew, just as did all the high and dry salesmen ignoring her did, that there was no sale to be had here.

The girl's name was Aiello, pronounced I-L-O. She was smart and completely serious about buying this car. We had all misjudged.

"Aiello received a workman's comp settlement from her three surgeries," her mom, who was the passenger, told me. She had been managing a Chili's Restaurant when a box weighing ninety pounds fell off a top shelf and seriously injured her neck and back.

Just before we took a test drive, Aiello showed me an envelope from her handbag that was as fat as a stuffed pork chop.

"I have $18,000 in cash with me."

There was nothing left for me to say except: "The keys are over the visor."

When we returned, Rich had to get up from the desk he had laid claim to and all the others migrated to Montello's office like a clutch of homing pigeons. I could tell Montello was furious by the way he summoned me to his office.

"What are you trying to pull here?" He motioned his troops to move along. They ignored him.

"I have a buyer for a car that you are spending a ton of money advertising, Mr. M. I should think that would please you on a bleak day like today."

"What's her name?" he barked.

"Aiello."

"Yel-low? Is she an Indian?"

"She's tribal," I answered, unwilling to give up all shreds of political correctness.

"That trade she drove in is a piece of crap."

"She doesn't have a trade."

"Then what are you trying to pull here? How much is she putting down?"

"She's not giving us a 'downy' today," I said. "Why don't you let me write it up? I don't have anything else to do."

"Don't you let that girl think she is going to buy that car." His voice couldn't have been more full-throated if he was an opera singer practicing scales.

"She doesn't think she's buying the car, she knows she's buying it." So this is what it felt like. The enjoyment Montello and Wade got each day making us all squirm when it wasn't really necessary. Squirm away! Wallow in it, Montello.

When I removed the slicker, gawkers gathered to see if my wet T-shirt offered any amusement as I wrote up the deal. I stepped to the back and gave my buddy Angel a heads up and handed her the keys so the car could receive its final detail.

"I'll make it look better than Wallace's Pimpmobile Cadillac."

I couldn't have stayed on the lot one more day without Angel. As I glided confidently toward the office, Rich stepped in behind me. "You really aren't getting the hang of this are you, Alton? The rest of us know not to waste our time on a customer like her."

"Gosh, Rich, please don't let your concern for my efficiency keep you and Bingham from shuffling through your 3x5 cards. I'm sure there is a diamond in that stack of rubble somewhere." He huffed and turned away. I entered the office with all the pages as well as the tattered but still sealed envelope with what Aiello told me was exactly $17,995. Wade and Stretch crowded in behind to see me squirm, up close and personal. Instead, I coiled up in front of Montello's desk and showed them my fangs.

"What are you trying to pull here?" Mike said for the third time.

"I'm selling a car." I hissed as I stared at the two onlookers in the doorway. "Isn't that what we're here for or are we here to gawk?" The crew didn't budge as they hadn't seen anything to make them

think I was not about to be canned. As I dropped the thick envelope on the wooden desk, Mike grabbed for it before I let go and
it split open like a cracked egg, with dozens of green bills fluttering
down, almost filling the ink blotter.

"It covers the advertised price. See, I've written it here." I pointed to the sales line on my perfect write-up.

"Where'd she get it? Was it stolen? We have to account for
anything over ten grand, Homeland Security you know."

"I do," I said. "It wasn't stolen. She just received a settlement for
a Work Comp injury." The two men behind me were now backing
out of the small office. The show was over, but Montello was still
blustering.

"She'll have to pay the documentation fee; you know we don't
ever waive the DOC." Mike was always the guy who could squeeze
one more dime out of the widows and orphans.

"That's why you're discounting this vehicle the $200 it takes to
cover the fee."

"We don't do that," he said.

"You do today."

"No, you need to get the DOC fee."

"All right," I said and with no argument. I stood up to go, "Let
me take this cash back and go tell her that, and send her on her
way." I reached to gather up the bills. Mike stopped me.

"She doesn't have another two hundred bucks?"

"She doesn't have two more dollars." I was determined to get
this concession for her as an apology for all the people that had sold
her short, just as I had.

———

Once again, I got to be the center of the ceremony that was putting the temporary plate on the newly sold car as the rain clouds
parted. *Cue the Sunshine!* Afterword, I returned to the sales floor
where I was now a total pariah. Only Clay made any comment or
spoke to me.

"You deserved that one," Clay mumbled as he headed out for home.

I silently agreed and waited patiently for my commission check and more importantly, this car had what the dealership called a "spiff" on the vehicle. A spiff was an amount of money offered as an incentive on certain models to light a fire under us salesmen to get it sold. It worked better on the most greedy, competitive types, but I wasn't above taking them. $250 additional pay. I needed it more as each paupered day went by. As I stared at the office, I was not sure, but I thought I saw Mike and Wade each pocketing some cash just before Wade sidestepped out the south door, looking over his shoulder to see who might be watching. If that was true, I didn't want to know, as long as some of it was mine. Mike handed me an envelope as he made his exit out the north door. He said nothing. Since I was the only one left on the floor, I opened it. The check for the $18,000 sale was, wait for it—$75. That's right, I had just given Montello 180 $100 bills, and in return, he gave me less than one. Amazing how an unexpected sum can seem like a delight and the same amount feels paltry if you were expecting more. I was indeed disappointed. It wouldn't be the last time.

Mike popped his head back in the door. "Oh, just so you know, that $250 spiff? That ended yesterday."

CHAPTER 16

In the evenings at home, I just went through the motions, eating, and a lot of sleeping. A damp dishrag would have been better company. So, when Grams told me she wanted me to meet her friend Geneva and Geneva's daughter Dana, I was pleased to break the spell. I wondered if Grams was holding them back just as the dealership was not ordering business cards for me to hand out, both wondering if I was here to stay. I wanted to tell her that I would get on my feet and get moved on soon to let her have her life back but I was too scared it might not be true.

"Dana's in her early forties. I'm sure you'll like her," Grams told me as we left the house.

"Those words usually introduce a bad blind date," I said. "We aren't meeting David again, are we?" She ignored me as I helped her into the passenger side of her vehicle.

"Dana works at the police station," Grams continued, "I think she actually runs the place. She's the one that helped me set up the scanner." Then she calmly added, "Her mom has cancer and is no longer in remission."

The intel on Geneva took a moment to find its way into my consciousness.

"Oh, Grams, I'm so sorry to hear about your friend."

"I know. It sucks." The juvenile word "sucks" seemed strange coming from Grams, but she was right; cancer sucks. She was old enough to have lost more than one friend that way.

When we arrived at Maria's Mexican Restaurant, I held the heavy carved wooden door as Grams slipped through heading toward the table where she saw her friends. I trailed along behind, slowed by the weight of what I had just heard. Grams made introductions and I did not hesitate to order.

"Bud Light Draft, tall," I said to the waiter as soon as he presented his cherubic face.

"Make that two." said Dana, with proper enthusiasm and a large toothy grin. I liked her instantly. "No, on second thought, make mine Red Beer," she said.

"Mine too," I parroted. Dana had bright mischievous eyes under her square-cut bangs. In my teaching days, when I would see that look from the little Madisons, or McKennas in my classes, I could tell they were in for a life of merriment. Dana seemed able to have fun, even with Geneva so sick. I admired that.

The women asked about the dealership and I made them laugh by recounting the idiotic shenanigans I'd already encountered, but then I did something I rarely did since I arrived in the Springs—I listened. Before me were three strong women from different generations who handled adversity with humor and grit. Grams shared tales I'd never heard before of the looniest Rexall Drug Store customers from the old days and Dana shared hilarious antics by the many wannabe policemen, never women, who had circled through the revolving doors of the Copper Springs station. Her mom, Geneva, regaled us with her account of being a big-haired young woman from Kentucky married to a Fort Huachuca Army Sergeant in the early eighties even as she sat before us wearing a turban having lost all the big hair she had to her treatments. The stories were light-years removed from those of the privileged, preppy, over-educated professorial types of my previous life and just as far from the nasty, gossip-addicted, pettiness of the crew that was my new work life.

Here at Maria's Mexican Food was a table set with the priceless porcelain of authenticity and deep friendship. We feasted for several hours, enjoying each other's company.

"I'm ready to call it a night," Geneva finally said. "This chemo really takes the starch out of a person." This was the first mention of her illness, and she obviously didn't expect any more to be said.

———

"I told you," Grams said later. "There's nothing like a friend to make life seem more worthwhile—friends and granddaughters." She put her hand on my forearm and gave it a squeeze.

"Well, Gramma Lou, with as many folks as you call your friends, your life must be pretty darn wonderful."

"It sure got a lot better when you arrived." Her sweet proclamation turned on a faucet; I had trouble seeing my way as we neared the bungalow. What if I lost my dear Grams the way Dana was going to lose Geneva? What would I do then?

I was still gazing out at the children's park across the way two hours later. How easy those summers of my life were before my sixteenth year when it all changed. I slipped on my Levis, sandals, and a light jacket then tip-toed out through the kitchen to the garage, and on to the moon-lit tilted merry-go-round where I felt like I was twelve again. The metal grab bars were cold but the wooden decking was surprisingly warm. Instinctively, I began to use my left foot to propel the flat wooden platform round and round as I lay down and watched the brilliant Milky Way swirl in the sky above me like a slow-motion video made by the scientists at the Kitts Peak Observatory. The swirling high-low motion, the dampness of tears on my face and the squeak, click, squeak, click, of the twirling carousel almost lullabied me to sleep. I had good reason to know that people in my life wouldn't be around forever but somehow, up until now, I always thought an exception would be made for my Gramma Louella.

CHAPTER 17

After life in Nebraska, the rugged treeless peaks of southern Arizona still astonished me. The El Jefe Mountain to the east delayed the actual sunrise in Copper Springs for almost twenty minutes, but the sky was bright red with anticipation. It gave the morning ritual of "keying" cars a Zen quality. Those words would of course never leave my lips. The boys already considered me a nut job.

To the uninitiated, "keying" usually means a vandal has added a jagged, disfiguring pinstripe to the side your new Corvette. On the car lot, the term meant distributing each set of keys to the corresponding vehicle at the start of every day, then pulling them back every evening, leaving over two hundred cars open with keys inside. What could possibly go wrong?

"Everybody participates in keying," Montello repeatedly told me in my non-interview. Did I strike him as a shirker? However, there was a loophole. Salesmen with car deals late in the day did not have to key, which had exempted me three nights running and since I completed those sales that explained the total freeze out that I was enjoying from the entire sales force. Even Clay had steered clear. They thought that I milked those deals so I didn't have to join them. Maybe I did. Maybe I didn't. But I wouldn't be the first to do it, even if I'd intended to. Either way, on the fourth morning, what was designed as a two-man job was once again—me, alone. That is, except for the tow truck guy and his banged-up doggie, Juicebox, who were mysteriously following along about twenty paces behind, watching me wrestle the heavy ring.

The gangly Stretch, who had a smoker's cough, but was built like a distance runner, oddly appeared out of nowhere and snatched the key ring as though it were a baton being passed in his last relay. Had he come to help me? Well, how unusual. Maybe I misjudged my coworker?

"Mike said to show you how to get done faster. We've got a meeting this morning." They left me out here to solo then they call me inept for it. Stretch's acne looked far more pronounced when the sun finally peeked over the mountain. He was hung over too. *I'll be damned, he has a cigarette over each ear.*

The key organizing system was crude. The large wire ring weighed about as much as a five-gallon bucket full of slop that we fed our pigs back in Nebraska. I was glad he was slinging them.

As I opened and shut each door, I realized that most buyers who visit the pre-owned lot assume they're looking at trade-ins. They're not. The used lot was actually filled mostly with lease returns— purchased at auction—but trade-ins are what the dealership would prefer you to think. That's why most vehicles on the used car lot were some variant of gray, fifty shades of gray, just like most rentals ever produced. By comparison, the new vehicle lot was colorful and paved of course. There were acres and acres of heat reflecting blacktop all lit up twenty-four hours a day, brighter than the wall at the Mexican border. Unlike the border, it curiously had no fence and no cameras either. Weren't we looking at a couple of million bucks sitting here? And every car spent the day with its key in it?

Stretch's gait and leg length were even longer than mine. He was moving fast, randomly tossing keys on hoods the same as a flower girl might drop rose petals along a church aisle.

"It's already pretty warm," I said as I passed him coming back down the row next to me.

"Warm?" he bellowed back, By now he had a cigarette dangling from his lips as he talked. I was making banal weather conversation and he overreacted like I just said his blind dog looked like a des-ert-weary pack rat.

"Honey, if you think this is warm, you might as well quit now." He said this as he was running away behind me as fast as his extra-long spindles would propel him.

The "why don't you quit" suggestion was a constant irritating theme. Don't need to waste time training her—she won't be here long. They were hoping that was true since I just kicked their butts the previous three days. When I made it to the end of the row, I looked up, and my partner Stretch was already back up in the smoker's circle. I was halfway through with my part of the task. Hell, maybe I was slow.

It was a rule, I'd been told, that no one could leave the lots in the morning until all the keys were in the cars. From my vantage point, that was more like a guideline than an actual rule. *Quit, huh? You'd love it if you could get me to quit wouldn't you, you pencil-legged, acne-faced—Okay, that's enough, Birdie.* But if he thought I'd quit now, clearly, he hadn't sized Birdie Alton up properly. If I were a quitter, I wouldn't have taken fourteen years to get out of a lousy marriage. My mind wandered to Peter. I wondered how many co-eds he nested before he decided to fly away to Barcelona with one.

I concentrated so hard on the task at hand that I was startled when a pearl-colored one-ton Escalade truck the size of West Texas pulled between my last two rows. The big door opened and a short bow-legged cowboy wannabe in a Toby Keith hat, a red shirt, and new Levi jeans covering his ample rump slid down to the ground followed by a familiar-looking rambunctious pooch.

"Howdy, Miss. Birdie, is it? I'm Wallace Winchell, but they call me Wally. That's Orbit. We're both happy to finally meet you." I didn't bother to tell Wally, the biggest boss, that Orbit and I were acquainted.

"Yes, sir," I said. I straightened my back and gazed straight forward like an army one-striper with a four-star general stopping by on inspection. I stood at attention. *Don't salute. Don't salute!*

"I know Louella," he said, referring to Grams. "She sure speaks highly of you."

"You too, sir," I emphasized sir. Was I Richard Gere in An Officer and a Gentleman? "I mean Mr. Winchell." *Birdie, relax.*

"No, no, it's Wally. Call me Wally, will you please? Say, are you out here keying all by yourself, when I can see as plain as that sunrise that the rest of my crew is up there with my General Manager smoking and shooting the shit?"

"I, uh, usually key by myself," I said thinking that would diffuse the situation.

"We'll have none of that," he boomed. His remark was amplified to try to get the guys to hear. They didn't. He excused himself to drive his truck the last fifty feet up to the dealership windows. Orbit stayed with me. Wallace hollered back from his open window: "I hear you're a golfer. We'll have to go play a few rounds before the tournament." I had sold four cars and I still couldn't get out from under my little white golf lie. I remember my dad saying once when it comes to golf, your lie can be important.

Great, I'm going to be late and they will start the meeting without me. No sooner had that thought popped into my head when I looked up to see all the other salesmen come hurtling at me like driving range golf balls toward an unsuspecting gopher. Someone should've yelled, "Fore!"

"What help do you need?" "Which cars have you done?" "Which direction are you going?" And just like that, my used car lot chore got accomplished with the snap of a finger. So, this is how we do the teamwork thing.

CHAPTER 18

was expecting gems of wisdom from Wallace as the pope might give when he visited the peasants. Would we be blessed with heavenly sales skills instruction and become disciples? St. Michael Montello seemed to worship Wally, at least it looked like it. He practically kissed his feet before the meeting. I didn't notice if Wally had a Papal ring.

What I got, what we all got, was a long-winded diatribe. It turned out our Wally was loveable, generous, thoughtful, and did an impressive impression of a javelina for the TV ads, but his description also had to include wordy, dull, and repetitive. The gathering went far past the usual half-hour mark before Jason called Wally away to film commercials. Clay told me afterward it was the eleventh time he'd heard the loyal collie story from Wallace's youth.

"That must have been some collie," I said to Clay. "I wonder if Orbit's jealous."

"I know what you mean. Trying to keep up with the specter of the long-lost brother. Orbit's probably in some doggie therapy, but, don't sell him short. He's smarter than half the guys here," Clay said.

"And equally as smart as the rest of us," I added.

The dog stories were all schmaltzy and sentimental, but I thought it was rather sweet even if it pre-empted the Super Bowl trophy acceptance moment for the most car sales this week that I had practiced in front of my bedroom mirror. *I want to thank the members of the Car Lot Academy.* The others were giving me the silent treatment so I figured they had already given my success a commemoration of sorts.

"Birdie Alton—Manager's office." The demand was reduced to shorthand and blared inside as loud as outside, where it often had to roust sleeping salesmen out of cars three acres away. The GM was looking right at me as the system echoed the announcement—I could hear his actual voice better than the loudspeakers. I took two steps and stood in his doorway feigning respect for authority. Then I noticed Wade.

"Are we having a manager's meeting?" They glared for a moment then got to their point.

"The guys are not keying with you." This was a revelation? Mike who spent half his time out smoking with the offenders enjoyed their making fun of me as much as they did, which he would deny vehemently if accused. I was already getting acquainted well enough with him to know that if it would be beneficial to Mike to have not said something, it could be unsaid. He could have a career in politics.

"Well, I didn't say anything to Wallace if that's what you mean." I was keeping my eye on Wade twitching his mustache. He scared me.

"That's not the way it's done here," Wade said. All evidence to the contrary. "No one comes into the building until all the keys are placed."

"It won't happen again, "Montello added. A flick of his head and I was dismissed. He served me his over-baked platitude with a side of witness, then he went back to his computer monitor looking at adorable poodles dancing the Cha Cha on their back legs. This was my greatest difficulty with this place. Unless Wallace was in the building or threatening to stop by, then selling cars or training to sell them was the last thing on anyone's mind. Then I realized that neither of those things was more important to Wallace than a loyal childhood collie. Were dancing puppies very far removed from that? Wallace's current puppy love, Orbit, it turns out, was smarter than the management too.

CHAPTER 19

By noon, Jason's donut delivery was reduced to a single ring of rubber, with pink frosting and yellowed coconut on top. I ate it anyway. As I attempted to dispose of the box, the flimsy cardboard corners un-tabbed themselves and rained chunks of dried frosting and sprinkles all over the sales counter and onto the computer keyboards on the desks below, sending the two receptionists into major fits of annoyance. Why not, I may as well get the rest of the staff on board with the hate Birdie routine. I couldn't feel like more of a loser. It was getting worse.

It took me twenty minutes to snag an Up on the sedan lot—a man in business clothes who wanted to look at a light-colored sedan. Light-gray I hope. He decided, with my urging, to drive a low mileage Taurus.

"It's for my wife, Barbara. If I like it, she's going to come down and meet me here. May I drive it?" Bingo! Was this job getting easier or was it my imagination? Sure, he was one-legged this time but what about one-legged Jeffrey? I sold him and I had just illustrated one of the Holy Grails of the car salesman's Bible: Get the customer to drive the car. I was feeling smug, sale number five coming up.

I reached above the visor, retrieved the keys and handed them to Randy, my enthusiastic customer. He tried the key in the ignition and then tried again. He turned the key upside down and tried a third time.

"It doesn't fit. Doesn't work," he said. I reached awkwardly for the jingling mass dangling between his legs and tried to start the car. *What the...?* Did Stretch put the key on the wrong car? I looked closer at the tag; the keys belonged to the pickup parked right next to us.

"I'm so sorry; these must have gotten switched," I said. I hopped out, silently cursing Stretch the entire time. I made the trade then hopped back in, handing Randy the correct set.

"These don't fit either," he said. This time the key fob indicated that they were for a small truck three vehicles away. I hadn't even looked. Was the key mix-up deliberate? I lost control of Randy, another big no-no. He got out while deciding he needed to "look further" and skip the game of cat and mouse. In my embarrassment, I felt relieved to watch him drive off. Was Wicked Wade watching? Of course, he was. Thank God Wade didn't know that Randy was ready for a test drive and then I lost him. That would be a hanging offense.

Wade motioned me in. Too bad, Wade. I know you are far too lazy to come out and make your point. Wade fancied himself as a puppeteer pulling strings from up in his tower, only in our case they were chains, not strings, and jerking them was his life's work.

I hid out on the lot for the next hour bouncing around like a pinball between rows—straightening the key mess out. As the day came to a close, Rich and Clay had deals going and Bingham went home early so once again, I found myself keying alone even though "that's not the way it's done here." I always looked over one shoulder to make sure the ConMan wasn't in the vicinity. He was the one car lot inhabitant I would go in to avoid.

The keys in our one luxury car were missing. Gone. The gleaming black BMW with red leather seats and a special Bentley Grille was open and keyless. Wally was selling this four-wheeled conquest from his personal collection, dumping it like a guy might trade in a first wife with too many miles on her for a new revved-up trophy model. As the boys say, everything is about sex, especially cars, but Wallace had several new trophies in his garages. No keys. Had it been Rich who had been showing this vehicle and took the keys? I left it open and went inside.

"Mike, there's no keys in the BMW. What do you want me to do?"

"Were they there this morning?"

"They all had keys," I said. Was that true? "Do you know where Stretch is? I could ask him if he remembers putting one on that hood."

"Just go back and lock it up. We'll deal with it tomorrow," the boss said.

"What if we can't find them tomorrow? How will we get in?"

"Just lock it up!" He was not in good humor so I backed out of his office and was more than glad to lock it and get the hell out of Dodge.

CHAPTER 20

Until the previous day, experiencing the beauty of the morning sky and the Zen-like mindless keying were my favorite parts of the job. Montello announced that he had switched us all around for the keying chore so I didn't go back to the lot where the BMW was. He gave Clay and me one of the new lots in front of his window.

"You fuckin' abandon her out there again and I'll fuckin' fire you!" I heard Mike say, supposedly out of my earshot. Clay glared at me as he passed by, clearly not pleased to be linked up with the village pariah. Well, who would be?

"Stretch didn't come in today," Clay told me when he finally felt like talking. Clay was a jabberer so it was hard for him to keep quiet very long. "No one seems to know where he is."

"He was hung way over yesterday," I said. "He looked pretty bad."

"He always looks bad," Clay said.

"I mean worse than bad."

The days at the AutoMall were beginning to run into each other like a prison sentence. A run-on sentence I thought. It was three days before anyone missed Wally's BMW.

The vehicles in the front line were in such disarray again they looked like dominos thrown down on a felt table, some sideways, some backward and all the rest crooked. There were so many empty spots that no one really knew what should be here or there. Technically, it was Wade's job to keep track of inventory but blame was one of the few things he didn't take for himself. But it was clear the BMW was gone.

At last, some excitement. Grand Theft Auto! I sneaked into the smoker's circle; no one even noticed. Between puffs of Spirits and Pall Malls, several theories were bandied about.

"Someone kyped the BMW keys during the day and came back for the car in the middle of the night," said Bingham. The group let out a collective "Duh."

"Schoolboys took it for a joy ride, and we'll probably find it out in front of the movie theatre like the last two times it happened," offered NewKid.

"Does it happen often?" I waited for someone to say, "Who let you in?" But they didn't seem to notice.

"Every few months," Clay answered. I was shocked to learn that despite repeated events, there wasn't a single camera to record the theft. Everyone talked at once, and I was actually enjoying myself when I heard my name on the loudspeaker summoning me to Wade's office.

"Who do you think did this, Birdie?" Wade asked in his favorite accusatory tone.

"Has anyone seen Stretch?" I said, thinking Wade might make the connection I had made, but he didn't take the bait.

"You were the one with the key problems." Was he really was accusing me?

"Why are you singling me out? Stretch was there." Wade! Put two and two together here. A guy like Stretch, proficient with a Slim Jim, certainly has some car stealing experience.

"I think your customer has our BMW. Do you even have his phone number?" Wade managed to get his dig in.

"I know he's not from Copper Springs," I said.

"Hell, that really narrows it down, doesn't it?" Wade attempted to roll the end of his handlebar, but it was still too short. All he could manage was a limp Yosemite Sam.

"But he didn't have the demeanor of a thief," I said, defending my unknown suspect. "He has a family. He didn't even look at the BMW." I made my case but the judge wasn't listening and the jury smoking outside the window would no doubt convict.

"The police will be talking to you," he said. So, this was how he'd get me to quit. Bingham was right.

"Me? What about Stretch?" I whined.

"What about Stretch?" Wade shot me one of his patented sideways glares, with the half-opened eyes.

"Shouldn't we talk to him about the keys, too? He put the keys out that day. We should ask if he saw anything." Wade sat still, but his mustache twitched like a rabbit's whiskers.

"Stretch is in the county jail," he said, as though he was telling me one of our lucky clan had won a Maui vacation, then he added, "DUI."

"What was he driving when he was arrested?" Wade missed the overt link I'd finally made for him. Wade was a man of few words, and yet he shared more than he had ever done before.

I walked over to Clay. "Is Wade telling everyone that I lost the BMW?"

"Pretty much, but don't worry about it. It'll probably turn up with a local high-schooler behind the wheel. He'll be cruising the drag in another day or two. We always find the cars. Your problem with the Beemer is that it belongs to our illustrious owner."

When the place cleared out, I grabbed Angel's arm and guided her out the side door.

"Stretch is in the County Jail," I told her, delighted that for once, I had the good gossip. I didn't give a single thought as to who knew it came from me when she repeated it later.

"No shit? What happened?"

"DUI! I was hoping that Stretch and the BMW went missing together and that book chapter could get closed, but it looks like he was otherwise engaged. Mater towed his Kia back here."

"With all the work we give him, that tow guy's probably got a couple of million stashed somewhere, but he's not wasting it on wardrobe, is he?" I said.

"Maybe he's the smart one," Angel added. "Don't tell Linda in the office that I told you, but she kind of likes him."

"She likes who? Mater?" I felt like I was back at my junior high.

"And she thinks he's sweet on you."

"What! Sweet on me?"

"Hold your voice down."

"You mean Linda actually thinks that I'd go out with Mater?"

"Well, you're single, pretty and they're saying, well… they're saying that if you got laid maybe you wouldn't be such a sourpuss all the time. Did I say, sourpuss? I meant bitch."

"However true that statement is, it sure as hell wouldn't be Mater, now would it?" Angel flashed me a huge grin.

"God, I hope not because that would break a lot of other hearts around here."

"Especially my dear friend Wade's," I said.

"Indeed! Especially Wade's. You're right, he and Mater just might have a thing going." We laughed, but I couldn't help but think how far my prospects had actually fallen.

CHAPTER 21

"Little Deuce Coupe," was my current ringtone, annoying enough that it startled me out of a robotic stupor as I let my car drive itself to the grocery store after work. "Little Deuce Coupe, You don't know what I got." Nothing, I got nothing, I answered.

"Hey you, Mom and Lou went into town tonight to play Bingo. You want to get a beer and a burger at The Dback and swap some news?" Dana said.

"Depends, you got the good stuff? Because I have some good stuff."

"That settles it then. Meet you there in ten. I'm already on the way. We'll trade the contraband information over the hood of your Mini Cooper," she said.

"No! I'm hungry; we're going to have to go inside." I was happy to hear Dana sound upbeat. All the worry about her mom had taken a toll.

As I pulled into the Dback parking lot, I saw a Lone Pine pick-up parked near the front and my heart lilted. Really, it was lilting! Perhaps my heart thought I needed to get laid too. The wooden door opened toward me as I got near and two cowboys emerged and I saw them climb up into the Lone Pine truck. *Stand down, lilting heart.*

Dana had already set up shop at the far back booth.

"I was just headed to the grocery store to see if I could find organic vegetables somewhere in this town." I said as I arrived at the table, "I'm glad you called."

"Honey, the only thing organic in Copper Springs is the Wurlitzer in the choir loft at the Baptist Church. I'm surprised you don't know that already. What you need is some good home-grown Arizona Angus to keep your strength up." Dana motioned for the waiter to come by to take our orders. When he left, Dana asked, "What the heck is going on at your place?"

"I was hoping you would tell me. Did your guys arrest Stretch?" I asked.

"No, that was the sheriff's office, but we share the same lock-up. He had priors so it's taking your guys a while to get him out."

"What priors?" I asked.

"I probably can't tell you that, but let's just say, he was a busy boy."

"Okay, then, my turn," I said. "Did Wade report the missing BMW?"

"No. Now you've lost a Beemer! Losses never end there."

"One of Wally's personal vehicles; Of course, he has fifteen or twenty. I guess he drove this one quite a bit before he threw it over for his new pickup obsession so it's caused more of a stir than usual. Wade has been telling the whole staff that I lost it."

"You have it, huh? Great! Is it outside? Let's take it to Tucson for a joy ride."

"I wish. Then at least I'd have air conditioning that works. At any rate, I'll be more than happy when it finally turns up." Our waitress put our Rattler Special cheeseburgers with pickles, lettuce, and mayo down in front of us, and I poured us each another glass this time from our second ice-cold pitcher.

"We'd better slow down or Stretch will have to share his quarters with us." There it was… my over-protective schoolmarm had surfaced. Her priggishness was arriving later than usual.

"Hey, lookie there, who just walked in. It's Burke Buchanan. Do you know who he is?"

I took a moment to turn around but when I did, I was thunderstruck. Welcome emotions flooded back in. Every woman in the place had eyes on the tall cowboy, including Dana, so she didn't notice my reaction. Burke was politely bending down to chat up a couple at the bar. Did his mother pick out the teal blue and a navy plaid shirt that made him look like a model that just stepped out of a Winchester ad? Dana interrupted my thoughts.

"He's the most eligible bachelor in town now that his son's off to school."

"I heard he lost his wife a while back," I said, demurely, trying to tease more personal details out of Dana to fill in the gap of lost years.

"That was sure sad. I had just moved here from Tucson when the accident happened, so I didn't know her, but I guess she was pretty important in town. She was on the school board and she worked in the county offices. Folks really rallied around him and his kid when she died, but mostly the two guys just kept to themselves. You never saw them out anywhere unless it was a school function. They were phantoms. Everyone's glad to see him out more. I know I'd like to see more of him," she said with a cheesy grin as she took another big swig of her Bud Light.

"He comes to the dealership," I told her. "I've seen him there. I actually knew him many years ago." As I talked, I watched Dana's eyes widen like she just saw Mamma kissing Santa Claus and before I could follow her gaze, I felt warm breath at my ear.

"You ladies mind if I join you for a beer?" Burke asked.

"Hello, Mr. Buchanan," I said as he slid his slim hips into the big red leather booth across from me, right next to Dana who hardly gave way. He had to scooch his butt toward her to get her to move over. Dana giggled.

"Mr. Buchanan, is it now?" he said, fixing me with ever-so-sexy eyes that were taking on the color of his teal blue shirt. "I didn't realize the sales crew down at the dealership had such formal training."

"Burke, do you know my friend Dana?" I asked. She was practically sitting in his lap. He reached around to take the beaming

Dana's hand and said, "Nice to see you again, Dana. How are things down at the Copper Springs police station these days? I heard it doesn't run without you there." Her face flushed.

"It's more exciting here," she said, then winked at me.

"That's because Miss Alberta has moved back to town. Everyone wants to take a gander at the last best girl to get away from the Springs. We lost the prettiest girl in town and the captain of the golf team."

Dana's Bud Light brain wasn't following.

"Who's Alberta?"

"Alternate on the golf team," I corrected. "Hardly the captain."

"That's how she got the nickname Birdie," Burke said to Dana.

"Too bad I wasn't any better or I'd have been called Eagle."

"Or Double Eagle instead of Double Al," he said.

"Double Al?" Dana said, trying to keep up.

"Or any worse and you'd all know me as Triple Bogey."

Burke grinned at me, a smile so wide and sparkling that he looked like he was eighteen again and had just won the 4-H Blue ribbon for his prized calf. All it took was a little beer and an old friend to roll back the clock. He seemed relaxed and engaged in our conversation. I never pictured an encounter like this with him. All I could ever think of was the look on his face when I left.

"Wait. Are you Alberta?" Dana said. "Who's Double Al then?"

"When I was a kid, my family called me Bertie, short for Alberta. Some, like Burke here, called me Double Al because my dad had made himself quite famous with his TV ads inviting folks to Double Al's Auto Emporium, but that was back in Nebraska." I told the story to her but Burke and the million-watt smile had all our attention. I had forgotten about the dimples; they were a bonus that was making my heart feel jumpy. Even from across the table, I could tell that Burke smelled like new-mown hay. Was it even hay season?

"So, your dad was a car dealer? And you call yourself Birdie because of golf?" She made it sound like I'd given myself an alias.

Have I given myself an alias? Am I hiding out here in Copper Springs? I ran like a chicken right out of Midvale and I have no intention of going back.

"It's a golf term, and it sounded like Bertie so the name just stuck." I wanted to tell Burke the truth, which was that I was, in fact, several different people. I wasn't the Alberta that he knew all those years ago. I hope he thought someone better took her place.

"Birdie, huh? Like Tweety bird, right? Dana said. "So, that is why your license plate says "Tweety?" She was catching up, pleased with herself like she just put the last piece in a 1000-piece jigsaw.

Burke said, "And I'm sure because it's bright yellow like a canary. Speaking of your car, I saw it outside; that's why I stopped."

"It'll be hard to get away with anything in this town, won't it?" I said.

"I have news for you; with, or without Tweety, there are many people curious enough to keep track of you."

"What might that mean? This town can't be that dull can it?" I said. He rolled his eyes and shrugged.

"Say," he said, "I'm going to bring my truck into the AutoMall on Thursday to leave it for a few days, or however long it will take that idiot Conrad to figure out what's wrong with the electronics, anyway. Are you working that day?"

"I am," I said.

"Good, I'll see you then." He was already taking his leave. He said goodbye to Dana and just like that he was up and headed for the front door with every woman in the bar watching his Wrangler-clad rear end. It was like someone pushed a pause button on the entire gathering. As soon as he was out of sight the din of conversation started up again.

"Okay, come clean, how well do you know this guy?" Dana asked.

"We dated in high school; that's it. Then we both went off to college and went different directions. I honestly never thought I would ever be back here in Copper Springs and be talking to him again."

"If I had to guess, I'd say he never got over you," Dana said.

"I broke his heart once upon a time," I confessed. "Broke it and I never talked to him again. Peter wanted my undivided attention and I was willing to give it to him. That is how dumb I am or was. I didn't know Burke had married or that he had a son because I made Gramma Lou promise not to tell me anything about him. After a while, I wasn't sure she even remembered that we were sweethearts. I didn't know his wife had died, and that makes me feel like a lousy friend of any kind."

"I think you may get a second chance," Dana said, repeating Gramma Lou's sentiment.

For some time, I had been the star guest at Gram's Airbnb. It was high time I contributed, so I shopped on the way home, then cleaned my non-organic veggies and chopped my little heart out prepping like a chef for the next night's dinner. It felt cathartic, wielding a cleaver and slicing and dicing. I got to thinking. Would Burke like to be invited?

As soon as Grams arrived home, I made my suggestion.

"Say, should we invite someone over tomorrow to enjoy this feast with us?"

"That's funny," she said, "because I've actually invited someone for tomorrow."

"Who?"

"It'll be a surprise." A surprise? I hoped it was the one I had in mind.

CHAPTER 22

Finding common ground with our customers, or 'making a friend' as it was called, was sometimes embarrassingly difficult, as I discovered with one old, cranky cowboy named Frank whom I Upped in the truck line.

"You just march in there right now girlie, and get one of those sales men out here to sell me a vehicle, or I'm taking my business to Tucson. I've been buying here for forty years." Behind him, Frank's wife mouthed her apology. It was the first time the sexism was so blatant—from a customer; I got it every day from the crew.

I knew from previous scoldings that I either coaxed a guy like Frank into the building to meet the managers or I turned him over to someone who could. Mr. Curmudgeon would have none of it. The only contender for a turn in the vicinity was the Purple Tie. I was pretty sure Rich knew less about the trucks than I did, but he had the requisite penis the rancher required. Two hours later, I had half the commission on a truck sale just for handing him over. Sweet! I loved earning money the easiest way, just like the rest of the troops. I got a whopping ninety-seven bucks, which I actually did nothing to earn but get rid of an old crank. Woohoo.

But for me, the script was never that simple. It was more like a complicated old classic, Commission Impossible.

By morning, the easy money I had made needed extra effort to shake it out of the piggy bank. Montello informed me that some-one from Finance, the department I disliked only slightly less than the Service Department, had not gotten all the right signatures and he commanded that I drive out to the ranch to have the correct papers signed by the irascible rancher.

"You got half the deal," he said. "That means you drive."

"You don't do this to the guys."

"Will you quit whining for once?" he hollered back at me. "I treat everybody here the same." His male-pattern amnesia had kicked in; it was a serious condition.

"But I don't leave signatures off of my paperwork," my Goody-Two-Shoes protested. "So, nobody has to run these errands for me. I had to give the old fart to Rich because he didn't like me. Remember?"

"You're not near as perfect as you think you are." *What did that mean? Perfect, I hardly think I'm*—He interrupted my inner analysis. "It's the wife's signature we didn't get." I was half relieved, but it didn't mean the cantankerous spouse wouldn't be looking over her shoulder.

"Go. Scoot. The sooner you leave, the sooner you'll get back." I couldn't help but think I was being set up again. What deal will I miss? What life changing event depended on me having both feet firmly planted in the showroom? Little did I know that wouldn't happen until I returned.

I scooped up the folder and marched outside where I picked a newer Ford Focus with a sun roof to drive. True to form, no matter what I chose, Wade, the catfish-resembling bottom feeder, didn't like it. He sent Rich to halt my departure and instruct me to take a beat-up, little three-cylinder engine Geo Metro that had seen its best days in the late nineties. It was sitting on Wade's side of the building where ConMan had lined it up with the other heaps for Mater to haul away. *Great, he's shoving me in a P.O.S headed for the junk pile.*

"Will it even make it out there and back?" I asked Rich.

"I doubt it," he said. "Be sure to take your cell phone, but there's not much coverage out there so you better hope you don't need it." The piece had slicks for tires and no muffler.

"Muffler noise might get you arrested, but that's the one he wants you to take."

"No cell coverage, no gas, no shit!" I said.

The headliner fabric of beat up P.O.S. was hanging low enough off the ceiling in back to obstruct the view, and the back seat looked as if it had been haphazardly thrown back in. Why would someone take it out just to put it back? Since I had worked at the AutoMall, at least six of these cars had been lined up then hauled away by Mater—all wrecks, both inside and out. It was hard to believe that we had any reason to take these as trades, let alone spend money to send them to the Phoenix auction, especially when there was an Auto auction in Tucson.

The keys were thrown on the seat instead of over the visor. That usually meant that the driver's door had no hope of working. It didn't. I had no choice but to enter on the passenger side, climb over an old-fashioned stick-shift jutting right out of a rusted floorboard. It was easier to climb across than a newer model might have been. Of course, a newer model would've had a door that opened.

With this heap's three banger engine, the $10 gas voucher could get me all the way to Mexico, if I were so inclined. In fact, that might be a better idea. But instead, I headed toward Rancho Cranky Pants.

As the Arizona countryside passed, I realized I was riding alongside the Buchanan Ranch, with every fence post straight, tall and well kept, like Burke himself. Mr. Crusty Cowpoke, it turned out, was Burke Buchanan's next-door neighbor.

It was obvious that everyone used the back door of the ranch house so I stepped into the vestibule looking over my shoulder at the barns, hoping the rancher was out there. On the wall near the back door were eight wire wall-hooks above my head overflowing with Carhartt jackets and coveralls, all stiff with mud and dirt. I felt as though I was back at the farm in Nebraska. Thoughts of the Sander's Farm were seldom good, but this sensation was pleasant, especially the smell emanating from the kitchen on the other side of the door. I knocked and hoped it was just Mrs. Curmudgeon on the other side.

"Hi. I'm Birdie, from the AutoMall." I said. "With the papers to be signed?" I held up the folder.

"I'm Bonnie," she said, "Please let me apologize for my husband. The old guys are pretty set in their ways. I hope the younger men are getting better at accepting women in the workplace."

"The nation's AutoMalls would certainly be the last hold-out." I told her.

"I just made a coconut crème pie earlier and I'm dying to have an excuse to cut into it." Bonnie's kitchen floor was spotless, despite the caked mud in the entry. How did this gracious woman end up with Cowpoke Frank? I joined her at the table for coffee and pie. One small piece shouldn't take too long.

"So, isn't that the Buchanan place next door?" I sheepishly asked. Bonnie took my lead, and I frittered away the next half hour savoring coconut pie and Burke Buchanan gossip. I almost forgot to have her sign the papers.

"Yup, that's the Buchanen Ranch," she began. "The old home. My friend Mavis lives there with her son and grandson, only now the grandson is away most of the time."

"I heard that," I said.

"Mavis lost her husband right about the same time her son Burke's wife was killed in an accident quite a few years back. There were some pretty terrible sad days in that house with a widower and a widow both under one roof.

"Doesn't Burke have his own house?" I asked, not believing he had lived all those years at his mom's place.

"He did; I mean he and his wife did, but that house is on his Uncle Kenny's property now. Mavis is ready to move over to California with her brothers; who aren't in the best of health. As soon as Burke finds someone to settle down with, then she'll be gone and it will be Burke's house then."

"Is he looking?

"Why, honey, he's just about your age, I think. Do you want me to introduce you two?"

"Oh, golly no, Mrs. Granger. I was just wondering how Mrs. Buchanan was doing. I met her a long, long time ago." I pulled out the papers, and she affixed her lovely cursive signature right where Montello had indicated with a yellow marker.

As I left, I took a long look at the two-story ranch home of the Buchanans. It had a wide veranda on three sides with two wooden swings that had served as the venue for some serious conversation between Burke and me. We talked so much then, but not a word between us the twenty years after that. And whose fault was that?

As the junker Geo putt-putted along the fence line, a Lone Pine truck came into view from out amongst the cattle. It could be anybody, I told myself, maybe even Burke. Either way, I needed to get back to the office with Bonnie's signature, but that didn't prevent me from taking in the bucolic scene.

I cut across the back way because I felt pretty unsafe driving the beat-up Tin Lizzie. As soon as I pulled up at the dealership, I found out just how unsafe it was at any speed.

CHAPTER 23

The Service Department manager was waiting by the side of the building when I returned and he was livid. He greeted me by grabbing at the door handle on the passenger side to open it and yanked the only remaining handle right off the car and broke that side too. There wasn't enough baling wire on a new spool to hold the heap together. How could it have any auction value?

Conrad's anger issues were beginning to annoy me. Now I was stuck, so I attempted the impossible by climbing out the passenger door window hole backwards as if I were an entrant in a demolition derby.

"Who the hell told you that you could take this car from my auction line?" Conrad screamed. As the top half of my body got out, I managed to sit my rear on the window and balanced by holding the door frame with my right hand. I stretched my left arm out over the top of the car, still holding the signed paperwork in that hand. This was completely awkward, as my fanny was resting on a half inch of sharp window sticking up in the door. It felt like it was slicing me in two. The race car drivers made slithering out look easy.

"I don't need your permission to drive a car off the lot. What's the big deal about these junkers with you, anyway?" Of course, my legs were too long to pull one up and out while I sat in the window hole. I had no earthly idea of how to proceed but still, I kept up the angry dialogue.

"You running a chop shop with these?" *Wasn't that sort of funny, ConMan?* The thought of any single part of these heaps was worth a plug nickel deserved a courtesy chuckle but apparently ConMan didn't agree.

Why did I forget the first rule of combat? Never turn your back on a snake like this guy. I sensed him coming up behind me, but there was no defensive posture that I could assume. He put both hands on me and grabbed two fistfuls of the fabric shoulders of my poplin shirt like he was a linebacker pulling down a quarterback. My legs seemed endless as Conrad dragged me backwards out over thin air until the backs of my shoes caught on the sharp top of the crank window where I had just been sitting. However bad pulling me out a window was, what he did next was unbelievable, even for him. He dropped me! Both hands deliberately let go. My shoes were still caught on the window so I twisted as I went down, falling first on the heel of my right hand. The left side of my face hit the ground next. The moment my face kissed the cinders, my first gasp took desert dust into my lungs and I began to cough as I wriggled on the ground. NewKid came running from the showroom and loomed over me as I lay on the ground choking and spitting out gravel.

"Birdie, are you hurt? Are you okay?" He bent down to try to help me up.

"What kind of nut are you?" he said to Conrad. "You can't do this kind of shit to people and get away with it."

NewKid was the most alert person on the lot. I'm not sure the others would have even noticed. I brushed my face and realized I was bleeding, with probably a few Arizona agates embedded in my cheek as well.

The aggressor ignored NewKid. "Give me that key," he demanded. I instinctively pulled it back from him. What the hell? Was I still thinking I was going to continue to fight?

"I'll give it back to Wade who told me to take this car out on a signing,' I said, "and no one else." He stood looking down at me like I was a cigarette that he was about to stub out with his boot. My right hand clutched so tightly around the key that later when I finally let it go, my flesh looked like the wax impression a thief would use to make a new key. The signed papers from Burke's neighbor were strewn across the gravel, and a few were under the crappy car that ConMan was so enamored of.

NewKid stepped between us, so Conrad backed off, then fled through the service bay door saying, "You bitch, I'll take care of you." I would have thought he already had. I've had similar things said to me by middle schoolers when I caught them in compromising positions, but it had never unnerved me. ConMan was not a young boy. He was a horrible ogre and I was as scared as I've ever been.

"It's okay," NewKid said. "I'll help you in. Now I see why you clocked that guy in the nuts the other day. He's a rabid bastard." My sharp neck pain told me where I had taken the brunt of the throw down.

"I think we might be even now," I said.

NewKid went to the tower and told his pal, Wade, about what he witnessed, and I could tell Wade was unfazed by it. Shouldn't he at least be concerned about a hostile work environment law suit enough to interview me? But it wasn't his business, and he didn't want me there any more than ConMan. Did they both think this would run me off? Well, it might. This time it might.

Angel appeared like an apparition of Florence Nightingale clutching the first aid kit.

"You've got to stay away from that guy. I'm not kidding." she said. "Not a safe guy to be around. He's done stuff like this to me."

"Why haven't you reported it?" I said.

"I can't afford to lose my job. You know how the guys all stick together." Then she looked me straight in the eye and said, "I've never had a witness like you did here today." Did she expect me to stand up for all of us? Look at me. I could barely sit, let alone stand up. Her look gave me pause until she applied the cure.

"Ouch! That stings." I jerked away, making me aware my shoulder was sore too. Angel taped a large bandage on my elbow and one across my palm, nearly depleting the stock of gauze in the kit. She stuck a stupid brown Band-Aid on my cheek.

"This wrist wrap makes me look even more depressed than I actually am, you know."

"Stay away from him. I know what I'm talking about. Really, somebody should get rid of that guy." Me. She meant that I should file a grievance, or call a lawyer and take down the menace, like some sort of muckraker. Screw that. He let me fall to my doom. Who knew what else he might have in mind?

Montello was out of town until Monday. I decided to take it up with him when he returned. Filing a complaint was nothing I had ever done before—nothing I'd ever had to do either. I waited out the clock until it was time to leave. The rest of the crew told me that they would do the keying. Clay walked me to my car.

"I'm sort of scared," I said.

"Don't blame you. You two really don't like each other." What? Had Clay placed me as half of this problem?

"Didn't NewKid tell you what he did?"

"I just don't understand why you keep provoking him," he said, then walked quickly toward his car before I could set him straight on the subject. He was one of the only guys here that I trusted to understand, and clearly, he was thinking that if I weren't such a bitch, Conrad and I could be buddies.

As I headed for home, I remembered that we had a dinner guest coming and it was too late to call it off, and added to that, I was supposed to be cooking. Great. I resolved not to tell Burke or Grams what happened, but I was not sure how I would explain my appearance or if I wanted to admit that the AutoMall was finally getting the best of me.

CHAPTER 24

I parked Tweety behind Gram's faded blue Plymouth. Despite my lateness, Burke's vehicle was not there. Through the kitchen door screen, I saw Austin Stein, the oil change kid from work. I felt confused, but then, I had fallen on my head.

"Hi, Austin." Maybe the news hadn't gotten to him.

"Geez, I heard my boss really took you out today," he blurted out. Even the oil change kid heard about my humiliation. Gramma Lou came rushing out of the living room.

"Alberta, dear. Oh my. What are they doing to you at that place? Honey, you're bandaged everywhere. Austin was telling us one of your coworkers roughed you up today." Us? Burke was here?

"It wasn't quite that bad," I told her, thinking it was worse.

"That guy doesn't get along with anybody," Austin said. "So, I wouldn't feel too bad if I were you." I didn't feel bad at least not that way. "Although, you look pretty scraped up. I don't think he's done that to anyone else."

"I'm sure Mr. Montello will do something about it when he gets back on Monday," I told them.

"Good luck," he said. "He kind of has a habit of ignoring stuff like that."

"Well, aren't you wise beyond your years." As I finished the sentence, two dark-haired, tanned and very attractive men walked toward me from the living room. Neither of them was Burke Buchanan.

"This is Mario Stein. Do you remember him, Bertie? He owns Stein's Hardware downtown." I remembered the little Mexican man who used to help Grampa with window screens and plumbing supplies. This Mr. Stein was fuller, older, mustachioed, and with a twinkle in his eye that I had never noticed when I was young. Funny what you don't notice until time and experiences widen your worldview.

"And, this is his son Jack. He's a parole officer." The tall good-looking guy planted a big wet kiss on Gram's cheek. Jack? Wait… It isn't? My first-kiss Jack? And now he's kissing my Gramma! Jack was much taller than Mario, with perfect posture. He had a full head of almost shoulder length dark, wavy hair and the same gorgeous dark brown eyes that I remembered from when we were eleven. His nose looked like it had been broken more than once, but it was still pretty much in the middle of his handsome face.

"We've met," he said with a gregarious grin. "I go by Cuervo now."

"College nickname, I suppose."

"No. No college. Just a bit too much of my favorite tequila," he said as he shared a look with the others.

My faux pas embarrassed me. I no longer ran with the professorial snobs of Midvale, Nebraska, who were ever-at-the-ready to list their advanced degrees, but I had just made myself sound like a perfect snob.

"The boys are here for dinner." Grams picked up the conversation. "Mario has been here this afternoon cooking with the vegetables you cut up. I hope you don't mind. I made a German chocolate cake today, too." Wonderful. In case this dinner went as badly as the start at least there was more medicinal coconut for me.

"You go on into the living room, Bertie, and sit down to rest and get acquainted with Cuervo and Austin for a while. Mario is doing the cooking." Since when did Grams let one of the neighbors come in and commandeer her kitchen?

"Dad, I'm going to run back down to the house and get my iPod," Austin said and out the front door he skedaddled leaving me alone with a guy I barely knew a hundred years ago.

"You haven't changed much," Cuervo said, "That is, you still look all banged up like you just fell off your roller skates."

"The sidewalks in this town are still hard to skate on," I said, both of us knowing full well the town had no sidewalks. I was relieved not to retell the real story. Cuervo was gentle and helped me to the well-worn green velvet sofa. Stiffness from the fall was starting to set into my back and neck.

"I thought you had moved to California with your mother," I said.

"I did, but I'm a desert rat, not a beach bum. You know, you can take the boy out of the desert but you can't take the cactus thorns out of the boy. I stayed in California long enough to get married and get divorced—it's a family tradition. But I'm a changed man now."

"Don't play all nice with me. You're the kind of guy who looks for trouble."

"Me? Who told you?" He had that "Look at me; I just won the lottery" grin going.

"Nobody had to tell me. I could see it in the way you waltzed in here and grabbed Gramma Lou and kissed her."

"Wait. You're jealous of Louella. I love that."

"No. I didn't mean that. I just meant I could tell by your swagger that you look for trouble. Why aren't you one of those shoot-em-up cops with the shaved head, instead of a parole officer? I bet you never even get to shoot a gun."

"First of all, let's see, you think I'm the one of us who looks for trouble? Miss all-scuffed up-and-nowhere-to-go." He was getting his dander up. I could see the veins in his neck sticking out. "Second of all, why would I want to shave off beautiful locks like these?" He reached up with his left hand and fake-tossed the hair on his neck as a fifties Hollywood starlet might. "Those low testosterone guys have to shave their heads. I don't. And thirdly, I pride myself on not using deadly force in my chosen career field, and it's not because I can't hit my target. Do you want to come to the firing range with me and see my name several times on the trophy wall? I have deadly aim, my, dear. Deadly, in all things that I do."

"The target range isn't real life. How do you know you can use a gun in real life?" Why was I deliberately baiting a friend of Gram's and being a jerk like the rest of the AutoMall crew? "I just mean that being a parole officer doesn't make you sound that tough. That's all."

"Well, who's looking for trouble now?" he said. "You're trying to get a rise out of me and I'm not in the mood, and you clearly aren't in the mood for discussing meeting me out at the merry-go-round for old time's sake. I think I'm going to the kitchen to see what Dad and Lou are up to." He stood and walked out of the room without looking back. I heard them talking and laughing while I sat a room away in a pool of shame. In a few minutes, Cuervo came back with lemonades for both of us.

"Louella told me you're a heavy drinker so I spiked yours with gin."

"Gin? Everybody knows lemonade's supposed to be spiked with vodka." He smiled. "What brought you back to Arizona?" I asked in a less accusatory manner.

"Austin. He was running with the wrong crowd in Cali."

"And you think the crowd at the dealership is a better one?" I said, holding out my bandaged palm.

"Well, Wallace is a good guy. But, no, you're right. There are some who aren't on the right path, that's for sure."

"I don't suppose you'd care to elaborate?" I said, "Maybe to let me know who to watch out for next?"

"Watch out for everyone. That's my best advice. I don't talk about my clients or investigations, but I heard all about your tough day today. Do you want to talk about that?"

"No." I changed the subject. "Let's see, when did we last see each other? That one time in the grocery store, wasn't it?"

"That's not the meeting I remember most," he countered. "No, not by a long shot. Until Austin said you were living back here, I almost thought I imagined you. Did you know that you were the first girl I ever kissed?" he said with a shy, boyish grin.

"I'm your first, huh? Well, isn't that something to put in our diaries, then." He looked disappointed. "Tell me about what it is that you really do. Then I'll tell you about the rough and tumble car business."

"I shadow criminals to make sure they're following the rules of the State of Arizona that allow them a bit of freedom as they make their way from prison back into society. They follow rules perfectly or they go back to jail."

"Since you are sort of in the cop business, you haven't seen Wallace's black BMW in the wrong hands, have you? It disappeared and Wade wants it to be my fault."

His expression turned serious. "A BMW? What day did it go missing?"

"You have seen it. I knew it would turn up."

"No, I haven't seen it, but I'll look out for it now. Do you know if it was reported missing?"

"I was told it wasn't. My friend Dana said it was because it was probably a high school kid that took it. I guess I should be asking Austin."

"Or maybe it was because the dealership was using it for something they don't want the police to know about."

"Now that could be a sinister plot turn. Maybe you should be a writer."

"I am a writer. I turn reports in every day, and I know more real-life plot turns than you could ever imagine."

"Well, I told Dana and she works at the police station so the cat is pretty much out of the bag anyway. I thought it was maybe Stretch, one of our slimy salesmen because he went missing at the same time, but then I heard he's in jail so probably not."

"Yes, he's in jail. That's public record."

"I guess you know him?"

"Afraid I do." Cuervo's voice was low and had a hypnotic quality. He told me he was working with border patrol agents to bust a drug ring. "A stolen car might be just the clue they're looking for," he said.

"Not to change the subject," I said, "but I saw people walking in the dry river bed today and lights flashing. What was going on?"

"They're illegals," he said. "I mean undocumented. They're escaping a terrible life in Mexico or more likely Central America to get into the U.S. and they probably got caught. None of that is my jurisdiction. Be careful, Birdie. Don't get your nose into places that could get you in trouble."

"Me? Trouble? I'm a middle school librarian," forgetting momentarily that I wasn't. "How much trouble could I get into?"

"Those scrapes on your arms and face tell me otherwise. That was no fight in the schoolyard," he said, as his warm hands helped me up to go into the kitchen for dinner.

We made small talk over Mario's dinner. It was a delicious concoction—a sort of stew but flavored with cumin and a bit of pepper but not too hot. My brawl had made me hungry and I asked for seconds while the men made pleasant conversation. The three generations of Stein men were warm and engaging. I could see why Grams liked them.

After we finished, I took two Excedrin and headed back to the living room couch. I heard Austin say, "Good night." Cuervo popped his head around the corner and said, "Nice seeing you again, merry-go-round girl."

"You too, Cuervo." He nodded and turned to go but I called to him.

"Cuervo? It really did make my diary that night."

"Good to know," he said and gave me that grin that was already becoming one of my favorite things.

I heard Grams packing up some of the dinner to go home with Mario. He was the last to leave. And then, as I watched through the arched doorway, I saw Mario give Gramma Lou a kiss. It was not the big show kiss on the cheek that Cuervo had planted on her earlier. This was a real kiss—more like a peck really—but on the lips. I felt the heat in my cheeks rise. I looked down and feigned reading when Grams came in the living room. Grams and Mario?

"Are you feeling all right dear?" she asked. "You look a bit flushed. You might have a fever."

I was beginning to ache.

"I'm sorry, Grams, I wasn't very good company. I didn't mean for them to leave early."

"It's okay, they'd been here this afternoon for quite a while, and we all knew that you had a very bad day. We'll have them over another time," she said as she served me delicious German chocolate cake piled high with homemade coconut pecan frosting. Then, she kissed my forehead and touched my skinned-up cheek. Bless her heart. I could be a cold-blooded killer and my Gramma Lou would be certain of my innocence and never waver one little bit. But, Grandma and Mario? Does Cuervo know? This little town was becoming a lot more interesting than it used to be.

"Grams, can I ask you a question? Why are three guys who are obviously Hispanic named Stein? I always wondered."

"Mario was adopted by the Steins when he was very young. He told me his mother was Mexican and worked in the Steins' home. Her husband was in Hermosillo and came up to see her quite often. Mario has photos of the two of them holding hands at the Catholic Church, here in Copper Springs, really a beautiful couple. Her husband spoke no English. When she got pregnant, she made sure she had the baby in Arizona. A month later when she had to flee from authorities, she left Mario behind. He ended up being Steins' only child.

"Not so different from what happens to kids today."

"True, only now they'd throw the boy out, too."

As I headed to bed, I pondered that kiss, not Cuervo's, when we were kids, but that smooch between Gramma and Mario. It frightened me. I better make this car sales thing work better than it has if I am to move on and give my dear grams her life back. And, if Grams has Mario then who do I have? Who has me?

CHAPTER 25

The pain I felt was more akin to being hit by the jalopy, not merely "falling" out of it. My drop to the dirty gravel not only scuffed me up, but it also wrenched my neck, back, and shoulder. I could very legitimately have had the day off, but I felt compelled to show up to prove that I could take it. I imagined the boys would have some measure of sympathy for me, but Clay and Rich steered totally clear. Wade and Bingham were off, which was another reason why I felt I had to show up. My job loyalty knew no bounds. In reality, I was darned if I'd let anyone scare me off. I'd made good money, finally and I needed to continue the streak so I could get out of Gram's home and her hair.

"You look like shit," NewKid said. Well, someone at least noticed I'm in the showroom.

"Birdie Alton. Please report to Mr. Montello's office." He had used his great loud-speaker announcer voice. The noise of it gave me a headache. If I went in there, I knew it could mess up my say nothing plans, but I couldn't ignore the summons.

"What's going on between you and Conrad?" he asked. Not, "how are you" or "are you sure you should be at work today?"

"I'm fine, Mr. Montello, and how are you today?" I said, noticing for the first time he had a man in his office with him. "Is this the best time for us to talk about it?" I suggested, nodding to his guest. He ignored my hint.

"Why are you provoking him?" he asked. I stood in front of him bandaged and this was his greeting.

"I think Wade set me up."

"What the hell does that mean? Now you sound paranoid," the boss said.

"Wade made me park the car I had chosen to drive to the Granger Ranch and insisted that I drive that auction car last night. Every time I get near one of those rattletraps, it flips some psycho switch in ConMan. Every time. So, I think Wade deliberately sent me out in that rig so the Service guy would flip."

"That's a bullshit theory. Sounds like a New Jersey wise guy tale." Here we go. Wait for it… wait for it.

"When I lived in Jersey—" he said as he began regaling his office guest. Bingo! There it was. "I worked for a haberdasher." The guy sitting in front of him might be the one living being to be hearing it all for the first time.

"What's a hab-er-dasher?" the fellow asked.

"Only the best clothier in all of New York City. We were at Teterboro Airport in New Jersey." Really? This is where we're going to go today with me standing here in bandages? I had heard this several times, so I was ready to be testy, guest or no guest in his office.

"A little New Jersey airport? That seems an odd location for a fancy men's store and how is that in New York City?" He looked back at me, his brows knitted.

"Well, our clientele was from the city and it wasn't like it was on the runway. And it was a tailoring shop, not a store.

"You need to get your story straight."

"Teterboro's for private jets. It's in Moonachie." He was blabbering. None of us here in this dealership or in Arizona would know Moonachie from Moon pie or Moon Landing. Moonachie might as well be the moon for all we cared.

"I have a deal working," I lied. "I need to get back to it."

He hardly took a breath. "All of New York City's finest Wall Streeters, politicians, even the police commissioner, let me measure their balls for an inseam before they got on their jets to go skiing in the goddamn Alps." I finally realized that this was a new mechanic he was interviewing. Mike was trying to impress him with his exotic story.

"By the way, their balls weren't as big as they thought they were." A little haberdasher's joke? Mike fancied himself a conspirator giving away a secret. His secret was more like Victoria's. If you had spent more than two hours on the car lot without hearing Montello's worsted wool history, then you hadn't been paying attention. The balls he was referring to were from thirty years ago and are long dead or seriously shriveled now. Mr. Montello knew a lot about the Wall Street life of the eighties, the era he lived in still. Once, when he told NewKid that he looked like Don Johnson, NewKid said: "Who?"

"You know, the Miami Vice guy!" Mike told him.

"Is that a punk band?" NewKid said, then winked at me. Later, at the curb outside the showroom, NewKid stated our management situation.

"Montello is bolivious," he said, using a dubious term Rich uttered a few days earlier.

"So true," I responded. Mike Montello was indeed "bolivious" and he was the captain of our ship. A perfect storm.

———

I sold a new Ford mid-sized sedan in the late afternoon. It wasn't a spoon; it was a lucky answer to a random phone call. The matte black vehicle had an identical twin from a screwed-up dealer trade that was priced $2000 more, so there was no hope of trading away these little headaches.

My buyers' research told them exactly which one they wanted—two vehicles with a combined year and seven months on our lot and carrying enormous spiffs of $500 each to finally encourage them on their way. You're looking for a 4x4 ¾ ton pickup? Come look at this fabulous little two-door Focus. This time the "deal of a lifetime" wasn't just car lot hyperbole and I had the customer who wanted just that vehicle.

In the course of my sale write-up, Michael and Cindy, my buyers, both quizzed me about my white gauze wrist accessory.

"I had a fall on the lot yesterday," I awkwardly explained. "But despite the injury, I can still wield a mean pencil," I said, using car lot jargon for writing a great deal. The couple turned out to be lawyers buying a vehicle for their college-bound daughter. Before they drove off, one following the other, Michael made an observation.

"You're obviously a tough cookie Birdie, but you look to be banged up pretty good, almost like a domestic abuse case I had recently." If he was trying to compliment me, it wasn't working. Or wait, did he think I was married? And abused? "I would be glad to represent you if you decided to make a claim for your injuries. I specialize in that, and, if I do say so, I'm pretty good at it."

"Thank you so much, Michael. The way things are going, I 'd like a couple of your cards." I made sure one of the crisp white cards was sitting in plain sight for the rest of the day.

Montello wrote out my $500 spiff check without blinking an eye or saying a word. I snapped up the check saying, "Michael is a personal injury lawyer. He gave me his card."

It never did me any good to get on the Haberdasher's bad side, but it was difficult to know which side you were really on. In less than an hour, the GM spoon-fed me a deal that sped through almost as fast as the lawyers' deal had. It was a '05 Porsche Cayenne station wagon that sold for $4900. As stunned as I was about the price the thing pulled, imagine my shock when Mike wrote me another check for $760 for two hours' worth of work. That lawyer's card was indeed valuable. It was also the boss's way of saying that he knew my altercations with Conrad weren't my entire fault. I held the check and stood in his office for a while.

"Mater's sort of a weirdo, isn't he?" I asked Mike, as I saw the overall-wearing tow guy come through the outside door toward the Service Department. This was none of my business, but it was starting to bug me that he was always loitering about.

"Weird with a capital W," Mike said, "And he spends too much time here. It's starting to annoy me." Wow. That was more info than I expected. "I was going to talk to Conrad about him but you sort of sidelined that, didn't you?"

"I beg your pardon?"

"Because of you, I have some more pressing things to visit with him about. Our discussion about his friends who hang around out there will have to wait."

As soon as Mike said, "You sort of sidelined that" I knew he was using me as an out for not doing his job. Conrad would not be fired as he should be. Bingham might be wrong. Maybe a woman did have a place here, to serve as a handy scapegoat.

CHAPTER 26

My body healed rather quickly. I wished my psyche would mend as fast. Only the scrape on the side of my face still had a scab. Perhaps out of concern for me, Gramma Lou was baking every day now.

"I'm making a few things for Mario," she told me but there on the counter were my favorite coconut macaroons made with liquid sin—Eagle Brand Sweetened Condensed Milk. She had a reason to be pushing calories at me. My rapid weight loss had Gramma Lou worried.

"Grams, I'm walking a million miles a day now instead of sitting at a desk in a library. Dropping a few pounds is nothing to worry about." But I was tipping the scales fifteen pounds lighter than when I arrived. I took Gram's worry as permission to stop by Bernadette's Bakery and buy myself two coconut-topped donuts on the way to work, two maple bars each for Clay and NewKid, and a bear claw for Angel. I didn't feel the need to provide sustenance for any of the others. Upon arrival at the dealership, I bee-lined for the Detail Department.

"Hey, there, Angel girl, I brought you a bear claw," I said to the figure removing white plastic from the windows of a pickup fresh off the transport.

"It's not Angel," a deep voice said. The words were from our favorite MIA, Stretch, back at last. Oh, how I've missed you.

"Stretch? Why are you back here?" He looked rough but had better color than he had a week ago. Let's face it; I didn't look too great either.

"What does it look like?" Hmm, Color improved, personality, not so much.

I found Angel in the small bay she termed her office. A wall bank of rusted school lockers narrowed the space. They harbored her menagerie of scrub brushes and 100% cotton polishing rags, not to mention the gallons of magic green cleaner and whatever other potions Professor Snape had conjured up for her.

"You've really spruced up the place," I said, gesturing to the recent locker addition. "What do you call the décor, chamois chic?" I held out her favorite treat from Bernadette's. She devoured it. For a moment, I thought she was going to eat the bag along with the pastry.

"Stretch wasn't my idea, but he can't drive a car right now, so where else are they going to stick him?"

"I guess I assumed he wouldn't be coming back." Hoped was more like it.

"Yeah, he's back. I've had to lock up everything." She gestured toward the old lockers. Three had oversized padlocks added to their louvered doors. "He's a klepto."

"I was told on my first day to lock up my handbag, and I gathered that Stretch was the reason."

"I have to lock up my pistol now. How much good would that be if I need it?" she said.

"You bring a pistol to work?" Why did I suddenly feel less safe?

"Everybody owns a gun, even Montello; he keeps it in his bottom drawer. You need one too."

"You're the second person to tell me that. I better sell an extra SUV, so I can afford one."

"I know a guy who sells them really cheap and there's no record," she said. I'd stepped into the front end of a Law and Order episode. I changed the subject.

"Gramma Lou is worried I'm losing too much weight, "I said, before taking a sizable bite out of one of two donuts I'd purchased for myself.

Angel reached in one of her hinged metal stash boxes and extracted a pedometer that she pressed into the hand not holding the donut.

"Here. Check your mileage. I snagged it out of a yuppie Outback that was traded in a few weeks ago," she said. "I bet you do six miles a day."

"Is there anything you don't have in there?"

"Seriously, Birdie girl, you'd be surprised what things I find in the back of these heaps. Some of it they didn't intend to leave behind." She waved a stuffed baggy in front of me.

"Weed?"

"No, oregano. I wouldn't keep it here if it was the actual stuff."

"Sounds like you know the difference."

"Oh, I know my drugs." She smiled then headed back to her work task. Angel readily admitted that she ran with a tough crowd most of her life. She seemed sober and street-wise since I'd known her. Now I also knew that she was armed.

My new accessory was clipped to my hip as we walked into the showroom. Angel, whose arms had the circumference of a pipe cleaner, didn't need a pedometer to tell her that she ran her ass off. I should've gotten her two bear claws.

I stood at the doorway and surveyed the showroom. There they were, my cohorts—Lackluster Row. They didn't need a pedometer to know how much exercise they were getting—none. Bingham took the "big sit" a step further. He used his office chair like an Amtrak recliner on the Southwest Clipper—his seat doubled as a sleeper. He was snoring so loud he was keeping the office girls awake.

"My gosh, you men are stupid," I said to Clay, the person I thought was walking up beside me.

"Who are you calling stupid?" The low sexy voice startled me. I turned around.

"Hi Burke," I said. "Does the shoe fit?"

"I don't know about shoes because I wear boots mostly, but yes, I'm stupid. I like it better when I call myself that rather than hear it from a pretty girl, though." Clay was just beyond and had heard enough sweet talk, so he excused himself and headed out the side door as Mater came in. Burke turned back to me and threw his pickup keys on the desk.

"I'd love to take this discussion further," Burke said, "but I have someone waiting outside to give me a ride back to the ranch. Say, are you going to eat that donut?"

I hesitated and then offered the plate. "It's my favorite," I said. He helped himself to the pink pastry. The gesture felt familiar as if we had done it a thousand times before in a previous life.

Burke downed the donut in a couple of bites. "Delicious. I didn't have time to eat today," He looked out the window and waved toward his driver. "Would you do me a huge favor? I'm not in the mood to hassle with your Service Manager. Would you turn in these keys so they can work on my truck in the morning?"

"As you know, Conrad and I aren't on the best terms, either."

"I do know. That's why I'm calling it a big favor."

"I think you termed it a huge favor, and it will cost you dinner." I was definitely getting more comfortable with the owner of the Lone Pine Ranch.

"Okay, you're on." He held open the door and said, "Sunset dinner then?" Just then, Uncle Kenny stormed through.

"Is he offering to cook for you, darlin'? I'd think twice about that if I were you. He cooks about as well as he dances and dancing ain't his long suit." Kenny grinned from ear to ear and gave me a little peck on the cheek. No wonder everyone in town loved Kenny.

"What would his long suit be then, Uncle Kenny?"

"Damned if I know, but he's almost gotta have one, don't you think?" Kenny fake-punched Burke's arm and hustled him out the door. Burke smiled back at me before they both climbed into Ken's stock truck to get back to work. A yellow shop tag with Lone Pine's name on it still marked Burke's keys from the last misguided attempt to fix it. I slid the ring near the edge of the desk. I needed to wait until the Service Department promptly put out the closed sign at five p.m. on the nose. I didn't need another ConMan confrontation, either. By the time Burke and Kenny pulled away, Mater was standing beside me.

"You look to be interested in cowboys. I saw one give you his keys," Mater said. I decided not to pick up on his inference.

"Who isn't?" I said. "They're very popular. They've even made a movie about one. It was very successful; maybe you've heard of it—Toy Story?"

"Hmpf," he said. "That was about a spaceman. I'm not so fond of cowboys." He made it sound like I'd implied he had the same interest in Burke that I might have. "Cowboys and Coyotes, they are both trouble," he said.

"Ky O Tees?" I said.

"Sure, you know those guys that look like cowboys but instead they haul illegals. They get paid big bucks to do it." Was he lumping Burke Buchanan in with a group of outlaws who extort money from people trying to cross the border? *Don't engage him Birdie. Don't engage him.*

"Surely, you're not implying that a prominent local rancher has anything in common with an extortion artist at the border?"

"Oh no, not really, but they both wear Levis."

"Wranglers." I corrected him. "That cowboy wears Wranglers." I'm all about accuracy.

CHAPTER 27

The late afternoon heated up with car buyers overrunning the showroom and the new car lot. This had to happen because I had a date to go to Tucson shopping with Dana. It was Birdie Alton's Universal Law of Inversity—if I didn't want it to happen, it was sure to happen. In fact, my thoughts seemed to fuel the car lot gods to manifest the opposite. It certainly was in effect on the days where I prayed for a sale. As I had learned from my first actual customer, Karen, an afternoon sale more often ended up with a next day delivery. To avoid watching Stretch steal another commission, I didn't want to write up a sale that would just slip away from me tomorrow. I had begun using the stupidest logic.

When I spied the first Up, I woke up Bingham, napping in his chair. He snorted and jostled, but he was the one guy here who pursued an Up like a bulldog did a bone, running out to the lot and beating all the guys half his age. I'd lost foot races to Bingham already and when it happened, I didn't know if I was mad at him or mad at myself for letting the old, short-legged, fart beat me to the punch. I trusted him to scoot out to the lot as soon as I pointed, like a retriever, to what looked like a sure winner of a prospect. The Bulldog didn't disappoint. He ran out to greet a middle-aged couple in a clean six-year-old Buick. It's trade-in time! The naps did him a world of good. *Was a day off really worth it for me to pass this perfect Up off?*

When I saw the next prospects drive in, I hid behind the Pepsi machine until Rich finally turned up to talk to the family in the beat-up hatchback. One of the kids, still wearing his footie PJs, was pushing buttons on the soda machine when he saw me and ran crying to his mom. What? Was I making myself totally repulsive?

By five o'clock, I'd had enough of hiding out in the ladies' bathroom, so I filled out the rest of my day's dance card by slinking out to the Detail Department.

"Where's Angel?" I asked the reprobate Stretch who was trying to get a seat out of an SUV for repair. Was he actually working?

"She was just here," he said. That was all the help I was going to get. I wandered out the back of the building to see if I could find her and to see what great gossip she had turned up during the day. Angel was my favorite person at the dealership and yet if she had been at the same high school as me, she would not have been in my group. After all, I was in the popular girl category but, my status as "popular" was wobbly at best. Angel led the badass group. No wobble. She would have been part of the gang that had street smarts and weren't afraid to use them.

"Angel, are you out there?" I didn't expect an answer, but from a vehicle parked thirty feet from the wash bay, I heard her talking from the back seat of a ¾ ton Ford that had seen better days.

"He fired me!" She couldn't help herself. She had a rag in her hand and, fired girl or not, she was still cleaning grime off the back of the truck's front seat.

"Hey, leave some upholstery," I said.

I opened a door on the other side of the old truck and jumped inside so that I could hide out with her. "Okay, I'll bite. What happened this time?"

"This isn't funny. I refused to clean his personal car today, the asshole! I had six details to do for actual customers! Is Stretch working in there?" she asked me, clearly worried about the output of a department she may no longer be running.

"Certainly, that decision will get overturned by Montello, just as it has before."

"ConMan wants me gone. He doesn't want me spreading rumors about him and his Chickie—Miss No Tits—over there."

"What are you saying? ConMan's having a fling?" With some-one in our office? I must have sounded too surprised.

"For Christ's sake! You see them together 24/7, don't you? Now you're going to act like you don't know?

"You mean Maggie? I just thought he was very bad at the com-pany paperwork." Angel shook her head.

"He's bad all right, and he's very bad at knowing how to use a condom too," Angel said as she was collecting her things.

"Is that your personal information, or hers?"

"That was mean. I wouldn't get near that son-of-a-bitch. If it was up to me, he'd be the one not working here tomorrow, not me. That isn't the only scam old ConMan's running either, and he knows I'm on to him." She dropped her rag in the truck and hopped out. "I'm headed to the Rusty Spur to get plastered. You want to come with me? Come on, I'll tell you all about it."

The Rusty Spur was the only authentic dive bar left in Copper Springs. It was rowdy, loud, and smelled like forty years of spilled beer. I started to say no, that I had to work tomorrow to the lady with no job. I forgot for a moment that I had done everything humanly possible to keep my day off.

"I'm sorry. I'm dying to hear more dirt on the ConMan but I can't go. I'll talk to Montello tomorrow for you; he'll straighten it out." I forgot again that I wasn't supposed to be in the next day.

"Good, you do that, will you? Oh, fuck it, forget the bar. I'm going for a drive on my motorcycle tonight. I can use some time to myself right now." She stomped through the service bays to her shop project of a '92 Yamaha and zoomed away in a cloud of exhaust. Angel's three kids were almost grown, and together, they lived on the very edge in every way. Her earnings were used to the penny on the last day of each month, sometimes a few days sooner. Her motorcycle, as she called it, was a conglomeration of sheet metal and parts that she had cleverly reassembled. It was amazing that it actually ran, but it probably was not a great idea to take it very far out of town.

So, ConMan was doing the nasty with cute little Maggie. Does everybody but me know about them? I looked over at Jeannie, the office manager, who sat with her back to the window. Jeannie knows then, and Mrs. ConMan, Juanita, I bet she knows too. That explained delicious burrito lunches for the rest of us. We couldn't run this place without Angel. For that matter, we couldn't do without Juanita's burritos either.

I managed to shirk all duties and avoid customers for more than three hours, knowing there were plenty other salesmen around to take them. Still, I never thought that I would be that employee. I could now say proudly that I did nothing and avoided everything. Slacking off—just another useful new skill that I've learned at the Copper Springs AutoMall. All this, so I could go shopping in Tucson with Dana on my regularly scheduled day off and find some new clothes that actually *fit*. *Is that so much to ask?* I checked the pedometer. Without giving the day a solid work effort, I had walked five and a half miles.

I was so busy worrying about Angel and dodging all possible customers that when I slipped out the back door to my car at exactly 5:30, my Roomba Robot Vacuum of a brain forgot all about the huge favor I'd promised Burke. Gram's bridge playing friends, Jean and Carol, were coming over for homemade soup and cornbread. I headed home straight away.

CHAPTER 28

At home, I found Dana lounging against the half wall in front of the bungalow reading on her cell phone because Grams was not home. She followed me into my bedroom to visit and plan our next day excursion.

"Girl, you're hiding a lot of salesmanship under that padding," she said, referring to the nude-colored cotton bra with the extra wide four-hook back that was folded on top of my dresser.

"You're really becoming a nag, you know that. This is the way I've always dressed." At least since I became a middle school teacher.

"Haven't you heard the news? Sex sells! It was in all the papers. You're a woman, aren't you? You're covering up your best advantage."

"Okay, now you are laying it on a little thick."

"I guess you know thick," she said, holding up the padded bra. "Exhibit A," she said, but I was more of a B minus than an A.

"That is not what I sell. I sell transportation, not cleavage."

"Oh, honey you are so misguided! You're putting a valuable part of your selling arsenal in a locked vault." She was becoming annoying. I had acquiesced to the shopping trip to Tucson just to get her off on a different discussion, but truth be told, I was very excited about it. My clothing choices were hard habits to break, and everything in my closet was now too big. At Midvale Middle School, no one had to lecture me on keeping my B cups wrangled and padded over. I knew it by instinct.

"Certainly, we have more to teach our sixth graders than ogling," our portly Principal Jackson used to say. I was no prude, all wardrobe choices as evidence to the contrary. It was just easier that way.

When I arrived in Arizona, dragging fifteen extra pounds of divorce weight, I bought two sizes larger Granny panties and bras with enough padding to insulate a Minnesota Icehouse. After fourteen years, I'd forgotten how or where to shop if it wasn't J.C.Penney, so Dana had stepped in to show me. The difficult part was getting a day off; we had already postponed our trip twice.

After Dana left, Grams and I enjoyed dinner with her buddies and we turned in early. It would be my last restful night for a very long time.

CHAPTER 29

Songbirds chirping incessantly outside my window and the fragrant smell of cinnamon and butter woke me up when I could have slept in. To verify what my olfactory senses were telling me, I skated out to the kitchen in my oversized leather-bottomed slippers. Every level surface was covered with pans of cinnamon rolls! The smell reminded me of my high school years in Copper Springs and that reminded me of Burke and that reminded me...

"Shit!"

"What is it dear?" Grams had overheard me from the living room.

"I forgot to turn Burke's keys into the service department."

"Did you see Burke yesterday?" She immediately glommed onto the most interesting tidbit.

"Yes, he dropped his keys by so they could work on his vehicle today. I told him I'd turn them into Service." I had been so busy avoiding doing anything that would cause me to go in and now I had to do just that.

"I'll be back in twenty minutes, tops. Dana isn't picking me up until 9:30."

"Can't you just call?"

"They don't answer the phone until the office crew comes in at nine, and that'll be an hour late. Damn it." I grabbed the smallest cinnamon roll from the tray that Grams had just put on top of the stove and flew out the door.

In case you hadn't already noticed, my abnormal Roomba brain worked in circular patterns like the Roomba vacuum model. It went over some real estate ad infinitum then skipped chunks that needed serious attention, like turning in a customer's keys. I drove emergency-fast. *Slow down, sister!* It wasn't even eight AM yet. The oil change boys had the side door unlocked and slightly open, so I slivered through it and headed toward the door into the show-room. The oil bay room to my right was lit up like a stadium ready for a Friday night game, so I trekked by in the dark unnoticed. I was so intent on getting to the desk where I left the keys that in the relative darkness of the service area, I almost didn't notice that Burke's truck was already parked over the first work pit. Someone was about to work on it, but why weren't the overhead lights on? It wasn't hoisted up, just simply parked and ready to go up. Who knew the key was on that desk in the showroom? Did they have to call Burke to ask him? Oh, God, I would be so embarrassed if they called him last night after we left because they were looking for that set of keys.

The driver's door of Burke's rig was open, and the biggest wrench that Snap-on tools makes was sitting on the seat. Was someone working on it already last night? Maybe this was the exceptional service that we advertised. Even though the wrench was heavy, I lifted it and put it back on top of the mechanic's metal chest. *I think that's Frank's tool box, but still locked? No mechanic ever leaves tools, he must be here.*

I knew a hundred reasons why I shouldn't, but I thought; what the hell. I was there alone with Burke's pickup and the door was wide open inviting me in. I climbed up in the driver's seat of the ¾ ton truck to have a look around. I'll just have a peek, maybe look at those receipts littering the dash. Hmm, Burke, you have been eating a lot of burgers at BurgerTown drive through. The catsup on the seat was also a dead giveaway pointing to fast food. Polo Cologne was in the glove box.

I leaned over the gear shift rifling through the papers in the glove box, pausing to inspect every receipt. What did I expect to find?

"What are you doing?" a voice said. I snapped back up so hard and fast that I hit my head on the gun rack in the truck's back window.

"Oh geez, Birdie, I didn't know it was you. What're you doing here in the dark"? Austin said. "I thought you were off today."

"I am," I said, trying to exit the truck like maybe he wouldn't notice that I was ever in it.

"You don't have to tell anybody you saw me, and then it will be like I wasn't here. Burke left me the keys last night and I wasn't sure the guys would find them on my desk so I… I just came in to… " I could tell that Austin was anxious to get back to his job and was getting antsy with my long, embellished explanation.

"Can I help?" he said.

"There was a list in the glove box that he wanted me to give them too," I said, coming up with a feeble explanation as to why I might be snooping in the owner's jockey box.

"I can do that for you," Austin said in his ever-helpful manner.

"Oh, no, that's okay. I think Conrad has had words with Burke about getting his truck fixed, so he probably knows what it needs." They had words all right, I heard them. As I went back outside to head for home, I looked around to make sure no one else saw my mad dash. It was the last thing I would like Mr. Montello to know because it made me look… What? Too forgetful? Too schoolmarm? That I came in early to correct my mistake? At least I knew I could trust Austin. It was our secret. The very idea of one of the guys watching out for me and then turning in those keys? That was a new one.

CHAPTER 30

I sped home before Dana pulled up in Geneva's elegant new four-door sedan with the leather seats and spoke wheels. I noted that it was not a car brand available at our dealership.

"Your folks aren't AutoMall shoppers, I see."

"No. Mom and Dad decided to buy at the other end of town this time," she said, as we both got in. "They don't like your Service Department."

"Who does?" The more I was at the dealership, the more I would think about shopping elsewhere too. As she stuck it in cruise control on the I-10, I began to regale her with tales of the numerous little two-bit jabs from my cohorts, then worked my way up to the part where they stole from women and children and I was one of those women. She shared similar stories of her tenure as the only woman at the police station. I realized as we talked, I hadn't had a real friend in years, and the idea flashed in my head that Peter's life-long buddies had ostracized me long before the day I actually left.

When we reached Houghton Road, at the edge of Tucson, I said, "Now, don't let me say another word about that Godforsaken place."

"Deal," she said, but she never made me feel like she didn't want to listen. Even with all the things I had told her since I'd known her, I left a few things out. I didn't mention Angel. I supposed that Angel and the police department might have a professional relationship. I didn't tell her I had to go back in today because I was a forgetful idiot yesterday. I wanted my friend to think better of me, but I had no idea how hard that would be by the end of the delightful day we were about to spend together. I also didn't tell her about my run-in with ConMan because I was trying to forget it ever happened. For now, I felt tremendous appreciation to have someone I could trust and confide in, and I began to relax.

"Oh, look, my cell phone isn't working," I said with my finger on the off button. Gramma Lou had Dana's number if she needed me.

As our car descended from Interstate 10 exit onto Congress Street, we were sounding like a couple of giggly teens. We traipsed around downtown and filled our car for about an hour then we were off to lunch. Dana maneuvered the sedan into the parking garage above her favorite eatery on Pennington, where heavenly aromas met us at the front door along with background sounds of the rock band Coldplay blended with the conviviality of the patrons. Our waiter was a U of A student named Kolby, who served us piping hot plates of tortilla-filled bliss. We relaxed and devoured our first bites.

"Birdie," Dana, more gregarious than most, spoke slowly and seemed to be choosing her words carefully. "It's not any of my business, I know that, but I'm curious. May I ask what happened to bring you to Copper Springs when you were sixteen? You've never said and I'd really like to know."

Here was my life's trickiest question, and I had good reason to be reticent to tell it. If I told a prospective new friend too early in our relationship, it threw a bucket of cold water on it. I had doused several fledgling friendships out of existence. If I held the story back too long, it took on the even bigger specter of—what's wrong with her that she wants to keep it a secret? But Dana was ready to hear it. She was fast becoming my friend and this was as good a time as any, so I began the short version. We could discuss the longer version later. I began as I always did.

"In a way, you could say that I lost my mom because she loved fashion. She was tall and gorgeous like a runway model. And—I lost my dad because of how much he loved my mom." Dana stared, inviting me to continue.

"One month short of my seventeenth birthday, Mom and Dad were on a quick trip to Omaha to buy her a lovely formal for my dad's installation as the Grand Poohbah at the state Masonic Temple. They were social to a fault, and they looked amazing when they were all decked out. Everybody remarked about that."

"Since they had an event the next day, my dad decided to fly them in a small plane that he shared with his banker friend. He used it to get to the statewide meetings he attended; it was a Cessna 210. Mom shopped in the morning while Dad had a business meeting, then they had lunch together in downtown Omaha. When the new dress and shoes and bag were stowed in the back for the trip home, the latch on the cargo door was somehow not secured properly." Dana let out a long breath. She probably knew what was coming next.

Whenever I tried to talk about it, it was hard for me to get through that part of the story. I could picture that rusted latch as if I had just seen it the day before. Did it break? Did the rust finally build up and prevent it from closing properly? The first time I noticed it was when I saw my dad load my hard-side plaid suitcase on my very first trip with them. Should I have mentioned it? I didn't because they always thought I was a worrywart.

"When the hatch opened after they took off, it created a drag that the engine couldn't overcome no matter how hard it tried. It just stopped in midair. It was Friday, the First of September, at 1:45 p.m. It was a beautiful funeral. I think everybody in the state of Nebraska attended. There were white freesias, Mom's favorite, everywhere. I don't much like the smell of them now. I have never been to another funeral since, although I've been lucky and haven't really had any that I had to go to."

Dana sat in silence, so I continued. "In less than two weeks, I was sent to Copper Springs, to finish out my last two years of high school, to live with my grandparents who owned the Rexall Store."

"No wonder you and Louella are so close," she said.

"Yup, the closest. But even so, I headed right back to Nebraska the moment I could, as though being in Nebraska would bring them back. You know, I just now realized that I was never happy on the Sander's Farm, not even one day in all my time there. What I wanted in Nebraska didn't exist anymore, and I lost so much with what I left behind here." It was the first time I'd told the story without tears. That surprised me.

"Well, you're here now!" she said. "Let's get you more acquainted with the old Pueblo!" Bless her heart, she didn't ask more. There would be other days for that. Ironically, we followed that story with shopping where, without fail, I always missed my beautiful mom.

––––––

We moved on to Fourth Avenue, a hubbub of busy streets, light rail activity, and shoppers, then headed off down Broadway to the mall where we began assembling the parts of the new me. It was like playing with Legos. I gathered up the colored pieces, and then Dana, my personal stylist, fit them together until I looked alluring, or at least until I shed my schoolteacher armor and frillied up a bit. By the time we were done, our trunk and half the back seat were full. We were exhausted.

"I hope I haven't spent the rent money," I said. We both laughed, knowing I didn't have rent payments, but it made me think. Maybe some of the month's outstanding earnings should go to Grams for housing me. Geneva became the central subject of our conversation for the ride back.

"They've given her six months," Dana said with a quiet voice that indicated she'd stoically accepted the sad news.

I didn't know what to say to her and I should have. Hadn't I lost two parents? But I kept quiet the way she did when she listened to my story. I put my hand on her arm, and we rode silently for a few minutes until I finally spoke.

"She is surrounded by a lot of love with her family and so many friends," I said, but it was a flimsy comment for such a serious moment.

"That she is." Dana agreed. "That she is."

By the time we passed the turn to Sierra Vista, our mood was back to the fun of our excursion, and we were positively giddy when we arrived at the bungalow. We hauled all the bags in. She insisted that I try things on to make sure the total effect was what she, as my personal style maker, was after. I just hoped that I hadn't spent my limited funds on things I wouldn't have the guts to wear.

"If you can't be a harlot working at a car lot, where the hell can you be one?" she said, as she held up one of the two lace bras she had encouraged me to purchase. Dana provided friendship and philosophy. I zipped up short leather boots after shaking myself into stone-washed, skinny jeans, and I topped the push-up lace bra with a colorful peasant blouse. It was lower cut then I was used to, but I felt great in the new outfit.

"Aren't you forgetting something?" Dana held up a lacy thing that I thought maybe was supposed to replace underpants.

"I told you that I wouldn't do that thong thing. No way! And still, you bought it anyway?"

"They sell them by the pound" she said, opening the first package to let three bounce out. "They're cheap."

"It isn't the price that I object to. This isn't underwear," I said holding one up and swinging it around on my finger. "This is a slingshot!" She picked up a pair of my full-sized cotton jersey panties that were folded on top of my dresser and mimicked me by swinging them around her head and said: "These aren't either. These are as big as T-Shirts. These are huge, cotton, ass T-shirts! You could hang these up and show a movie on them. Hard Rock Café could sell these with their full-sized logo!" The idea of printing Hard Rock on my dumb underwear sent us into peals of laughter. We melted onto my bedroom floor in uncontrollable mirth. Life is so much better with a best friend that thinks like you and shares secrets and listens to yours. Before I left, my Nebraska social circle had distanced themselves completely from my pathetic self. They were worried that infidelity was communicable. Doing girl stuff with Dana made me happy, maybe happier than I had ever been.

As if in a distant room, a muffled cell phone rang. Dana realized it was her phone buried in the bottom of our first shopping bag.

CHAPTER 31

"**N**o wonder we weren't interrupted," she said. "My phone was in the first bag we put in the trunk when we were downtown."

She answered, and then the smile dropped off her face like snow avalanches off a mountain, leaving a cold serious stare behind.

"Is it Geneva?" I asked. It was clear that our wonderful day had come to an abrupt end. Dana glanced at me then turned her back and continued her conversation. A man's voice was on the other end. I wasn't able to eavesdrop, but I was pretty sure it was not her father. Was it a doctor? Should I get Grams?

Dana was the heart and soul of Copper Spring's police operation, so she often got calls from her boss, Jeff, or the deputies when they needed intellectual or emotional backup. It was Dana who saw to it that all the town-related activities such as holiday parades, talks at the local grade school, and various other "show off the patrol cars" events ran smoothly. Still, I was hoping the call wasn't about Geneva.

Her cell phone ringing reminded me that my phone was still turned off. As soon as I turned it on, it began pinging like a microwave when a frozen pretzel has been left too long. Ping, ping, ping—six new messages, followed by the pinging of five more. What the heck? That's more messages than I got in two weeks. So out of the blue I'm Miss Popularity? The first three texts were from my customer, George, who, by virtue of the fact he couldn't reach me, was now overly eager. Just two days before he was wishy-washy, but since I wasn't available, it threw him into a frenzy. More messages came through and then the buzzing indicating another phone message was waiting. Was a nuclear bomb dropped on the Mexico/Arizona border? Did the wall in Nogales fall down?

"What's happened?" I tried to ask Dana. Dana held her hand up signaling just a moment. Her eyes were signaling alarm. Copper Springs had its share of police-involved events but most were car accidents on the Interstate or bar fights.

My messages sound rang again. This time it was Mr. Montello asking me to call him. Maybe he actually wanted to give me that deal after all. Too late. Half a dozen messages from Clay, who had never messaged me, all begging me to call him, saying, "urgent" and "Where the hell are you? We've been calling all day!" And, four messages from Angel. Oh shit, Angel! I forgot to talk to Montello for her. Damn it. Not following through was becoming my M.O.

I opened my text feature of my phone again and read her texts carefully, then re-read them. I slumped down onto the bed. I felt like someone who had let go of a huge breath, then couldn't take it back in again. I had no air to use for questions that were forming like monsoon storm clouds at the front of my skull.

"Okay, I'll be right in. Yes. I'll bring her." Dana set her phone on the dresser. She stared down at me with the seriousness of an oncologist.

"What are they saying?" I asked because I already knew what had happened and it was unbelievable. I held out my phone and showed her my texts from Angel:

OMG Call me. Call me!

Where R U?? They are asking a lot of questions.

Birdie, they found the ConMan DEAD!

In the mechanic's pit near his office.

Please don't tell them about what I said last night.

"Have they talked to Angel?" I asked Dana.

"What did she say last night that she was so worried about?" Dana had already moved into detective mode.

"Oh, that. It was nothing." I hoped it was nothing. "Is it true? He's dead then?" I asked, changing the subject back to what? A murder! I had an instant urge to crawl under the covers but instead, I started babbling.

"He's been giving me a hell of a tough time since I started work there. Nobody likes him. It isn't just me." I heard myself trying to sell her my "it isn't just me" story, like I had tried to sell Clay. At least her family didn't like Conrad either. Even so, I didn't want her to think, like Clay did, that I was the instigator. *Instigator my ass—the guy is dead.*

"A few days ago, he pulled me out of a car and then dropped me on the ground." As I told her this, it sounded absurd and it sounded that way to her, too.

"That's a crazy ass story. Why didn't I hear that earlier today?" she said. "How does someone pull you out of a car? Why didn't you just open the door?" Why did I leave this out? I'd told her everything else.

"Because we said we wouldn't talk about work." Dana gave me that head-cocked to the side like a Labrador signifying no understanding of my explanation. Of course, all I talked about was work angst the entire way to Tucson. I wanted to tell her, but the whole thing was so strange. I decided to forget about it only to have it flood back into my consciousness. Now the thought had an added tinge of guilt.

"Don't tell anyone else that story, especially not now."

"Everybody at work already knows; several of them watched. Was that Jeff? What did he say?"

"It gets more complicated. Conrad was apparently found in the bottom of the mechanic's pit all right but, it was Burke Buchanan's truck that was parked right on top of him. They found him when one of the mechanics backed the truck out."

"Burke's truck?" Oh, God, Burke's truck was parked over the body. The body was underneath while I was in it this morning? Oh Jesus God.

"Is Burke a suspect, then?" Dana didn't answer my question.

"Dana, is Burke a suspect?" I asked again, grabbing her arm more strenuously than I intended.

"No honey, he isn't, but I think you are."

"Me?" I jumped up and stood straight, letting the clothes I'd burrowed into drop to the floor. My mind was so into Burke and my friend Angel, who I thought was probably already behind bars at the city jail, that I didn't think I heard it right.

"Me?"

Dana nodded yes. Once again, I slumped back down on the bed, this time pulling the frilly spread up around me. Why was I cold? I started to shake.

"Jeff wants to talk to you tonight, and tomorrow it will be the Sheriff's Department doing the inquiry."

"Talk to me. About what?" My mind reeled. It was holding onto information in bits and pieces and then randomly releasing them as though they were trivia answers from the "everything else" category. I was a suspect in a murder? This wouldn't look good on my background check for my next librarian job. After this, I'd be lucky to get a bookmobile.

"Dana, I was in that truck this morning," I said. "Could he have been dead underneath it then?" I wasn't really asking her this question. It was just one of the bits and pieces swirling in my head while my whirling Roomba-vacuum mind picked up on all the dirt.

"What were you doing in Burke's truck?"

My mind heard her question as if from the other end of a tunnel. Why was I in that truck this morning? I didn't have a good answer. What? Was I going to admit that I was snooping through wadded-up receipts to see where he bought his burgers? I was too embarrassed to tell the truth.

"I was looking for my lipstick," I blurted out. "I think I dropped it in the truck the other day when I went to lunch with Burke." A lie. Did it sound convincing? She looked puzzled.

"Burke stopped by the dealership and took me to lunch last week." I had deliberately not told her about the lunch. Why?

"Why didn't you just ask him for it?"

"I hadn't seen him since." Another lie. I saw him last night when he gave me the keys. My God. I couldn't believe my brain was conjuring this shit up. I had no good reason not to have told this to Dana.

"You'd better get dressed. Do you want me to take you over to the station? Can you hear me, Birdie? Do you want a ride to the station? They want to talk to you."

So, this is what abject fear feels like. I observed my hands shaking as though they were someone else's appendages. My teeth started to chatter uncontrollably, and it was hard for me to answer Dana. Fear is a whole different feeling than anger. Anger, I was familiar with.

"Honey, you don't need to be so scared. They just want to ask you some questions. I think I should let you settle down for a while, but you need to get dressed." Gramma Lou appeared in this scene like it was a dream. She and Dana exchanged looks of concern. Did they think I couldn't see them?

Dana pushed some of my new things toward me, but I pushed them away. I wanted my comfort clothes, including my knit bullet-proof polyester black pants, my cotton "ass t-shirt" underwear and my red cardigan sweater. In my stupor, I kept looking at the bedroom door, as if expecting Mrs. Larsen, my mean third grade teacher, so she could start yelling that she knew I was a troublemaker. It's true; I was then, but not now.

"Dana." I heard my voice call her name as if it was emanating from a small child. "Dana, there was a big wrench on the seat of the pickup. I picked it up and moved it."

She looked at me and took me by the shoulders. "We'd better do your hair, honey. They might want to take your picture."

CHAPTER 32

Grams drove me, which never happened. We should be home, enjoying the Chili Mac casserole she had fixed for us tonight, but I'd lost my appetite.

"I bet you never thought you would be accompanying your darling Alberta to an interrogation about a murder," I said.

"It's just questioning, dear, not a trial. You didn't murder anybody. This is just a formality. I bet every person on the staff of Copper Springs AutoMall will be questioned just like this," she said. I could always count on Grams.

We pulled into a downtown side street where a two-story building made from local rock stood alone surrounded by ample parking, but the lot was mostly empty. Above the door, the words "Let All That Enter Here Be Free" were carved into the red-colored stone. *Odd.* My Roomba mind observed, "Isn't there a jail downstairs?" Dana was standing on the curb.

"The outside's beautiful, isn't it? But downstairs is pretty much a shit hole," she said. "The town leaders don't want the pokey to have too many comforts. Come on, I'll take you to our offices." When we got to the lower level, Dana turned her attention to Grams.

"Luella, will you sit here? I'll come and get you after the questions. Okay?" Gramma stepped forward and gave me a heartfelt hug of immense proportions. I was ashamed to have caused her this concern. As Dana led me to the back, I realized that Grams had probably heard this whole event play out on her scanner this morning and couldn't get in touch with either Dana or me, but she never mentioned it. What a lousy thing to put you through, Gramma. I'm sorry.

"Dana, will I have to take a lie detector test?" I asked as we walked down a dark hall.

"Hell, no, we don't have the capability to do much more than to ask a couple of questions. When it gets to that point, the Sheriff's Office at the county will be involved. This is just a get-acquainted. Don't worry; you were with me all day, remember?" Then she asked for my I.D.

We entered a space too small for all the desks crammed into it. I couldn't see actual jail cells, but I was pretty sure they were in back. Funny, I expected the cells to be right in the room like Mayberry's jail. Thank God Stretch wasn't still there.

"Jeff, you've met…" she began, but for some reason, she needed to look at my driver's license to read my official name, "Alberta Kathryn Alton."

"I'll get a copy of her license while you two visit." Visit? She made it sound like a tea party. "Would you like some tea, Birdie?" she said. It was a tea party.

"Hi Alberta, nice to see you again," Jeff, the city police chief said. Nice guy; he was a Nickelodeon style cop from bygone years.

"You too, Jeff," I said. "Nice to see you." I mumbled the words evenly, with the intonation of a memorized grocery list.

"Birdie, whereabouts have you been all day?" he asked. "People have been trying to call you."

"She's been in Tucson with me," Dana interjected as she handed me back my driver's license and a cup of lukewarm tea.

"Dana, you know the drill. These questions here are for Birdie to answer. You better go on out front there and check on Mrs. Alton." Dana gave me a thumbs-up that Jeff didn't see as she exited.

"Alberta, what time did you leave Copper Springs for Tucson?"

"About 8 a.m.," I answered. "We started early. I haven't had a day away from the car lot in weeks. We went out for lunch and we…" He stopped me by putting up his hand as a crossing guard at a school might use to stop traffic.

"I'm sure you two ladies had a fine day. I guess what I want to know is where were you at 7:30 a.m. this morning?" I knew this question was coming. It would have been way too hard for a young kid like Austin to keep our secret, especially if it were cops asking. I just didn't think it would be the third question. I mustered all the truthfulness I could gather and then answered.

"I made a quick run to the car lot this morning to make sure that the keys that were left on my desk last night found their way to the service department."

"Was that key for the pickup truck of the Lone Pine Ranch out here south of town?"

"Yes, it was." Perry Mason TV reruns that I've watched with Grams came to mind. Did I need a lawyer? Should I halt this and ask for one?

"Did you find those keys this morning? If so, where?"

"Yes, I found them in the pickup parked in the service bay at the AutoMall."

"Did you get into the truck to check if the keys were in there?"

"Yes," I answered. That was a much more plausible reason for me to be in the truck. "Yes, I was looking for the keys," I said again.

"Did you drive the truck?"

"Oh, gosh no. I don't know when it was moved there. It was sitting outside the window last night." I knew I should say as little as possible, but my brain just continued to dump everything that appeared at the front of it.

"Did you touch anything other than the truck?"

"I don't think so," I answered, trying to think of something other than the fact that Conrad was probably dead under that truck all the while I was snooping through Burke's jockey box.

"Did you by any chance see a tool on the step?" Again, I felt gut punched. This time it was by a wrench!

"That's right, there was a large wrench, but it was on the seat," I said. I knew this would be his next question if I didn't just haul off and tell it up front. "I moved it in order to get into the truck. I put it on top of the red metal Snap-on tool chest against the wall so that Frank, our head mechanic, would see it. I thought it was probably Frank's." But mechanics are totally anal about locking up all their tools before they leave for the day, everybody knew that. It probably wasn't his wrench. Did Angel have a wrench set in the Detail Depatment?

"Did you see blood on that tool or blood on the seat when you got in?" Jeff's question brought me back to the brightly lit room.

"Blood? No." There was some spilled Catsup, I think—Jesus God. Was that Conrad's blood and not Burke's last burger condiment? Was it on my jeans? I must have looked alarmed.

"Alberta, we believe that Conrad was killed with that wrench."

"You don't think I did it. Do you?"

"You know, we have to talk to everybody. That's how this works."

I could hardly believe what I was hearing. I was actually a suspect! Of course, I was a suspect. I'd picked the damn thing up. I could feel the color and heat drain from my face right down to my ankles. I stood up suddenly. The tightly wound anxiety of the last hour was springing loose with violent force.

"Here now, sit back down, you're looking kind of peaked. Try to breathe." Jeff was kind and he waited for me to compose myself. "So, help me try to determine what the murder scene looked like before you tampered with it." Tampered with it? Tampered with it. Tampering with evidence was at least a better line of questioning than creating the evidence.

"I didn't know it was a murder scene," I protested.

"I'm sure you didn't. We're about done." The uniforms in the room seemed happy for that news but he continued. "I have one more question. We've been told that you witnessed a woman named Angel Moretti having harsh words with the deceased. Is that true?" Angel. She was in this as deep as I was. I hope not the deepest.

"I don't know. She was kind of fired up, but she gets that way. She's no murderer. I can't even count the people who've had harsh words with the ConMan." The uniform's heads all snapped toward me. "I mean Conrad," I said.

"But did she argue with him last night, Miss Alton?"

"I didn't hear them argue." That was a totally true statement. I didn't hear it. I had developed a great big headache and I wanted to go home with my Grams.

"I guess I do have a couple more questions. Do you know of any reason why Burke Buchanan would've come back to the dealership last night? Was there any problem between Burke and Mr. Richardson?"

"Not to my knowledge," I answered, the picture of their screaming match looming up in my brain. "Nobody liked Conrad," I said, "nobody."

"Where were you after work last night?" My mind was blank. Where was I? It was funny how that seemed so long ago that I couldn't remember. I just stared at Jeff and nothing came to me. Where was I?

"Birdie, where did you have dinner last night?"

"Oh. dinner, dinner, yes, I ate dinner. Gram's good friends Jean and Carol came over for soup. Yes, Grams cooked soup." I let out a big sigh. Thank God, I had two wonderful ladies that love my Gramma Lou to corroborate that story.

"All right then, that's it for now. Will you be at the dealership tomorrow? The Sheriff's Department will probably have more questions."

"I don't know," I answered honestly.

"This isn't a request, Miss Alton."

"Okay, I understand." I'd rather be anywhere else tomorrow. Dana led me back to where Grams was waiting.

"This'll teach us not to screw off in Tucson again," she said. "I've got more info now, but I can't talk here. I'll call you later."

As soon as I got to the curb, I vomited. Grams hugged me, and this time, I returned it so hard I almost broke her ribs. I got in the passenger seat of Gram's old beater, being careful not to mess it up. We sat in my sick smell all the way home. I took a shower and threw my clothes into the washer. I made sure I included the jeans with what might be blood on them in the load.

Gramma made me my favorite Constant Comment Tea with milk. I drank it to choke down two Advil PMs. I fell asleep on top of my new clothes. In my dreams, Conrad was a circus barker with some sort of whip, and all the AutoMall workers were circus performers. I was a clown in a crowded clown car along with Clay and Frank the mechanic. Cuervo was juggling wrenches. Montello was swinging on a trapeze dressed head to toe in a performer's suit of the finest worsted wool. There were tigers and lions in the mechanic's bays and Angel was the high wire act. My sleep was unusually sound and I didn't hear Dana's call.

CHAPTER 33

I woke up surrounded by wrinkled clothing and crushed shopping bags. Everything was rumpled or smudged. I must have put my dirty shoes on the bed. Birdie! This is not like you. Hello? Where's the nerdy librarian with the perfect attendance record and the meticulously organized closet? The answer was simple. She vamoosed. Gone. She high-tailed it out to the desert and joined a band of misfits—pot and pan salesmen, "Pot and panners," as my dad used to say. She's mooching off her relatives and I hear she may have even be accused of murder. Oh, my God. It wasn't a dream.

"Birdie dear? Are you up? I cooked you some oatmeal." Maybe I am in a dream. That sounds like my Gramma Lou getting me up for school. I was waiting for the movie plot to tell me that I was Peggy Sue, standing in my baby doll pajamas, about to make all different choices from the ones I had made the last few days.

"Little Deuce Coupe," my cell ringtone, broke my imaginings and vibrated, rattling my bed stand.

"Dana, I passed out last night. I think Grams gave me a mickey." A little joke but she didn't chuckle. "I didn't hear your calls. Sorry."

"Just so you know, Conrad had a severe head and neck injury, but he was shot too."

"Shot? He was killed twice?"

"That's what they're trying to figure out; it may have been a ricochet bullet because of the place of entry. So, the case is more complicated than our guys can handle. It's already gone to the sheriff. They will be at the dealership today because it's hard to drag everybody to Tucson where the county seat is." I listened intently, still shocked at what I was being told.

"Don't get too relaxed," she said. *Is that a joke?*

"They want to know where that truck key was. Also, your prints are on the wrench. You have an explanation, but they don't like your story of why you were in the truck or why you went back to the dealership in the morning. They think you may be covering up for somebody, and they want to know more about the incident where you fell out of the car."

"I didn't fall out; Conrad yanked me out of the window I was trying to crawl out of. Then he deliberately dropped me." I was no longer anything near relaxed.

"I told you. Don't tell them that," she said. "Don't say anything about what happened a few days ago, unless they ask and then play it down. Tell them you fell."

"The guys saw it," I said.

"Then, let them tell it, but you play it down, understand?"

"Should I be calling a lawyer?"

"Not yet. But play it cool, Birdie. Act like you hardly knew the guy." I didn't know him and hadn't wanted to.

"Do they have a real suspect?" I asked. "If they think I'm covering for someone, who do they think that is?"

"They're all over the place with their thoughts on that. They'll talk to all the people who worked for him, like your friend, Angel, and the mechanics, of course, but right now Conrad's wife is their prime."

"The burrito lady?" I let out a sigh of relief "But, Juanita, a killer? I can't see anyone as a killer except maybe Wade or Stretch."

"They always think of the spouse first. These guys are none too creative. But that's not all—someone in your office, her name is Margie, maybe? Anyway, it turns out Conrad had been servicing more than what he was hired for. Apparently, it's been going on for a while."

"It's Maggie from the office. They're together all the time; I mean they were. I just thought he was bad at paperwork, but Angel told me about them. Grams heard that Maggie was arrested the other day for a fight with someone."

"Oh? Is she Margaret Holbrook then?"

"I don't know her last name," I said, "but that could be right."

"If that's your Maggie, then yes, she called us, because Mrs. Richardson was threatening her. I better remind Jeff about that."

"Grams said she heard on the scanner that Montello bailed her out, so he may know more too."

"I'm taking notes here. Get this, Margaret or Maggie is pregnant," she said. "She told Jeff that."

"No wonder they like the wife for the murder. That's a pretty serious motive," I said. "Maybe he was dumping her."

"They have also talked to several others including Burke, since the body was found under his truck. Birdie, Guess what?! The wrench was from Burke's truck! They found a set in the bed of his truck with that one missing.

"Where's Burke now?" I wondered out loud. I was back in anxious mode again. "Have they ruled him out?"

"Not completely, but he said he was out to dinner last night."

"Do you know who with?" I asked. "I mean, was it a date?"

"Nice try, sweetie. No, I don't know who with, but I might be able to see the full write-up of his interview. If I can get my eyes on it, you'll be my first call. At any rate, he has a solid alibi if it checks out. They have him on the list to be at the dealership today too. I just wanted to warn you in case you wanted to wear your sexy new duds that we bought in Tucson." Wardrobe was the last thing on my mind.

"Can I call you later today?" I said.

"Better not. Jeff knows we're friends. I'll call you when I go out to lunch if I have any more news. Don't sleep through my call though!"

"No, that won't happen again. Thank you." I said. "I mean it, Dana. I really appreciate all you have done."

"No problem." What does she think of her friend now? The friend who left out some important plot points in last week's story. Why didn't I tell her?

———

As the day passed, I felt more immersed in Gram's world of the bungalow than I have ever been before. In all my life, whenever I needed a sanctuary, it was my Grandma's home.

"Do you have to go to the dealership today?" she asked as we folded clothes.

"Dana called a while ago. The sheriff's deputies will be there, and they are even talking to people who don't work there, like Burke."

"Burke? Why ever do they need to talk to him?"

"It was his truck that was parked over that mechanic's bay, and the murder weapon was a wrench from Burke's truck."

"Why, I'd never believe that of him in a million years." Grams was as ruffled as I was when I heard the news. I didn't believe it about Burke either, but I was afraid it was not going to be as easy to say that about Angel.

CHAPTER 34

The back parking area of the AutoMall looked like it did the week before we shipped the fleet order for thirty State Highway patrol vehicles. Cop cars were everywhere, just not parked as square and tight as the fleet vehicles. There was even a Border Patrol truck, but it might simply have been in for regular service. All the spots were filled so the staff was relegated to park out along the road to the highway and hike in.

Rich pulled in and Clay swung in right behind him skidding his child-hauler minivan in next to me, almost taking out Tweety's black and yellow front panel. The auto boys loved to play like they were NASCAR racers and even family man Clay was no exception—unless his little girls were on board.

"Well, this will be a real shit show today, won't it?" Clay said. "Did you ever think in your ever-lovin' life that you would work at a murder scene?"

"Not usually a librarian's worry," I said, "although, I was exposed to a fair amount of crime novels so they might want me to help solve the case."

"I can't say I'll miss the guy one little bit, but it's pretty creepy that someone offed him right in the building," Clay said. "Birdie, if they ask me about that day when you clocked him in the nuts, I'll have to tell them."

"Clay, you don't have anything to tell. You didn't see anything happen, and anyway, they won't ask. But I do know they're going to ask me who took that set of Burke's keys from my desk. Do you know who picked them up?"

"No," he said, apparently feeling no need to elaborate.

"Rich asked me about it so I'm guessing that he gave them to Conrad," I said.

"Except that Rich left early, remember?" Clay was obviously thinking about the day and trying to piece it together as much as I was.

"That's right. He left at 4 p.m. I forgot that. I guess it's for the sheriff's men to figure out. Anyway, they aren't looking too hard; they think his wife was the one who did it." Clay, who had been walking ahead, spun around and leaned right into my face.

"How'd you know that?" he said. I was getting more info from Dana then I should be allowed to have. I wouldn't make that mistake again.

"They always suspect the spouse first, don't they?" I said, sloughing off the question. "So that's probably what they're doing this time, too, don't you think?" What I really wanted to ask everyone was, "What did you know about Conrad and Maggie, and when did you know it?"

All the commotion emanated from the icky blue-green walled conference room. Although there was a window onto the hallway right next to the door, we didn't see who was inside because one of the donut-eating cops was large enough to generally block our view. Orbit was running in and out through the legs of the onlookers. Orbit meant Wallace was in the room. Somehow, I never pictured the stubby little cowboy in this scenario, but naturally, he was present. His business will be devastated.

The back end of the building was completely cordoned off. Cops were still milling about. The staff were all hanging with their individual departments as though mixing with each other would change the recipe and we'd all end up in the soup.

It seemed everyone there had on their Sunday best; at least, the shirts weren't burrito stained or holey. I'd gone with the standard stodgy schoolmarm attire and left my new jeans and blouses hanging in the closet. Maybe I'd never wear them.

Maggie was missing in action. She had to be a suspect. Didn't she? Who wasn't one? And then I realized that Angel was missing too. Jeannie, the cranky office manager, sidled up to me—the first time she had ever directly spoken to me—and I was a bit taken aback.

"The business is closed today. I'm not sure why we all need to be here at once."

"Will Maggie come in?" I asked, trying to lead Jeannie to tell me what she might know.

"Don't we all have to be here?" She didn't take my bait.

"How well did you know Conrad?" I asked her.

"Well enough to know he was a pig, and that he didn't deserve Maggie." So, I just had to ask the right question, then she wanted to tell me all she knew.

"We all warned her to stay clear of him. He has a past, you know. He's been in the big house in Colorado. I tried to convince Montello not to hire him, but Mike, you know, well, you can't tell Mike anything."

"So, Conrad and Mater got hired at about the same time?" I said, leading her again.

"No, Mater doesn't work for us. I think he covered for Conrad and Maggie some, you know. Hell, we all did." Don't include everybody, I thought. Some of us didn't even know they were getting action. She didn't mention the pregnancy. Does she know? See there, who has the inside info this time?

NewKid strolled over to a box of pastries someone was thoughtful enough to supply. It wasn't the TV guy Jason but the way it was going he might be called in.

"This is a mighty fine breakfast but what will we all do for our lunches now?" he said. Clay told me that you said they think the burrito lady did her old man in."

"No, I didn't say that," I lied. I suppose I may as well get in practice lying so when I'm ready to tell the doozies I can make them sound more authentic. "I said that they always suspect the spouse first, don't they? And she had plenty of motive."

"She did?" he said. Did I just do it again? Certainly he knew— of all people here. NewKid was the sweet talker who had wiggled into every clique in the building.

"Oh, you mean because of the Maggie thing." He said between munching on a raspberry Danish in one hand and gulping it down with milk from a plastic cup with the other. I breathed a sigh of relief. "But Juanita found out about that ages ago. Why would she off him now?" The sentence trailed away as he headed back to Bernadette's boxes for another Danish or two before the sheriff's crew gobbled them all.

Orbit came bounding into the showroom. I bent down to pet him, but instead, he jumped full into my arms and licked my face. Even Orbit needed more petting in this time of trouble. Rich was clearly miffed that Orbit was showing me so much affection.

It was unclear what order they were using to call us in, but the mechanics were inside the office first and Angel's helper, Austin, was waiting outside. Where the heck was Angel? Milling about, waiting, the time seemed like an eternity. Noon became 12:30. Twelve-thirty became 1:15. Several salesmen were called in before me. They exited, appearing dead serious and chastened.

When Clay emerged, he whispered, "Don't worry, I didn't tell them to look for the bruises on ConMan's balls. We'll let them think the missus did it." He grabbed his coat and went out the side door.

"Aren't you the comedian." Their comments were making me more uneasy. Rich and I stood alone next to the windows, waiting to be called.

"Jeannie made up some bullshit story about her dog at the vet," Rich said. "So she and Linda got moved ahead of the rest of us." None of my encounters with the head bookkeeper had impressed me much and here was yet another example where she was pulling strings or pulling rank so she could get home earlier than the rest of us.

"How well did you know him?" I asked Rich.

"Know Conrad? About as much as you could know a guy who comes in late and leaves early and doesn't know shit from Shinola." I smiled at that phrase; it was one of my mom's favorites. "What do they expect us all to say? I doubt any of us will paint the picture quite as bad as it was, or we'd all be suspects now, wouldn't we? Well, you might be one anyway, right? With all the encounters you have had with him lately. You know, somebody's going to tell them that stuff." I realized, right at that moment, which somebody it would be. I didn't have too much time to chew on Rich's comment before they called him in, then me, whom they saved for last.

The sick turquoise tint of our meeting room spilled a cool hue out onto the tile in front of the door. Someone should have taken in some incandescent lamps. Everyone here looked like zombies—killer zombies. I sat in the one empty chair.

CHAPTER 35

Sheriff Anderson, leathery-skinned and stocky, appeared all trussed up like a Thanksgiving turkey in his khaki-colored uniform. It was at least a size too small, for starters. His ten-gallon hat rested upside down on the table top, and he had a yellow legal pad on the table in front of him. No one in the overfilled room was using an iPad or computer.

My Uncle Pat's sage advice, "Just because you are asked a question doesn't mean you have to answer," was great in theory but proved to be a lot more difficult in practice.

"Hello Birdie." Jeff, the police chief who scared the hell out of me the night before, was somehow reassuring. The sheriff covered the basics. Then came the tough questions.

"Alberta, can you tell us about an altercation out on the sales lot with the deceased? Do we have this correct? You climbing out a window of a car?" *Thanks Rich, I owe you for this.*

"We occasionally drive some of the old junkers that are on their way to the auctions. I guess Wade thinks it's best to put miles on them since…"

"What we are wondering is why were you climbing out the window and were you injured when the deceased tried to help?" *Tried to help? Tried to kill me is more like it.* I tried to calm down.

"Not really. The car I drove had a broken door, and I fell. That's about it."

"You don't think that Mr. Richardson, the deceased, meant for you to fall and get injured."

"I don't know, I guess you'd have to ask him that question. I mean if that were possible."

"Did you try to hit him with the vehicle when you drove onto the lot that day?"

"What?" *Did NewKid say that?* "No!" He moved on to more questions, seemingly not caring about the answers.

"Ms. Alton, are you aware that your fingerprints are on the murder weapon?"

"I thought he was killed with a gunshot." My mind raced. Did Dana tell me that and I was not supposed to know? Or, did Jeff tell me that last night? *Birdie, you have got to remember that the guy who talks first loses.*

"Yes, there was a gunshot, but we think that Conrad was hit with a large wrench that has your fingerprints on it and yours alone. Why are your prints on the wrench?"

I spoke slowly. "Actually, I didn't give the wrench much thought at all; I just knew it didn't belong on the seat. I guess it could have even been Burke's." *Jesus! Shut up Birdie.*

"Did you know then that it was taken from a set in the bed of the Lone Pine vehicle?"

"No, I didn't know where it came from." My knee was trembling. I had to hold it against the table with my hand.

"What were you looking for inside the truck?"

"I just wanted to make sure the keys were in it," I said with confidence as I had practiced the answer the night before at the police station.

"Why would you think that the keys would not be in it when you'd already parked it in the work bay?" The chubby sheriff had gut-punched me again.

"I didn't park it. I never drove it. I had forgotten to turn them in so I was just checking, that's all." My voice box seemed to be tightening and I was starting to squeak. "The truck was parked outside the showroom window when I left last night."

"Who moved it then, Ms. Alton?" The formality was starting to get on my nerves, but I was wondering that myself.

"I'm sorry sir, I don't know. Keys are often on the salesmen's desks, so it was not unusual for the managers to come looking for them." As I made my explanation, I looked around the room at each man on the interrogation team; their faces were all frozen into expressionless masks. I wondered what the faces would have looked like if I'd said, "Sure, I did it."

"Let's get back to why you were in the vehicle yesterday morning, Ms. Alton. When we visited with Mr. Stein, the oil change worker, he mentioned that you had told him that you were looking for some sort of list, a list that you wanted to turn in. What sort of list were you looking for?"

Darn it, Austin, you really can't keep a secret. Now I have to somehow spin that little fib that I gave just to cover up looking through my old boyfriend's garbage while in a truck sitting over top of a dead body, it turns out. Damn it.

"I don't remember anything about a list," I said. It was true; there never was a list. I looked straight into Sheriff Anderson's eyes and willed him not to pursue it further. He didn't. Instead, he asked me if I wanted a bottle of water. What I didn't realize was they were regrouping and saved the biggest question for last.

"So, Miss Alton, we are wondering, why a person would come into the dealership at 7:30 in the morning on their day off and go directly to a murder scene, move the murder weapon, disrupt evidence in the cab of the truck and then leave before anyone in the shop arrived, if you were not deliberately and maliciously trying to cover something up or tamper with evidence?" That all sounded bad, really bad.

"I wasn't tampering! I was looking for the lipstick that I had dropped in the cab."

"So, which is it? Were you looking for the truck keys or lipstick or some sort of list? What were you really looking for? What were you trying to cover up?"

"Nothing, I mean I wasn't trying to cover up anything." My answers could not have sounded more lame or unconvincing, and why should they, since most of them were lies.

I pulled myself together and took measure of the disbelief in the room, then said slowly and clearly as if my life depended on it: "I came in early yesterday to make sure the mechanics had the keys they needed. I was surprised that someone had found them and moved the truck." *Whew. How did that sound? Was it in any way believable?* My clammy hands stuck to the seat when I grabbed it to steady myself.

After a few moments the sheriff said, "Please stay in the area in case we need you for future questions." Just like that, I was dismissed. I threaded my way out through the little side rooms to the showroom area and when I looked up toward the front of the building, I saw the strangest thing.

CHAPTER 36

M ike Montello was alone in his fishbowl of an office without a single of his Marlboro men hanging over him. This was so rare that he almost looked like a wax figure of himself in Madame Tussauds's Museum sculpted in an awkward, unnatural pose.

"That was just about as awful an experience as I've ever had," I said, standing in his doorway.

"Imagine how uncomfortable it is for the murderer." At least he made it sound like he didn't think that was me.

"I didn't realize you were that close to Conrad," I said to him. "It looks like this thing's hitting you pretty hard."

"What, a gangland murder under my own roof? Are we wise guys from Jersey? Sure, I take that pretty hard." The suit jacket Montello never took off was hanging haphazardly on the back of his chair. I looked out his door; the showroom and offices were lightless and empty. I could hear the time clock on the wall by the office ticking.

"You talked to Angel that night, right?" he asked. I nodded but he wasn't looking because he was cleaning his nails with one sharp side of a pair of tweezers. "Did you hear Conrad actually fire her? Did you hear those words exactly?" *He knows.* I slumped down into the soft chair in front of his desk, like an over-roasted marshmallow slithers off a stick into the fire.

"No, I didn't hear them. Did Angel tell you? Where is she?"

"K.C. did," he said, referring to the five-foot-tall mechanic that I'd had several encounters with.

"Did you see her leave?" he asked, still deep in thought. He went under each nail again with the tweezers.

"I did. She said she was going to get on her bike and ride up to the mountain. I hope she has a better alibi than her old pieced-to-gether motorcycle can give her." Mike lifted his head and looked directly at me with a chilling stare.

"Does she have a gun back there? Back in Detail?"

"Not anymore, I bet." Wherever she was, I was sure the gun had left with her. Mike tugged at the bottom drawer of his oak desk. So now he's pulling out his own gun with all the cops here! I cringed and looked over my shoulder to see who was watching. As I turned back a bulging bottle of eighteen-year-old Glenmorangie Single Malt Scotch was lifted out of the drawer instead of a gun.

"My dad was a scotch drinker," I said.

"Care to join me?" What? A bonding moment with the boss?

"Yes," I said and took the top cup from the stack sitting on his desk and held it out with two hands as if I was Oliver Twist waiting for a serving of gruel. He poured two fingers of booze for me into an eight-ounce plastic cup. I took a good swig. In for a penny, in for a pound, as my mom used to say. I choked—I was an embarrassing lightweight when it came to hard liquor. Why did I agree to take the drink? I sipped again, coughed, but not so much. The third taste was altogether different. What was that taste? Vanilla? Like Gramma's pudding? As I was swirling and studying the liquid, I looked up at Montello. He smiled at me.

"Kind of grows on you, doesn't it?" he said. It was obvious the bonding thing was working. I was mesmerized by the scotch as though it was a reefer I was smoking. After a while the drink tasted smooth, even creamy. Weird. Imagine that—me and Scotch.

"My father was a scotch drinker. He loved the stuff." I said.

"You said that already. You know, it took me over six months to find a Service Manager who would come to this God-forsaken place," Montello said. "Conrad didn't know the first thing about cars or parts; all he had to do was make schedules."

"Maybe that's your answer then," I said. "You don't need a mechanic. You need someone who's organized and good at talking to people and making schedules. A woman maybe?" He glared at me.

"Actually, I need a mechanic, too. Frank quit. He doesn't want to go into that work bay again."

"If you want my opinion," I could hear the scotch talking because I would never have offered business advice. "I think you should get Polson's Ready Mix in here tomorrow and fill that hole. That way it would be gone—people wouldn't be staring down into it."

'Birdie, that's a rrright fine idea. That's exactly what we rrre going to do." Was the scotch filling up my ears? He offered another pour. I took it.

"Did they tell you that my fingerprints were on the murder weapon?" I said with all the casualness of a dental assistant announcing that she was ready to clean his teeth. I should have been a dental hygienist, I would have gotten onto a lot less trouble, especially if I was going to spend all my time down in the mouth anyway. I giggled. But hell, I'm a librarian and they're supposed to be completely trouble free. Look what that got me.

"They did," he finally said.

"Did what?" I had floated away on thoughts of my dad and forgotten I'd asked him a question.

"They told me that your fingerprints were on the wrench. You didn't do it, did you?" he asked. "Not that I would say I blame you if you did. He really had a dislike for you. That was a very bad deal out on the lot the other day." Was this a form of apology?

"I don't understand the gunshot," I said. Look at me; I'm Colombo, Dad's favorite detective.

"Nobody does," he said, answering me, but clearly his mind was elsewhere. "I should've fired Conrad the first time I heard about Maggie. For sure I should have let him go when his Mrs.

went after Maggie." He was now sharing secrets that I would never be privy to without the scotch.

"Could I have a bit more Glen-More-Angie, is it?" He barely dampened the bottom of the glass. Did he think I couldn't hold my liquor? I was just getting relaxed although I'd never done that before with scotch. At least it was the good stuff—the really delicious stuff.

"And you know Maggie's pregnant, right?" I said because I assumed he probably did.

"No, I didn't!" Good. I've shocked him.

"Well, hell, that'll give both Maggie and Mrs. Conrad a motive then, won't it? I'll probably be filling that position too then. Christ. How can one man cause so much destruction?"

I agreed. We were delivered from a menace who ironically would continue to cause trouble for both of us and who knew for how long? On top of that, we still had a murderer at large.

"What will this do to business?" I thought this was just in my head, but I must have said it out loud.

"Fuckin ruin it. At least in the short term, I'm probably going to lay people off and cut inventory. That's what it will do." This tidbit, I know, he would never have said to me. He lit up a cigarette—I'd never seen him do that inside his office before. He leaned back in his chair with his left leg crossed over the right, and he affectionately touched the large glen plaid cuff of his trousers, studying the fabric. "Do you know how many threads of pure virgin wool it takes to make fabric this sumptuous?" he asked. He wasn't bringing up men's fashion at a time like this, was he? 'Sumptuous'? From the old Haberdasher. Haberdonner. Haberblitzen. I giggled and watched as he flicked the ash off his cigarette right into the cuff of the trousers he admired so much. For some reason, the impromptu bonding, I guess, I decided to share a secret.

"Mike, did I ever tell you that my father owned a car dealership in Nebraska?"

Montello was instantly finished with his wayward visit to the land of ultrafine threads and inseam measurements. He uncrossed his legs, stubbed out the cigarette in his pencil holder, leaned forward and stared directly at me like he was seeing me for the very first time.

"Then you should be a hell of a lot better at this than you are, shouldn't you?" He looked over my shoulder and abruptly stood. The sheriff had come to the door of Montello's office behind me, and Mike knew it was his turn on the hot seat.

"Mike," I called out. He turned back. "Could I bum a cigarette?"

"No," he said and followed the man down the hall.

I took the cigarette anyway and lit it in his office, then sat quietly, finishing the last of my third serving of scotch. My eyes welled with tears. I wished I hadn't told him about Double Al. That should have been my memory, my secret. On Mike's desk, my eyes lighted on the day's issue of *The Phoenix Sun*. What do you know, we made the front page. Didn't the old adage say all publicity is good for business? Maybe not this time.

AUTO SERVICE MANAGER FOUND DEAD

The body of Conrad Richardson, Auto Service Manager at Copper Springs AutoMall, Copper Springs, AZ was discovered at 11:50 AM. Foul play is suspected.

Yeah, I'd say when you're beaten and then have a bullet put into you for good measure, foul play would be a suspect. I continued reading.

The sheriff has reported that the time of death has been established and a murder weapon has been recovered. He expects that a suspect will be in custody by this afternoon.

Is this today's paper and the sheriff already has an arrestable suspect? What the hell were we all doing here then? While I smoked the purloined Pall Mall, I read the article about the killing in the *Arizona Daily Star,* the Tucson paper, also on Montello's desk. I imagined our disaster had set every business in this town back to the great recession. C'mon into Copper Springs AutoMall—We'll make you a killer deal. A Deal to Die for!

The worst day at the AutoMall was finally over for me. I had no idea how long it would go on for Montello, but, at least he had some good scotch to keep him company. As I pulled out of the dealership, I saw Mater heading into the interrogation room. Were the NAPA auto parts delivery guys next?

When I got to the bungalow, Grams had gone to Bingo. Since I felt at loose ends pacing around the empty house and she had not left me cookies on the table, I decided I'd like to go hang out with a friend. So I made a difficult call.

CHAPTER 37

"Well, isn't this an unexpected surprise." Cuervo's voice was deep and rich like the scotch I had sipped in Montello's office.

"I think unexpected is a prerequisite of a surprise, isn't it? I, uh, was wondering, if you would take me out for a beer? I mean tonight." His hesitation stretched out endlessly. "Unless you're busy," I said.

"No, I'm not busy, but didn't you have a pretty tough day?"

"I did, but I'd like to go out for a while if you'd like to join me."

"I would. How about 7 o'clock? Should I pick you up, or would you just like me to bring a six-pack out to the merry-go-round for old times' sake?" I ignored that.

"Is the lounge open at the hotel?" I said.

"Hotel? Now we're talking."

"I'm not trying to imply anything. Don't make me sorry I called you."

"Okay, I get it, no jokes," he said. "Seven o'clock it is, at the lounge at the Dude Rancher Inn. Right?"

Grams was home from Bingo before I left and anxious to hear about what had transpired during the day. I told her what I knew but I didn't share the part about sipping scotch with the boss. I told her I was going out with some friends, not mentioning who, and we had some discussion over how wise that might be.

"I'm not working tomorrow," I told her, arguing my case.

I dialed Dana next and she was full of news.

"Jeff told me that none of them think that either Maggie or Juanita could wield that heavy wrench above their heads to hit Conrad very easily."

"Unfortunately, I can attest to how heavy it is," I said.

"The ballistics have to go to Phoenix and aren't expected back for a few days. Everybody in Copper Springs has a pistol so that ruled no one out. The bullet thing still has everyone baffled. It looks like someone shot into the mechanic's bay but not at Conrad. The bullet just ended up going through him. I don't mind telling you that is the weirdest piece of evidence in a murder that I have ever heard of. Why would someone shoot him after he was dead? And not even aim at him?"

"Did they find the gun?"

"Not yet," she said.

"The newspapers say they're ready to make an arrest."

"They hadn't done it by four p.m. By the way, I did find out who Burke was having dinner with that night." She deliberately hung it out there for a second or two.

"I'm waiting. Are you going to tell me?" I said

"It was Kenny and his family and Burke's mother. They all had dinner together."

"It's a relief that he has a good alibi," I said.

"It wasn't a girlfriend. That's even better, right?"

It would be if I didn't have something like a date tonight with Cuervo.

"How 'bout we take your mom and my Grams out this weekend and have some fun," I suggested, changing the subject.

"If Mom's up to it, that would be great," she said.

———

As seven o'clock approached, I laid out several of my new fashion choices—zippered leather boots, a thigh-high leather skirt with jean style pockets, a light lacy peasant blouse styled in ivory lace and a vertically ribbed vest sort of like corduroy. I eyeballed the thong on the dresser. Not tonight. I grabbed a pair of my regular ass T-Shirt underwear, but a bright red pair. *That's right, Birdie— live dangerously!*

"Gram, could I take your car tonight?" I asked. "My Mini is recognized by everybody. I'd like to lay a bit low."

"Anytime you want to, sweetheart. Mario is coming over to watch Antique Roadshow with me. I guess Cuervo is going out with someone, and Austin is out with his buddies too."

So Cuervo hadn't told his father? We all seemed to be getting more and more comfortable with leaving out details.

"Grams, would you like me to take you to the grocery store tomorrow?"

"I'd love that, sweetheart," she said, "and we can get lunch at Bernadette's."

"Even better," I said. I so loved my Grams. I didn't know what she'd think of my seeing Cuervo, but there was no need to find out tonight. There were no lights on our driveway and backing out in the pitch black desert evening in someone else's car made me feel like a snake slithering off. A snake that was lying to everyone. But why?

CHAPTER 38

The Dude Rancher Inn had a quiet western-styled bar and was one of those iconic, authentic hotels that turn up from time to time in "Sunset Magazine" or a travel article in the "New York Times" in stories featuring secret spots to really experience the Wild, Wild, West. The west, right here in Copper Springs, was getting wilder by the day.

Cuervo was participating in an animated conversation with two men at the bar when he saw me arrive. He excused himself to take me to a back booth. The duo gave me a serious looking over; one of them actually whistled. My attire and the situation made me feel something I hadn't felt in years. What was it—youthful or sleazy?

"Would you prefer a table?" Cuervo asked. He was wearing a hot pink, short-sleeved pullover shirt with a softball team logo. The warm hue set off the color of his well-tanned face and his amazing build. How is it I hadn't really noticed that before?

"Well, you made my day, Ms Alton. I'm thrilled that you called me, but I also suspect beyond wanting the pleasure of my company that you might think that I know a thing or two about what's happening at your place of work."

"Then I could get two for one." My mood was already improved by his dazzling smile. Probably good dental hygiene-He didn't seem like the whitening strips kind of guy.

"I'm more interested in the goings on because Austin works there and everyone in town is talking about it, but I probably don't know any more than you do. Austin told me he felt terrible having to respond to their questions about your being at the dealership the other morning."

"I hope not. He's a good kid, and he should answer honestly whatever questions they ask."

"How about you? Are you able to answer honestly?" he said. I stared at him, wondering where this might be going. My evening was beginning to resemble my afternoon, and it might be even shorter than I expected when I thought up the crazy idea of inviting him.

"Here's what I mean. Did you get all dressed up and invite me here to talk about a murder investigation? If so, I can think of quite a few people who would know more about that than me. Is it possible that we could take this in a bit different direction? Answer honestly."

"Neither of us has perfect track records," I said, avoiding his question.

"You mean because we have been divorced like fifty-one percent of the marriages in this country?"

"Is it that bad? Only a fifty/fifty chance?" I said taking a draw from my bottle of Michelob.

"Just to be clear, this isn't a marriage proposal," he said. "And fifty-one percent is better odds than a lot of things. For instance, what are my odds of buying you dinner tonight, say, at Bernadette's? It's not exactly an intimate candlelight dinner, but I'd say it would do for a first… encounter." I watched the soft curly locks of his hair fall over his collar as he talked. He brushed them back seductively.

"I suppose it would be too much to call it a date," I said. "Are they even called dates anymore?"

"No, they're called hook-ups. However, because of our advanced ages and for the sake of argument, the next time I ask you, it will be a date. Hopefully, the hook-up part might figure in later." He beamed.

"Oh, sure, I remember this macho attitude from the merry-go-round, now that I think about it. I would like to talk some about the investigation, though," I said.

"Let's do it over dinner, then," he said, paying our bill. The man at the bar whistled again.

Outside, Cuervo's eyes sparkled when he smiled. He helped me into Gram's Pontiac then he got into his neon-orange Dodge Power Wagon. I followed him a few blocks to Bernadette's, the little restaurant with the pink and white awning that we both knew closed at nine. A first encounter, but definitely not a hook-up.

All the tables were full, so Cuervo ushered me to our second booth of the night, again in the back under the huge sepia-toned photo of the Eiffel tower. Bernadette's was known for its breakfast pastries and chicken salad sandwiches on homemade croissant rolls for lunch so I was pleased to see that unlike other bakeries, Bernadette baked all day. The rolls that our waitress served with my baked potato soup and his white bean chili were fresh out of the oven. I was just thinking this had been one of my better ideas of late when Cuervo spoke.

"Hey, I hear you're a golfer like me."

"No, I am not. I'm not a golfer," I observed. Heads turned at my volume, way too high for the room. "I don't know why everybody thinks I can golf."

Cuervo recoiled and put up both hands as if I'd pointed a loaded Ruger at him.

"Whoa, excuse me, did I say golfer? I meant UFC fighter. Clearly, I got the wrong info about which sport you partake in. Remind me to wear protective gear before I get in the cage with you again." He turned his head away. He was probably wondering which me was Jekyll and which was Hyde. I wish I knew, Jack. Why did I keep picking fights with this guy?

"Okay, I used to golf, when I was a kid."

"Oh, no you don't. That subject is off the table now. Let's talk about something less violent, like, for instance, the murder at your place of business, and is it safe for my kid to continue to work there?"

"That's a good question. I personally feel safer there now that Conrad is gone, but don't tell anyone that since I'm one of the suspects in his dramatic exit and whoever did it is still on the loose."

"If you mean, am I going to call the sheriff with the news flash, well, I do have him on speed dial. See, right here." Cuervo held up his phone and gave me a big grin. I seem to have been forgiven. Golf was getting the best of me and I didn't even play.

"I probably shouldn't tell you this, but I have two of the prime murder suspects on my parole list." Cuervo looked around as he said this to make sure no one else was listening.

"I thought you might know more about it than you let on. Is Angel Moretti one of them?"

"She has had some scrapes in the past, but I don't think she is currently on any of the parole lists that I know about. Austin told me that you and she have become pretty good friends."

"Friends might be stating it strongly," I said.

"So, you're more like golfing buddies then?" That was adorable.

"Yeah, like that," I said, grinning back. "But seriously, she gets a raw deal half the time. She's a genius at car cleaning. She knows every cleaning product. What is the worst thing you have ever done to your truck?" I asked.

"In the truck or to the truck?"

"I'm just saying the girl's a genius."

"Businesses do continue to run even without detail girls and service managers, for instance" he said, "And those skills of hers might come in handy if she ends up in the big house." That image sobered me but not as much as his next statement.

"Unless it's you incarcerated, if not you'll be back to work soon." I know he meant that as a joke, but the thought startled me.

"Don't worry, Car Girl," he said, "they'll figure out it's not you."

We switched our conversation to lighter fare. Cuervo shared stories that were serious and stories that were silly and by the end of the evening, I found myself almost forgetting my own bad day. When he walked me out to Gram's car, he gave me a kiss on the cheek.

"Lucky we were only twelve, back then; on the merry-go-round, I mean." He held the driver's door while I got in.

"Or that you didn't actually invite me out golfing," I said.

"And lucky we both found our way back here. Hey, I almost forgot. Did that car that went missing at the dealership ever turn up?"

"No. That's one good thing about this mess; nobody's talking about my losing that Beemer anymore."

I followed my dinner partner home. He turned off first in Mario's driveway. I turned off in Gram's. She was already in bed, but she had left out a plate of her Rice Crispy Crunch cookies for me—her friend Maxine's recipe—they contained coconut of course. If I had to guess, there was probably an identical display of them on Mario's counter waiting for Cuervo too. I took a handful to my room and fell into bed. Arizona was proving to be measurably more interesting than Nebraska, just as Dana had promised it would. My brain was so occupied recapping the conversation of the evening that I didn't even miss my cell phone.

CHAPTER 39

As I awoke, the remnants of a provocative dream slipped off the edge of my pillow. Was that Burke I was kissing? No, No of course not—Cuervo, then? The man of my dreams was fading as fast as the real men in my life did. I almost hopped in the shower and dressed for work before I remembered the AutoMall was closed. There was no work to dress for and no one knew when we would return.

"We'll call you when we want you to come back," they'd said. What if there is no dealership to be called back to? Until that moment I had not considered the possibility that this murder might well destroy the dealership and that, of course, brought me, as it inevitably did, to my own self-interest. I'd had money worries from the moment I drove off the farm. Why should today be any different? But without income, my mountain of car repair bills, and even the Visa bill for my new wardrobe would cost a fortune in interest.

"Burke stopped by last night," Grams said as I stumbled into the kitchen in my sweats. "He saw your car and thought you were home. He got his truck back already, but of course, they kept the wrench—you know, THE wrench."

I nodded that yes, I knew THE wrench she was referring to— the one the cops said ConMan was bludgeoned with—the one with my prints on it. How I wish I didn't know. A plate on the counter caught my eye.

"What's with the coconut donuts?"

"Oh, Burke brought these. He said you like coconut donuts. Don't you like them?"

"I do!" When was Burke at Bernadette's? Had he seen me there with Cuervo?

"He's such a thoughtful and conscientious young man," Grams said.

"Grams, he's almost 40."

"Well, that's young to me, isn't it?"

Before I'd scarfed down both donuts and a tall glass of cold milk, Gram's ancient red phone rang. She was outside watering plants so I answered.

"I've got your cell phone," Cuervo said.

"What? How do you know it's mine?" My gaze shot toward the bedroom. I wanted to check my purse but the old-time receiver cord had me tethered to the hall outside the kitchen.

"The cover is Tweety Bird yellow, right?" he said in a singsong voice, "and it plays Little Red Corvette for the ringtone?"

"Little Deuce Coupe," I corrected.

"You still don't believe me." He sounded pissed. "Bernadette called this morning and asked if it was mine. I think I should be insulted. Anyway, how are we gonna do this without Louella being the wiser? I assume you're anxious to keep our dinner quiet."

"You're right, I'd prefer not to make a show of it," I said. "Is that a problem for you?"

"If we meet regularly it will be but, in the meantime, I really don't want my dad to know either."

A scheme formed in my head. "Why don't I go down to the Post Office and get my mail? In let's say, ten minutes?" He was right, I didn't believe him. I ran to the bedroom and checked my purse. No phone. My jacket pocket—no phone. I grabbed my windbreaker that was completely mismatched from the sloppy sweat pants. I glided past Grams in the kitchen and headed toward the back door while babbling my fib.

"Gram, I'm expecting some mail from Nebraska. I'm gonna make a quick trip down to the P.O," I said. "I'll be right back."

"Great," she said. "I'll go with you and we can get the groceries."

"Uh, you're not ready to go are you? I can take you when I get back. Then we can go right to the store and not waste time at the post office." I threw out excuses like a fisherman might throw chum into a lake, trying to get anything to bite.

"Nonsense," she said. "The store's right there; I'll get my mail too then we can go to Safeway. It is just right there," she repeated, shaking her head with exasperation that I would be so foolish as to make two trips.

"I'll drive," I said, once again grabbing her keys. We loaded her recycling in the trunk and headed toward town. "Let me get rid of the recycling first, then P.O., and then groceries." Even though the sequence was silly, she said nothing. If Cuervo was in front of the post office, I'd try to get his attention from across the street, so he could see that I had Grams with me.

By the time I pulled up to the P.O. on the right side of his truck, he had a plan.

"Hi Louella," he said through his passenger window, now conveniently open with me standing beside it, "And Birdie."

"What are you doing here?" Grams asked, "Doesn't your dad get the mail?"

"I, uh, had a package to mail." He paused. "For work." We were acting like kids passing notes in English class. As a former teacher, I could read this ruse so fast I'd have had a hold of his ear, and dragged him out into the hall before he could say 'old enough to know better,' but my dear grandmother didn't seem to tip to it.

"I have that magazine here I told you about." He winked.

"You do?" I said tentatively. Apparently, I was not so good at playing this side of the game. I looked in and saw him slipping my phone and a scrap of paper inside a folded magazine. He handed it up to me.

"Thank you," I said. Even though my back was toward Grams, I was sure that I was giving it away. Cuervo covered.

"It has an article about Nebraska," he said, "I told her about it the other night at your house." Cuervo's ad lib left no doubt he was pretty good with a fib. In fact, he was such a pro, I wonder how many lies I'd heard from him, maybe even the previous night.

"I'm sure I'll enjoy it," I said, and then turned to follow Grams into the Post Office. She was far enough ahead that she couldn't hear.

"Angel called you this morning," he whispered. "Can I give you some advice?" He waited for my nod. "Best to steer clear of her if you can." Which I was already doing, by virtue of the fact that I couldn't find her anywhere. As he pulled away, I smiled at the magazine cover. It read: **Successful Pheasant Conservation in Nebraska - Lessons for Your State?** Tucked inside the magazine was a note written on half a used envelope. "Tweety Bird—Next time will be date #3," it read.

Date number three and the mythical third date gratuity. No, no you don't Mr. Cuervo, there will be no sex on the third date. Don't you even begin to think that this meeting was our second.

———

I called Angel - straight to voicemail. I was just a moment behind in entering the store, but already I'd lost Grams. I stood at the crossroads of two aisles, trying to decide if she'd headed for the bakery or frozen foods, as perplexed as a tourist lost on a foreign street corner. All I needed was a big unwieldy map to unfold and some people walking by who didn't speak English.

"Hola," said a restocking boy crouched down stocking shelves. I almost tripped over him. The back of a pair of bib overalls standing in front of the bank teller counter at the other entrance of the store caught my eye. It was Mater with a healthy stack of cash in front of him.

Depositing or withdrawing? None of my business. Maybe he was going on a little vacation now that he'd lost his buddy, Conrad. When he glanced in my direction, I instinctively ducked my head, pulling Cuervo's hunting magazine out of my handbag to cover my face. Then, I motored to the opposite end of the store. Wherever

Grams was, she would eventually turn up in the hamburger and chicken wing department. Mater trailed me.

"Donut shopping?" he asked. "Those are usually in the bakery department down there."

"I'm more of a connoisseur," I told him, "I only buy them at Bernadette's."

"Conno what?" he said. Where was Grams? I nervously rolled the magazine Cuervo had given me like a megaphone, thinking of hollering for her with it. Give me a G! Give me an R!

"I see you read hunting magazines," he said. "What gun do you shoot?" He seemed genuinely interested. What should I say? Do I tell him I don't have a gun and it is not even my magazine or make him think that, of course, I have a gun—an AR-15—doesn't everybody? Thankfully, Grams appeared, walking out through the cold fog of frozen foods.

"Grams, this is Mater, the tow-truck driver for the dealership."

"Hello," she said, sizing him up. "Aren't you Jim Moore's kid?"

"Yes," he said, wasting no extra words.

"Wait, what? You two know each other?"

"What's your name again?" Grams said. It was not like her to be so interested or so bold.

"They call me Mater." He looked at me then tuned to Grams and added, "But my given name is Mason."

"Yes, I thought you were Jim Moore's boy. The oldest, right?" Mater nodded.

"I'd better be on my way," he said. Did he wonder—as I did— what question my grandmother would pose next?

Grams and I finished our shopping and, as promised, she took me to dine at Bernadette's. I was becoming a regular.

"How do you know Mater's family, Gram? You seem to know everybody."

"I don't know him, but his parents were customers of our Rexall store. The Moores are always on my scanner; there are plenty of them." Our conversation was interrupted by Bernadette who came by to greet Grams. We forgot all about Mater and whoever he belonged to. That was fine with me but looking at the grand sepia-toned photo of the *Arc de Triomphe* that covered the left half of the back wall made me remember the night before. I didn't want to think anymore about the tow truck driver, but thinking about Cuervo, now that was another matter.

CHAPTER 40

After three days, Jeannie was given the job of summoning us to return to the scene of the crime. As Cuervo told me, Angel had actually called. Despite his warning, I tried again to reach her. Still no answer. Then I called Dana.

"We hear they're making an arrest today," Dana huffed. "Jeff's pissed. They used us to do all the dirty work, then cut us out of the investigation when the press was about to descend, so now they get all sorts of coverage for their great detective work. Jeff is really peeved."

"I can hear in your voice how peeved Jeff is," I said.

"Hey, we're all pissed but a lot of good that will do."

"So, who's the killer?" I asked. Saying 'killer' made my heart quicken. I was afraid to say what I was really thinking: Am I still on the suspect list?

"You'd make a poor cop if you think the person we arrest is always guilty," Dana said. "But the County Attorney will make a good case for whoever they haul in. It still looks like the wife to Jeff and me, but we'll have to read it in the paper just like everybody else."

"Okay, so we wait for the paper then. This is my last day off and I intend to make the most of it." In all my fourteen years at Sand Hills Middle School, I never appreciated the time off like I had these few days, and not because I was relaxing. I did at least thirty chores; I cleaned the windows and fixed the bottom hinge on Gram's screen door.

"I have something to show you." Grams said as she led me to the mud-room by the garage and opened a homemade built-in closet door revealing some long-lost friends.

"My Callaways!" At first, I was thrilled to see the well-worn golf clubs still in the banana yellow bag. My mood soured when I remembered the golf tournament that Wallace seemed to think I could win for him.

"They look like antiques, Gram."

"I thought you might at least want to go to the driving range."

"What if someone saw me? Maybe we should hide these again."

"As I recall, you were pretty good at golf." My Grams was a never-ending source of encouragement.

"You think I'm good at everything, Grams. I'm not, you know."

"Nonsense, my Alberta Dear is good at anything she wants to be."

But that was just it, what in heaven's name did I want to be?

CHAPTER 41

On Tuesday morning the sales crew all arrived back to the dealership at nearly the same time looking refreshed and energized instead of sullen. We all avoided the back entry and entered through the clunking broken front doors. NewKid had arrived early and was the greeting committee.

"They filled up the hole." he blurted out. "They filled up the work bay where they found ConMan. It's gone." So, like a bunch of stooges, the lot of us attempted to squeeze through the door we had avoided earlier all at the same time to see it for ourselves.

"Did they take out the body first?" Clay said. Everybody groaned. Eventually, the entire staff, the office women, Greg and his Parts guys, and what was left of the Service Department all traipsed into the biggest room. Most of us had to stand. The bosses weren't in the room yet, and the rest of us were tapping on tables or scratching our heads or ears, or whatever we did to announce our nervousness to the world.

"It's quiet as a morgue in this place," NewKid said. Someone chuckled.

"Yeah, I hear people are dying to get in this meeting," Rich added. Crickets. Rich was always a half-bubble off when it came to making a joke, but he wasn't alone in being spooked. What were we going to be told? That the dealership was closing? That we were all looking for work? Our fidgeting continued.

Wallace and Mike entered from the rear of the room with a man that no one recognized. Where's Orbit? Wallace never ever went anywhere without his faithful pooch. Those of us standing took a step back, leaning on the walls for support.

"Well, thank you for…thank you for coming back, I guess," Wallace said. "What a terrible thing—for Conrad's family and for our family." He motioned around the room like he thought we, as a group, were a family. Could he possibly think we were his family? The "we put the fun in dysfunctional" type of family? Wallace was visibly shaken, so Montello stepped up to speak.

"The sheriff's office called us this morning: They've made an arrest." We all looked at each other as if to say, "Well it's not me, and it is not you." But what about Angel? I had yet to see her. Has one of the deputies uncovered her secret?

"They've arrested Conrad's wife, Juanita," Mike continued. "I know, our burrito lady, sort of a shock." I finally exhaled as did several others. Thank God.

"I told you," Clay whispered to me. He'd told so many people what I'd told him that he thought it had been his idea. All eyes seem to look toward Conrad's mistress Maggie Green who was sitting in the back of the room. I, for one, was surprised that Maggie was even in attendance but then I remembered the baby. She was working for two now, so she almost had to keep her job.

"We've rented two bays at Kmetko's Auto Shop across the way and will do much of our work there for a few days until things settle down," Montello announced. But where's Angel? Wallace took over the meeting once again.

"We need everybody to be on their toes. Our sales the next few weeks…" he spoke slowly and I hung my head, expecting the worst, something like, our sales will be in the crapper so be prepared, but that is not what he said.

"Our sales will reflect some big numbers." The sales crew looked back and forth at each other in bewilderment. What the hell? Did he say big? How could revenue be anything but horrible after a thing like this? Won't everybody in town get the creeps just to drive by a murder scene?

"We have permission from Corporate, for our biggest franchise, to offer the lowest prices in our history to get back on our feet," he said. This sounded like a come-on like our made-for-TV ads did when Jason the donut-man created them.

"This is Curt Larsen, from the Detroit office, for our largest franchise," he said, gesturing toward the tall, slim, and well-dressed fellow in a gray suit and Gucci logo tie. He could pass for a corporate lawyer or maybe a lobbyist—a greasy gritty car lot was the last place he should be. Curt stepped forward to explain why he was involved.

"It's in the interest of our corporation to help this dealership overcome this terrible event," he began, speaking with a formal air. "It's rare, but these things happen from time to time. We have thousands of dealerships, and we want our brand to get back in business here in Copper Springs," he went on about $1,000 discounts and another $500 thrown in by Wallace.

"Remember, as sharp as this terrible tragedy is in your memory, there will be people in the area who know nothing about this, and just want a phenomenal deal. We'll be drawing in customers from across state lines, maybe even from Mexico. Locals will stop in out of curiosity. They may even buy a vehicle when they see what prices you are offering."

Larsen, who looked to be in his late forties, was articulate and convincing. He was a fixer, like the mafia or politicians in Washington keep on retainer to clean up an inadvertent mistake they want to wipe away. I didn't think it was going to be very easy to clear it out of all our minds.

Montello was shockingly mute. Maybe he was grateful to have someone else at the helm, but that wasn't his style. The Parts Department people and office staff were excused, filing out in a somber parade.

"We're short on inventory," Bingham said. "When are we getting more?" This was the salesman's ubiquitous whiney lament: If we only had more inventory then we would be selling machines. As my dad used to say, "A really good salesman could sell the last vehicle on the lot to an unsuspecting fellow who just came in to buy an air filter."

Curt riveted our attention as he used numbers like $250 for the first and $500 for your second and this money was on top of our commissions, although Montello would wrangle a way to screw us out of those. Even the crusty curmudgeons of our merry band were smiling. "We'll have a similar program the following week as well," he said. Those of us with smartphones were scrolling down through our customer lists. Bingham and Rich were shuffling through their 3x5 cards, studying them like they were cheat sheets for a pop quiz. With his audience's attention now lost, Curt dismissed us.

I was more than anxious to commence with my astronomic earning potential, but first I had to account for Angel. Austin was full of news. Angel had been flown from Tucson to Ontario, California, twice to collect two hard-to-get vehicles from a distribution facility.

"She's driving back again. Can you believe that?" he said.

"She hasn't answered her phone," I told him.

"That's because she forgot her charger." He held up the end of a charger that was still plugged in the wall at the other end.

So, Angel was fine and I could get back to the job at hand—making money. First I left the path to riches and wandered through the workbay past the spot where Burke's truck was parked, past the still damp concrete floor that used to be the deep bay where they found the unfortunate Service Manager bludgeoned and let's not forget bullet-ridden. As I passed the Service write-up area, I saw the wire-rimmed glasses that Conrad wore every day, lying on his desk. Why were they not in the work bay? Why hadn't the investigators taken them? They gave the creepy aura of Conrad saying, "I still see you." I ran toward the showroom.

We weren't told of any plans for a funeral. In most cases that was the spouse's job and now Conrad's wife was otherwise incarcerated.

CHAPTER 42

Within the hour, the double glass front doors flew open welcoming a handsome young couple, the best looking "Up" that God had ever created. Bingham stormed the doors to greet them, but a moment later he hollered from across the room.

"They're asking for you, Birdie." He stomped out, leaving the air heavy with his rudeness. My vacant stare informed the two that I had no recognition.

"We're the Hancocks. You sold our best friends, Shani and Steve, a sporty little Chevy Equinox, and Steve told us that we must work with "Birdie" to buy our car. We're here to do a special order." My first true referral—Of course, I remembered Steve and Shani. No, really, I did. I was too new at this not to remember every single person I had talked to starting with 'Hell Hole' inhabitant Loretta. Soon I'd be remembering the Hancocks, all too well. But they didn't need to special order. I had their perfect vehicle already on my lot—I was completely sure they would see it my way.

By the time we returned from a drive, all the other salesmen had buying customers. The mood was effervescent. The first day back after a horrid, tragic, murder, and the sales crew was giddy. The Hancocks, however, were no longer happy and decided to go home to think about it. Montello was too busy to even notice, let alone scold me for letting them go.

By six o'clock, I had managed to fritter the entire day away. As I packed to leave, Austin drove up with a dealer trade he'd picked up in Tucson.

"Birdie. What's up? I just saw that couple I washed the SUV for this morning ordering a new car at the dealership in Tucson." The Hancocks? No, I won't forget the Hancocks, but I will try.

I was the only salesman with no sale and hoping Austin wouldn't blab that story to Montello. Then again, Austin did have a history of not keeping our secrets. Bingham had finished two sales, and so had the team of Wade and Stretch. Stretch's stint working in Detail was short-lived. He still couldn't drive, but he could, however, sit in the back seat and let a customer that Wade spooned him take the wheel. And look at that. Our new Detail boy sold two today! Eight vehicles were sold and delivered and even the dog killer Wade appeared to be happy.

Curt Larsen met me at the door and asked me to follow him to his make-shift office that he had stolen from Gordon, the finance manager. Anyone getting the best of Gordon pleased me no end as he was a world-class jerk as well as a thief. Whenever he could, he'd bilk a widow or an orphan. Gordon would make big bank with all this going on and that made me even madder that I wasn't in the mix.

"I thought you had a sure sale there this morning," Curt said, startling me. Had he already heard from Austin? Damn it. "Special orders can be tricky, but you probably know that." Since he didn't seem to know I'd lost the slippery Hancocks, I chose to keep my mouth shut.

"What do you need?" I said.

"Several calls have come into my desk and I'm sure there will be more tomorrow. If you come in early, I think I can help you start your day on a better note than today. Wallace said you're rather new here." I nodded. "He also tells me that you play golf." There it is. Not sixty seconds after I met anyone, they brought up golf. I stood to leave and looked back at Curt.

"So, what then? Do we have a tee time for tomorrow morning? We can get eighteen in before work? Is that the better note you mentioned?" I was moving out the door.

"No, Birdie, it isn't. Sit down." His measured tones were not as mean as mine, so I sat.

"I thought you were probably disappointed in your day. Also, I'm pretty sure I can get you a customer or two tomorrow for one of our vehicles so you too can be part of the action here."

"All right," I said, realizing he was just trying to help. "I'll look forward to it. Hey, Curt, do you think I could bum a cigarette?" He stared at me with an eyebrow lifted then handed one over. I surprised myself, by stealing his Bic lighter off of the desk and I headed out to see Angel. Montello motioned me into his office. What? No loudspeaker?

"Whatever Austin said I didn't do it," I said while I hid the cigarette behind me.

"What? No, I just wanted to tell you to watch out for Larsen. He can be trouble."

Was everybody trouble these days? I was certainly getting a lot of warnings.

"That's funny you said that since he seems like your kind of guy, Mr. Montello, white shirt, fancy tie, nice suit."

"It's polyester," he muttered.

"I beg your pardon?"

"He isn't my kind of guy at all; that suit he's wearing is polyester!" The interloper's suit wasn't worsted wool enough for Montello. Curt Larsen represented a world that Montello didn't know. What he knew was right and what he didn't know was wrong.

I didn't pick up the evening keys. The money earners can do tonight's ritual, I thought. Tomorrow, I'll have at least one of those lucrative sales. Angel was gone, so I smoked the bummed cigarette in the parking lot before I got into my car. Not much different than my sixth graders smoking the Cigarillos in back of my library. My new smoking habit—*Are two cigarettes really a habit?*—was nothing I wanted my dear Grams to know about, so I kept it out of my car.

CHAPTER 43

Curt Larsen with the unforgivable fashion faux pas of wearing a polyester suit was a man of his word. He bestowed three effortless sales on me the second day of our new beginning like gifts from the Magi and two more the next. The place was going crazy. Salespeople were using makeshift tables for write-up desks in the hallways, and all auxiliary rooms were full. Things were bound to get confused. By three p.m. a serious skirmish was taking place out in front of the dealership.

Rich, who'd been working with a couple from Las Cruces in the conference room, and Bingham, who had an officer from Fort Huachuca, had sold the same truck. Rich was taking the truck for gas when Bingham thanked him for helping. "I just sold this truck," Rich replied.

"You sold my truck? Why you son of a bitch!" Bing yelled as he commenced to drag Rich from behind the wheel. It played like a cheesy soap opera from the big screen of the showroom windows. Two potential suitors duked it out for the hand of the same femme fatale. The fair lady in question was an Electric Blue three-quarter ton GMC 4x4 with a sliding rear window and locking tailgate. Everyone watching the tableau would agree that the pickup in question might be a beauty worth fighting to the death over. But hadn't we already had one death too many here this month?

"I think they should duel for it," NewKid said. I didn't know whether that was a hip reference to a Broadway musical, or simply remembered from his eleventh grade United States History class. Either way, it was the most erudite thing said in this building since whatever his last remark was. Smart boy, what are you doing here, even for the summer?

"Richard and Bingham report to the General Manager's office immediately," the loud-speaker boomed. Duel averted.

Word of the incredible discounts had run a breakneck Le Mans style track up to Phoenix then all the way to New Mexico and back. Thanks to finance man Gordon, who received a substantial piece of the action, even with the great prices, customers were still getting their pockets picked in the Finance and Insurance department. ConMan's death was becoming Gordon Jenkins windfall. Gordon should be their prime suspect, I thought. I used the ruckus up front to escape to find Angel, but not before I stepped into Montello's empty office and borrowed another of his Pall Malls.

When I had nearly gotten to Detail, I saw Angel flick her head in a gesture that I understood to mean meet her out behind the building. Angel looked rough. Her hair was substantially shorter than she had been wearing it, like she had cut it herself with a dull scissors and not in her signature braid. Her clothes were covered with grease. Her cocky "I'm a lot cooler than you" demeanor was obviously shaken. If she was trying to hide some secret, she wasn't successful. Guilt was all over her face.

"Hey you, I'm not trying to be mean, but you don't look so good. Is it because Montello knows Conrad fired you? You know they arrested someone, don't you? Time to relax."

"No. He told me right away that K.C. told him. That damn guy anyway."

"I agree, the boys here are a bunch of squealers." I took out the lone cigarette that I had just stolen and lit it.

"What the hell! You don't smoke. Talk about me."

"I don't know, maybe I do now."

"Jesus, I thought you might be the one person who survived this place."

"Or not." I didn't tell her it was only the third smoke I'd had since my sophomore year of college. I took another draw. I didn't know I missed it. Smoking and college, things were much simpler.

"I can't get these junk cars out of here, and Mater has been bugging the hell out of me," she said. Jeannie told me they're impounded because the paperwork for them was part of what they confiscated from Conrad's desk. That's not all; when they let us back in here, my pistol was gone. I'm almost sure Stretch took it."

"Did you ask him?" I said.

"I don't like the idea of confronting a guy just out of the slammer. Maybe they wanted him for more than a DUI."

"Sure, maybe it was a stolen weapons charge," I suggested. "Did anyone else know where the gun was?"

"No, but Conrad made me give him the extra key to the lockers when I had them installed. He didn't know I had put the gun in there to keep it out of Stretch's mitts."

"What do you want me to do with the information? Please don't ask me to call the cops about this. I'm not exactly out of the woods on this investigation either."

"Nothing. I just wanted to bitch to somebody." She was polishing a radio knob that she was about to replace. With Angel, it didn't matter what heinous event had taken place; she still put work first.

"Let me have that," she said, pulling the cigarette from between my fingers.

"You don't smoke either."

"I don't know, maybe I do now."

―――

The rest of my day raced along at supersonic speed; I snared another good "Up" and sold one of our jazziest new 4x4 short-box pickups. Some friend—I completely forgot Angel.

When I came back to pick up my things, there was a pink and white striped Bernadette's bag sitting on the sales desk. Burke, you sweetheart, you got me another coconut donut! The contents of the pink-striped bag surprised me. It contained a maple bar. Rich walked by and said, "Mater left that for you. He said those are your favorites." Mater? What the hell? "It isn't the donut, it's the coconut that's my favorite." Rich shrugged.

I left the bag with the donut on the desk because I finally remembered Angel. It was dark in the Detail bays and locked so I headed for the calm and quiet of my grandmother's little bungalow. As I reached the parking lot, I heard my name over the loudspeaker. I chose to invoke my fifty-foot rule. If I was fifty feet from the building, I didn't have to go back in and answer. I got in my car and pulled away.

With the front and back windows of Gram's car open, my long blonde hair flew behind me just as it had when I was riding horseback across the plains of Nebraska. The farm and all I had left behind rarely entered my mind anymore, usually only when I had to pay bills and wished my lawyer would call to tell me a big check was on the way. No call had come so far. It was the first time I didn't have the chest-tightened feeling of a suspect. I had experienced a wonderful day as an actual car salesman, but I couldn't have imagined what was waiting for me when I got home.

CHAPTER 44

When I rounded the corner of Fourth Street by the household of three generations of Stein men, I gawked at the windows to see who was home. In my distraction, I barely avoided hitting the rear end of Burke's Lone Pine truck, the very vehicle tying me to the crime. The Mini Cooper, still parked in the driveway, made it look as if I was home. Had Burke now become an "I was just in the neighborhood thought I'd drop in" sort of guy? My heart once again lilted. I admit that I was ready, maybe even anxious, to get reacquainted, just not in front of my grandmother. Maybe we were going out to dinner?

Burke heard the screen door creak and was already standing when I reached the kitchen. I couldn't tell if it was polyester, but the brown suit and striped tie he wore were certainly not Carhartt or Cinch, which I would have thought were the only brands in his closet. I grinned at him but the look he returned to me was almost unrecognizable. His eyes were rimmed in red and he had a sullen, lost look. This was a Burke I had never seen before. I might have seen it long ago, if I hadn't run out on him and never come back.

"Burke's uncle died this morning." Grams helped him speak. Was Grams crying? Obviously one of Burke's mom's brothers had passed away. Does Grams even know them? I wondered.

"Oh Burke, I'm really sorry." I said. Burke, still mute, grabbed me before I could even get my purse set down, and we shared a long and heartfelt hug. It is always emotional to share a moment like that, even if I hadn't had one of these with him for over twenty years. But this was not the way I imagined our first embrace to go. We sat down together on the same side of the table where Grams already had a plate of macaroon cookies. No one was talking.

"It's always a shock, isn't it?" I said. Burke finally spoke.

"Birdie, you have no idea. My mom just left. I really needed to talk to someone."

I didn't know what to say. Was it me or Grams he needed to comfort him? His mom had already left to go to the funeral in California then, and I was surprised that Burke was so torn up what with the uncles so far away. Certainly, he didn't see them much, and obviously he hadn't gone with her.

"Did your mom go to California, then?" Gram said.

"Yes, she's moving there." Burke answered. I suppose Grams had asked all the same questions but for lack of anything better to say, I asked, "Won't you go to the funeral?" He stared without answering. He seemed so shocked he was unable to speak, so I asked a mundane question for lack of a better one.

"Did he have children?"

"Three. You know that, Birdie." I was a bit embarrassed and surprised that Burke would think I'd remember anything about his uncles in California after all these years.

"How old was your uncle?" I said, still making awkward conversation.

"He was just sixty-eight years old!" *Sixty eight? Now I'm confused.* It had been a long time since I thought much about Mavis or her older brothers, but I thought they were sixty-eight at least twenty years ago.

"Your mom's brother was just in his late sixties? I thought they were much older." He stared again –I just couldn't say the right thing.

"Birdie, it wasn't one of my mom's brothers; it was Kenny." When his words found their mark, they hit me somewhere in the middle of my chest like a wrecking ball.

"Ken! Oh my God! When? What happened?" Now I realized why Grams had been crying.

"Kenny was still your business partner, right?" Grams asked.

"And mentor and best friend," he added, tears welling up in his eyes.

"The entire town will be devastated," Grams said. I was finally speechless.

"We just had dinner the other night, all of us, Mom, too." He looked in my direction: "It was the night that Conrad was killed. My mom's moving to California," he said, "Did I tell you?"

I nodded. But he wasn't the one who told me; his neighbor did. I just hadn't realized it was imminent. Bonnie had indicated that Mavis was waiting for Burke to find someone to share his life with. Did she think he had?

"I remember how close you and Ken have always been," I said, hoping Burke would tell us more of what happened.

"The funeral will be Friday. You'll come?" he said to me.

"We'll be there," Grams said.

"Of course," I said. I hadn't attended a funeral for over twenty years but still I added, "I will." Then I changed the subject. "I'm sorry about everything with your truck."

"I can't help but think I brought that on myself, what with my run-ins with Conrad and all," he said. "I guess you could say that was the last big gift I got from Kenny—a dinner invite that night that proved where I was. I don't know how many nights I have spent at the ranch alone, and that night could have been one of those. I feel lucky that I'm not even more involved."

When the discussion wound down and the stories were starting to repeat, Burke stood to leave. My little Gramma gave the big cowboy a hug around the waist. I saw that Burke teared up again, and I decided to walk him out to his truck to say goodbye.

"I will have a lot of people at the house the next few days. But I want you to come out next week when everyone clears out. I'll cook you dinner." The house, as he called it, was now a vast empty void and I wasn't sure I was ready for him to pull me in to fill it especially filling a loss as big as his best friend Kenny. My heart certainly went out to him, even if the rest of me was more reluctant.

CHAPTER 45

My brain felt like wormwood looks—a million squiggling thoughts just under the surface chewing their convoluted paths to nowhere. I ached for Burke but I wasn't sure I was ready for a relationship with him. With anyone?

As the day progressed, my squiggly thoughts evolved into a simple question: Should I have even come back to Arizona? There, I heard it again, every thought in my head started with 'I' or ended with a 'me.' Every now and again a stray thought sneaked in about Angel and the cars out back, and of course, Kenny. Every local who came through the door, from the Napa parts delivery guy to the printer bringing new forms, stopped to talk about Kenny and how much he would be missed. One man told us that the Ranch Supply was closing so all their staff could go to the funeral. I was constantly reminded of Burke. It had been two days since he came to Gram's bungalow and he had sent only one text with three lines:

PEOPLE EVERYWHERE
I WILL CALL WHEN I CAN
SEE YOU AFTER THE FUNERAL

I'm not even sure where he got my number. I answered: "Yes C U then." And I was sure I meant it.

There were two local men dead in this town in one week, yet the mood in the showroom remained like a party. Conversations were a cacophony of laughter and silly jokes. Everyone was chatty except Montello, who was moody and cranky. If my count was correct, he had worked eight deals in one day, and that kind of mental gymnastics took a toll. In addition, he had to referee a monstrous truck fight. He had been so busy that I don't think he had duped a single sucker. It was after five p.m., so he was once again medicating with our liquid friend Glen. I thought of it as our cocktail now, and I was ready to two-time Burke with Glen. No, don't get ahead of yourself, Birdie. You haven't even one-timed Burke. I saw the golden bottle of scotch glistening in the late afternoon sun alongside the stack of plastic cups. The booze, once a very rare occasion, was now almost an everyday occurrence. I wasn't invited in.

Mater had been hanging around the building, in and out of the offices all day. Every time he looked my way, I got busy elsewhere. It was nice of him to bring me the donut; the only other gift I had received was the pedometer from Angel that I wore for less than a week. The donut, I would wear a lot longer. The tow guy was here because we had traded for at least a half dozen of the junkers that Montello liked to send to the Phoenix auction, but what should have taken an hour had kept Mater rambling around all afternoon. He was as crazy for those jalopies as the ConMan. What had he made of the death of his buddy? I willed Mater to get moving along and he headed out the side door.

I wandered into Montello's office. His glass cage felt like an oven ripening with a stale cigarette smell permeating everything. It pulsed off of Montello's hounds-tooth checked jacket. As soon as he caught me eyeballing the scotch, he opened the bottom drawer of his desk and dropped it in, out of my sight.

"That's for smoking. No more scotch until you quit," Mike said. Rats. Curt told on me.

"Everybody else smokes."

"They don't get scotch, now you don't either."

"What am I, tcn?"

"I guess not or we wouldn't be talking about hard liquor, would we?"

He looked as weary as a marathon runner nearing the finish line. His head bobbled and I thought it might drop right on his desk. Despite his scolding, he got the bottle out again and poured me a small snort, as my dad would have called it. I took a swallow then dropped into my usual chair. A warm relaxation came over me. It wasn't the booze. Or was that what they all said?

Mike was a father figure for most of the guys. Even though I knew he was somewhat of a shyster, I also knew the meaning of the word was to be shrewdly dishonest. I liked him anyway; everybody did and he was shrewder than most.

"Ms. Alton." Uh oh, that usually preceded something bad. I just sat back, sipped the warm golden liquid, and waited to get slammed with his critique.

"You kept your cool out there the last few days. Your paperwork has been good—no transposed VIN numbers, no forgotten fees. I wish all the rest of these yahoos had done as well." *Wow! Let me take this in! This was a compliment, right?*

"Your old man, what was his name? Double Al, the Nebraska car dealer? He would have been very proud of you this week."

His words were innocent—a simple, small compliment. Just a few short sentences, but the effect was cataclysmic. I couldn't stop it. A bucket of tears formed and rolled unbidden down my cheeks as I tried to blot them with the backs of both hands. Gooey snot dripped out of my nose.

"Jesus H Christ! What's wrong now?" Montello said as he tried to figure out what terrible thing his exhausted mind must have said to cause me so much trouble. "Hell, it was a fucking compliment."

"Nothing. It's nothing." I said and sprinted for the ladies' room where I balanced on the sink and released myself into ugly, shoulder-shaking, snot-producing, and headache-causing sobs. I could hardly catch my breath. There wasn't enough toilet paper on the roll to stifle my emotion. In a few minutes, Maggie came in to check on me. Montello had sent her.

"Mike wants to know if you're okay?" she said.

She was a sweet girl. I found myself hoping that all this stuff with Conrad would blow over soon so she could figure out what to do with her own life and the new one she was about to bring into the world.

"You know, I'm not feeling well. Will you tell Mike that I went on home?"

"Do you need someone to drive you? I can call Austin to take you home."

"No, no, no. I'll be fine if you'll just tell him. Thank you." The last thing I needed was Austin having another of my secrets that he couldn't help sharing.

As I drove out the alley exit, I focused my swollen eyes on the sheriff's cars and several officers wandering around in the tall grass in the acreage behind the building. I wished they would just leave us alone now, but they seemed to be a presence in our lives almost every day.

At home, there was a note that Grams went out to dinner and a movie with Mario and I started to cry again but it was just waterworks. I didn't have enough energy for more sobs. The thought that my dad would have been proud of me ripped me wide open. I had never dared to conjure up that image before. Perhaps I always knew that he would not have been too intrigued to have his daughter shuffle books around in a library all day. Mike was right. Dad would have loved seeing me succeed at his business—if that was what I was doing. One good week does not a success make. I cried with the deep sadness of the week combined with the pleasure that five sales had given me. I thought again of Burke who would most likely take the more traditional view of having a girlfriend who was a used car salesman. I made a mental note not to ask him. He had his own tears to cry.

Alone in Gram's house called for only one thing, and no, it wasn't Glenmorangie. I found the last can of Eagle Brand Sweetened Condensed Milk in the cupboard, opened it on a fifty-year-old harvest-gold electric can opener, then found the biggest spoon that fit inside the can. I headed for the living room to watch Hugh Grant demur to Julia Roberts for the thousandth time. It might have been be the first time in my life that I made anyone proud. I was going to relish it and spend the night with Hugh.

CHAPTER 46

Before I left for work the next day, Grams asked if we could go to the funeral together. I thought that maybe she had been thinking of going with Mario, but naturally, she wanted to be supportive of me.

"Of course," I said, "but I will need to go in to work this morning. Wade wouldn't hear of closing even just from eleven to one. I'm sure Wally will be going."

The ring of my cell startled me. It took me three rings to get it answered.

"Where are you?' I haven't heard a thing from you. Are you all right?" Dana asked. "Are you at work yet?" It was her habit to ask a string of questions and not wait for answers.

"They've released Juanita," she said.

"You mean let her go home until the trial?"

"No, they don't have enough evidence, Jeff said. The fact that the truck was moved over the body makes it look like it was someone from the dealership, he told me. Juanita's lawyer made the case that she would never have known where to find those keys and the murder weapon was too heavy for her to wield and she doesn't own a gun. That's what Jeff said."

"So what? I don't have a gun either, but I could get my hands on several, if I wanted to,"

I heard her suck in her breath. "For God's sake, Birdie, don't offer that story up if one of our guys asks."

"It's just that I don't agree with that lawyer. Juanita was often back in the Service Department with Conrad. She could have observed how things are done there. She carried that heavy tray of burritos all the time. She's quite strong."

"Wait. What's with you? Why are you so anxious to convict Juanita?" Dana said.

"Hey, I like Juanita. I don't think she did it, but things are finally starting to settle back down at the dealership. We need to have this over and done with." This whole argument made me sound selfish and worse. Maybe it sounded like I was trying to throw the guilt off the staff to anywhere it would stick. Or maybe it sounded like I am trying to throw the guilt off myself.

"So, you're saying they don't think it was Juanita now?" I was trying to wrap my mind around it when Dana interjected: "For what it's worth, they don't think it was you, either. You're off the list."

"Why not?"

"What's with you? All of a sudden, you're acting like the dodgeball kid afraid to be chosen last. Did you listen to me? I said you are no longer a suspect."

"Well, what I mean is, why is that definitive—not that I don't like the sound of it." And I did like the sound of it. It was always good to hear something that sounded like, "Hey Birdie; we no longer think you might have committed a murder."

"This is good news, Birdie. They don't think you did it because the murder happened in the evening and you have a verifiable alibi. He'd been dead for many hours by the time you got in that truck." If my eyes weren't so sore from yesterday's crying jag I would have started in again.

"I saw the sheriff's guys last night roaming around in the grass behind the building," I told her. "I don't suppose they were looking for a picnic spot."

"They're looking for the gun. No luck yet though. Oh, by the way, have you seen Burke?"

"Yes," I answered.

"What a terrible thing about Kenny. I'm sure you and Louella are going to the funeral?"

"Should we all go together?" I asked, hoping to have more support in our group.

"Mom's not up to it, but I can come by and get you two."

"Good, 10:30?" Grams was nodding her agreement on the other side of the breakfast table. So, I would be attending Kenny's funeral flanked by my two favorite ladies. I wish that made me feel less anxious. Maybe they'd come up with the right words of comfort for Burke, and at worst they'd have plenty of tissues. It looked to be a sad, sad day.

CHAPTER 47

Assuming it would be a quiet day at the dealership, I decided to wear my dress clothes—heels and a shortish blue skirt and cropped suit jacket—so I would not need to run home to change. I really must learn not to assume.

Montello had the day off. *Damn it! He didn't clear that with me when we were sipping Glenmorangie last night.* I hadn't exactly hung around to discuss it either. Half page ads in the major Arizona papers had created a swarm of traffic that would ordinarily be wonderful except that Bingham had the day off also. Rich and NewKid already had people ready to drive but that didn't stop NewKid from giving me a cat whistle as he walked by and saw me in my Sunday-go-to-meeting outfit.

"Birdie, Birdie, Birdie - The ALTONator!" he called out.

"Where's Clay?" I said, praying that nickname wouldn't stick.

"I don't know, but if I see him I'll tell him that a stunning blonde is in the showroom looking for him."

"There is? Where? We don't often see those here," I said.

"Not often enough" he said. Then he whisked his customers out onto the lot.

"What's with the legs?" said Greg from Parts. "And who have you been saving them for?" He didn't wait for an answer. I was feeling conspicuous and too tall in heels to make hiding behind the pop machine again an option. So, I snagged the least likely Up— the one that would never buy. Some things are a dead giveaway. They had an SUV with Idaho plates, too new and too far from home for a trade. Uber-conservative clothing meant they weren't impulse people. There was a purebred, seventy-pound chocolate Lab in the back seat. They were out for a drive and weren't buying anything. Today's perfect customers.

"Just looking for a pick-up," the Cottinghams said.

It was late in the season for them to be snowbirds killing time as they appeared to be. So, we headed out to the lot to do some tire kicking that would have them on their way and me on my way to Kenny's funeral at 10:30.

We had only looked at one vehicle when the get-out-quick scenario started to go wrong.

"We really like it," he said, about the two-wheel drive pickup they were examining. They wanted a two-wheel drive pick up? That couldn't possibly be correct, no one buys a full-sized pickup with two-wheel drive.

"You understand that this isn't a four-wheel drive?" That would put an end to the discussion.

"That's what we're looking for," he said. "I haven't been able to find a two-wheel back home. Can we take it for a drive?" *Wait. Shouldn't that be my line?* I couldn't quit looking at the clock.

It took me only thirty seconds to understand why I didn't normally wear heels to work. I opened the back door behind the husband, thank God. He didn't see that my skirt was now up to the top of my thighs, and I had to spread so wide putting the first leg up that it was a darn good thing I didn't choose today to try out wearing that thong thing. My lady parts had never seen so much daylight, but there was no other way to get in without a step stool. Even in jeans and sneakers, I struggled to get up in these trucks. The snapshot of me attempting to mount this ledge wearing a short skirt would certainly be overexposed. While we drove, Burke and I exchanged texts.

I WILL LOOK FOR YOU

CAN YOU SIT ON THE LEFT SIDE OF THE CHURCH?

SURE HOW R U DOING?" I answered.

PRETTY SAD TODAY, he answered.

I was pleased he took time to think of me. I should've called in sick, it was near 9:30, so I needed to get this buttoned up with the Potato State folks and get them on their way.

"Can we have some time to think about it?" the Mrs. said.

"Good idea; take all the time you want." I thought they meant go home to think.

"You know, you can order one of these in Idaho," I added. *Oh my God! Did I say that out loud? Was anybody near enough to hear?* Wade or Montello would fire me on the spot if they had heard that I had driven a customer then suggested they cut us out of the deal to go back home and order. I'd probably be tied to the tailgate and flogged with a radiator hose in front of the building for extra measure, and it would be justified.

Instead, I had unwittingly turned this into my very first use of the "Why don't you just go home and think about it" closing technique. The one where we indicate we can take this sale or leave it. We just aren't very interested or have better things to do. All true at the moment. It's a rule. When the customer thinks we don't care about the deal, then they want it all the more.

"We've tried ordering," my customer said, "Our orders don't seem to get shipped. We live in a little town, and our local dealer can't get it. We even put $1,000 down one time." How could I have said the one thing that triggered his next pronouncement?

"Aw, hell with it!" he surprised both his wife and me. "Lets just get it! We'll drive it home instead of flying."

Words that would have thrilled me on any other day sank my heart down to my knobby uncovered knees. Maybe they had terrible credit? I could hope. Maybe they didn't have enough income. Maybe I could still make it to the left side of the Presbyterian Church by 11 am. Maybe not.

"My wife's a doctor, a veterinarian, back home," he volunteered. This intel made it clear that I wouldn't make it to the church on time. Murphy's Law. If I could have gotten my hands on that idiot

Murphy, I'd have wrung his neck but I couldn't help but think Murphy was doing this for a reason.

At 10:30 I took the new 2x2 truck back to Detail and handed it over to Angel to get ready for delivery.

"Where's Clay? I gotta turn this deal and get out of here and quick."

"You look like you're going to a board meeting in that getup. Do you realize how long your legs look in those shoes? Clay left a few minutes ago to do a delivery on one he sold yesterday," she said. "I wish I could give you better news."

"As always, good news is in very short supply around here!" I swallowed. I was cross, but it wasn't Angel's fault. I called Grams but I didn't know what to say.

"What do you mean?" she said. "I'm sure Wally would not want you to miss something as important as this. I'll call him."

"No, Grams. He's probably already there; he was a golfing buddy of Kenny's. If I walk out on this deal, I don't have a job. There's no one else here to finish it. We are short-handed and there are buyers everywhere here today. Montello is gone too. He would have helped me out and let me go, but I'm working with Wade. I've told you how I feel about him." I was rattling off my excuses, one after the other as a fast-talking bid-calling auctioneer might. I was thinking if I listed them fast enough, one would sound convincing, and I'd sell the idea that I had no choice in the matter. I was also trying to convince myself.

"I am so glad Dana is coming by," I told her. "You two go and I'll catch up at the reception at the ranch as soon as I can." I knew she was disappointed but probably for me, not herself.

The Idaho folks were all-out giddy with excitement awaiting their new perfect truck. They needed a lower 2x2 just to haul their lawn tractors to their different properties. "Why buy more vehicle than you need?" This was a very logical thought in a place where oversell is our stock in trade. At least they didn't have to spar with Gordon in finance because they paid cash—they were practical. I loved those folks. I just wish I'd met them on a better day.

Burke texted.
I DON'T SEE YOU
ARE YOU IN BACK?

I no sooner said goodbye to the first customer when Brian and his wife Kimberly appeared. He was one-legged the week before, looking at an SUV without her. Of course, he wanted to work with me again. Naturally. There I was, the lone salesman in the middle of the showroom; even weird Wade was missing. I had no choice, I silently told myself. It was my job. I was responsible. Anyone else would have done the same. But behind all those thoughts, I knew no one here would have stayed. No one with any feeling at all would leave Burke in this time of need. Just the girl that couldn't bring herself to go to a funeral when a good enough excuse could be used to prevent it, making this the bluest, red letter day I had experienced in my last twenty years. All the while, Dana was texting me.

BURKE WAS ASKING FOR YOU
WHAT SHOULD WE TELL HIM?
WHERE THE HELL ARE YOU?

I was the saddest person in history to have just had two new car sales for the second day in a row. It was unheard of, and I'd been unheard from the rest of the day. At 6:30 p.m., I was standing at my desk waiting for Wade to write my checks.

Wade never handed me my commission checks. He put them in an envelope and sent a messenger with them, anyone that was handy, but we were the only two left—just us dedicated servants, exceptionally loyal employees willing to give up every shred of our private lives to this company. One would almost think we could bond over that. Maybe he would say something appreciative but that would not be happening. He shoved the checks at me without envelopes and without comment. There was one for $75 plus $100 spiff on the truck and $75 for the car."

"There was a $500 spiff on all the cars today, wasn't there? You said so yourself in this morning's meeting," I said, struggling to keep calm.

"But you logged those car folks last week and there wasn't a spiff then."

"That's just totally wrong!" I screamed, not believing what I was seeing on the two checks in my hand.

"I don't give a shit," he said. "Don't you ever quit whining? Take it up with Montello tomorrow."

"I'll quit being whiny when you quit being a deviant, lying, cheating, asshole." I almost added dog killer. "You can't cheat me day after day and get away with it. I think I need to take this to Wallace." I pivoted on my heel and headed for the relative security of my Mini Cooper parked out back. Screw the keying! I was most likely out of a job, but since I didn't walk out nine hours earlier, I had lost so much, much more.

I hadn't had a day of more terrible decisions since I left Nebraska without a plan either personal or more importantly financial. I still had no plan. I couldn't drive out to the ranch not knowing if Grams would be there to protect me and she was probably already back home. I was humiliated at my own behavior.

At 7:15 my cell phone rang.

Where were you today?" Burke asked in a frosty tone more fitting to a juvenile correction officer or a creditor.

"I'm so sorry that I wasn't there, Burke." My excuses were too flimsy to offer. When I tried them out in my head, they made me sound greedy and shallow and I didn't have enough honesty to tell him the real reason—that I'd spent my whole adult life avoiding days like today. From this late part of the day as a vantage point, I saw it had been a terrible mistake not to walk off the sales floor and the error was not forgivable. How could I tell him that after my parents died, I had vowed that the next funeral I attended would be my own?

"You knew it was important, right?" he said.

"I'm so sorry," I said again. "Was it a nice service? I hear almost everybody in town was there."

"No, not everybody." He said this slowly and firmly and with enough ice that a hockey player could slam a puck at a spectator from it. "Some of the most important people in town were not there. I'll talk to you later." He hung up without waiting for a reply.

I am sincerely sorry, Burke. And I truly was.

CHAPTER 48

I took two Aleve PMs and nine hours later, I woke up with a face problem. I didn't want to face either my Gramma Lou or the slimeball Wade Winchell, my boss, who was likely to have a pink slip waiting for me. I especially did not want to face Burke or even Dana. I quietly dressed and tiptoed out to drive Tweety to Bernadette's Bakery so I could take a booth and hide away until the car lot opened. Then, I'd drag myself in and beg Montello for a reprieve. Maybe he'd take pity on me. Wade probably called him last night. They were thick as thieves. Why not? They were thieves, if not with customers, at least with the salesmen.

Tweety wasn't as ready to wake up as I was. My beloved yellow Mini Cooper made cold dark morning outings uncertain. It wasn't her fault. I wasn't trusting her care to the Service Department at the AutoMall but it wouldn't be long and she would be under AAA's care if I didn't manage her health better.

As soon as I pulled open the front door of Bernadette's bakery, the moist, yeasty smell confirmed I'd finally made a great decision. If ever there was a day for comfort food, this was it. I took a seat in a booth under the gigantic sepia-toned photo of the Eiffel Tower at the left rear of the café and positioned my phone next to the fake flower arrangement in front of me, in case Montello called. A pink and white-clad waitress delivered coffee and guessed my order.

"Two coconut donuts, right?" She was sassy. So was I now a regular or just utterly predictable? When she stepped aside, the next thing I saw was Cuervo. He was a real, honest-to-goodness regular. *I couldn't catch a break.*

"Ready for a refill, Cuervo?" The young woman said. *Yup, he's a Regular.* He held out his cup and gave her a warm smile as she poured. "Thank you, dear." In no time he and his coffee cup had moved to the other side of my booth.

"You weren't at the funeral," he said. This will be the opening line anyone will use with me for the rest of my life.

"I know. Was it nice?" I didn't really care.

"It was big," he said." I wasn't actually inside, but I didn't see your car or Louella's there. Shoot. He didn't see Grams. I could have lied.

"Dana picked up Gramma Lou, and I was stuck at work."

"Wow. I didn't think you would ever become so devoted to The Copper Springs AutoMall."

"Why were you there, lurking in the parking lot of funeral?"

"I was just keeping an eye on some of my charges. When they miss their meetings, I need to check their excuses."

"Just like a teacher," I said. "A note from home not quite enough?"

"I'm more like a hall monitor. Just making sure they really are going to the boy's room and not smoking out back. You don't look too great," he said.

"Maybe you need to go back to your booth over there under the *Arc de Triomphe*," I told him. He ignored my suggestion.

"I know how to cheer you up. I can tell you a secret." His voice was seductive and gave the impression that he was really giving something away that should be kept in a locked box.

"You have to promise not to tell anyone. I mean it. You can't tell anyone!"

"Are you sure you should tell me then? I don't seem to be very trustworthy these days."

"Hell, no! Of course, I shouldn't tell you." With that, he had my full attention.

"I think. I think," he said again as he looked around making sure the booth behind him was still empty.

"What? What do you think?" I had no patience with his reality show lead up.

"I think I might know where Wally's missing BMW has gotten to."

"I thought I already told you, that nobody cares about that car anymore." I hadn't thought of that car since the last time Cuervo mentioned it. "I don't care about the damn Beemer!"

"Even if you don't, I might have found it. One of my parolees can't seem to give up his thriving drug business, and we're thinking he's stealing cars to use so he can't be easily trailed. Car lots that don't actually report thefts are a good place to get them."

"If you are trailing him, why don't you just go get it then?" I asked.

"I will in due time, but I have a detective working with me too and we think there is a ring of suppliers from Mexico that the car might lead us to. Anyway, as you said yourself—
Wally has a lot of cars."

"Is that even legal? I mean not to report it?"

"It isn't my job to bring it in now, is it?" There was no irony showing in his voice.

"Why are you telling me this?" He was annoying me.

"Because you look like you have lost your best friend," he said. "I thought it might perk you up."

"I lost my best friends and my job. I may have lost just about everything."

"No kidding. Sorry about the friends but that job didn't last long. You're kind of a job hopper."

"No. I am not a job hopper." His accusation made my blood boil. "I was at my last job more than fourteen years. I am not a job hopper." I stood to leave. "I'm on my way to the AutoMall to find out whether it is the guillotine or just another workday." My elevated blood pressure was giving me a headache. I was so anxious to leave that I didn't bother to check around to make sure I collected all my things.

"Remember, it's a secret." He called to me as he stood by the booth, holding up the very same phone I had left at Bernadette's before. He treated me to his little smirk as he watched me come back for it.

I was not a job hopper. It wasn't job hopping if a person attempts something that is far too difficult for her intellect, her gender or her fragile personality. She might be considered stupid but not a job hopper.

"I hear they are looking for a teaching pro at the golf course," he hollered after me.

Asshole.

CHAPTER 49

I sat hunched down in the Mini Cooper parked behind a one-ton truck hiding out in the Detail lot instead of the employee parking places until Angel drove in. No one had picked up the car keys the night before. It was a wonder any cars were there, but the lot was still full. When Angel saw my car and came over, I moved the junk mail on my passenger seat so she could sit inside.

"I'm probably fired. I'm here early to see what Montello says, but if Wade has any part of it, I am sure it's a done deal. I finally told him off royally last night."

"I'm thinking none of us will be here long," she said. "I need to tell you something."

"What am I, the priest at St Michael's?"

"Don't flatter yourself. When was the last time you were even in a church?"

"Too long, but it just seems like it is my day to take confessions."

"This is serious, damn it. I was on the Internet last night, just nosing around, and I put in Conrad's name." Angel had a sharp tool in her hand and while she talked she was picking at the crevices of that gold ring that she wore every day.

"Why do you wear that ring to work?" I asked. "Aren't you afraid you'll lose one of the stones or ruin it?"

"I never take it off," she said. "It's my mother's ring."

"You wear your mom's ring to work in a grease pit?"

"No. It's my ring. The kids bought it for me. There's a birth-stone for me and one for each of them." She continued to pick away at the debris that had collected in and around a small ruby, an emerald and what looked like two sapphires. "They gave it to me two years ago for Mother's Day, and I promised them I'd always wear it. They'd be very alarmed if I ever took it off." She continued picking at it while she talked.

"Won't they be more alarmed if you wreck it with cleaning solvents?" Angel gave me the "you don't understand because you don't have kids" glare. I've gotten that many times over the years. I looked down at my own hands—no jewelry of any kind. There was no golden symbol of undying love with or without gemstones—just broken fingernails and new calluses.

Angel broke the silence. "You know he lived in Colorado, right?"

"Who did?" She'd lost me to my self-pity.

"Conrad! I was just wondering if he had any family and all what with his wife in jail. Birdie, he was convicted of selling drugs and not just marijuana—the hard stuff—coke. Why would Montello hire him with a drug record?" she asked, incredulity creeping into her voice.

"You are so good at research you could have been a librarian," I told her, "but you need an update. Juanita isn't in jail; they released her. They don't have enough evidence."

"What?" Genuine alarm came over Angel's face. I hadn't meant to scare her.

"Montello hired him because he was desperate. He told me he had a terrible time finding Conrad. I guess he was desperate enough to look in jail cells for a service department guy, and I think he was the one to spring Stretch out of the slammer, too."

Angel wasn't listening. "They let Juanita go. Who's next? You or me?"

"That's not funny," I said.

"And what about Mater?" she said. "He and ConMan came here together. I couldn't find out anything about him. Something's wrong with him. I can feel it and all those other guys too that hang around them."

"Did you know Mater is not his real name?" I said. "He told me and Grams that it was Mason. For some reason that sounds familiar."

"Mason?" She was more surprised than she should have been. "Mason Moore? I can't believe I didn't recognize him. You know his sister, don't you? Her name is Loretta."

"My first customer Loretta? Loretta's kid's drug-dealing uncle? Jesus. Can that be true and we didn't even know it? Now what? We have to tell Montello." I looked up to watch him pulling his classic Crown Vic into his designated spot.

Angel left and I slipped in the door behind him a few moments later.

"You can't pull shit like that," Montello admonished as I followed him into his office. I intended to trap him in until I got the answer I wanted.

"You mean I didn't earn the $500 spiff then?" I said.

"No, no, you'll get the $500, but you can't talk to a boss that way." He caved easier than I thought he would. "Wade was just pulling your chain. You've got to quit telling him off. Wallace is very sensitive about his only nephew."

"I'm getting a little sensitive too. You don't understand. He deliberately screws up my deals; he makes derogatory statements in front of the sales staff, and he only gives me a lead when he thinks it's a loser. He plays favorites, and that's putting it mildly."

"And yet you're still here."

I bristled. "What are you getting at?"

"He's trying every way he can to get you to quit and yet you're still here." If that was a compliment, my dad would have called it left-handed.

"I don't quit. I'm not a quitter or a job hopper."

"I know." Montello sat and wrote out a $500 check with my name on it. "Get back out there and get to work." So, I wasn't fired. I stepped back in to ask one last question: "By the way, have you heard anything about Wally's missing Beemer?"

"Are you F-ing kidding me? With all that's happening here, you think anyone is still looking for that used bucket of bolts?"

"Just asking," I said. The thought that poor Catfish face Wade spent time thinking up ways to aggravate me made me smile, then I realized he didn't have the ability to think. Meanness just came instinctively, without any extra effort.

"What about Juanita?" I said.

"What about her?"

"They let her go." Mike looked dumbfounded and picked up the phone. I guessed it was to tell Wally that the nightmare wasn't over—far from it.

I left without mentioning Mater, or was it Mason?

CHAPTER 50

Several days went by and the dealership was slowly getting back to normal. Normal? I used to think of the middle school library as normal. The drama there was Hello Kitty. The drama at the AutoMall was King Lear.

Rich and Bingham had been too busy to complain. How could one call that normal? A day without Bingham and Rich complaining felt like the earth had toppled over and was bowling down the Milky Way. I couldn't complain either. I had sold, with various help, so many vehicles that unless I got totally screwed, a distinct possibility, I would make more money in the last few days than I had previously made in six months. Hell, it would be more than a whole year's salary when I started teaching.

Two service managers had actually come in to interview for Conrad's vacant position. I wouldn't have, what with the last guy murdered and the killer still on the loose. In the meantime, the short, blockheaded mechanic, Frank, the tank, had not quit and had managed to dole out the work to the rest of the guys, all of it still taking place across the alley or elsewhere. Repaired vehicles turned up parked out front. I wrung it out of Frank that another of the Lone Pine fleet was due, and I lurked around the intake area to see if I could catch Burke to try to apologize again. Instead, his hired hand, Jim, dropped off the rig. Maybe he would come to pick it up?

It was getting hotter by the minute, and we were required to be standing out on the lot. Even the ridiculous prices we were offering were no longer filling the sales desks, so, as I said, we were getting back to normal.

My personal Axis of Evil, Wade, Stretch, and Gordon, the finance guru, were plotting and laughing. They had their own dealership inside of Wallace's, and it ran for their exclusive benefit. Clay brought me the news that Montello had told the others out in the smoker's ring that he may have paid me the spiff this time, but now none of the spiffed sales would count towards our quotas, making me persona non grata once again. At the AutoMall, the payment plans got made up along the way, and just for fun let's throw Ms. Alton under the bus while we're at it. Both Montello and Wade knew we had all made excellent money this month thanks to Curt Larsen and company, and now they didn't want to hold up their end of the bargain. Wade managed some shitty comments toward me in front of everyone about how bad my paperwork had been the night before. He couldn't run me out, but he could put maximum effort into being a more perfect prick.

Bingham motioned me to his desk to give me one of his "It's all right to quit" lectures. "After all," blah,blah,blah, "I have never seen a woman make it in this business." Guess what, Bingham old man—today was the day. I was tired of his belittling negative bullshit. Sweet Birdie was signing off, Badass Birdie was here.

"You need some new material, Mr. Down-in-the-mouth. This is the fiftieth and last time you have given me that lecture." Bingham's eyes widened. "What are you going to tell the next woman you harangue if I happen to succeed and stay? Huh? What are you going to do then?" My voice grew louder and I inched closer to his face. "You'll have to rewrite your monologue, won't you?" This was the first time I had turned it back on old Bing and he was thoroughly flummoxed. My goodness, it was fun. No wonder the boys reveled in belittling me. It was a hoot.

"How many deals have you tallied this month?" I continued.

"I'm retiring." He spit the words out at me. "So, I won't have to worry about that." The normal Birdie would have stopped there and taken pity, but the new Birdie was all out of pity.

"Can I quote you on that, Mr. Bingham? Have you actually given your notice? I didn't realize. Does everybody know? Should we put it out over the loudspeaker so everyone can hear? Maybe someone will want to bake a cake." The tirade spewed from my own lips, but I was still surprised. I stood my ground and took the intercom phone receiver in hand, as Bingham screwed his face into a scowl. I pushed the intercom button.

"May I have your attention, please." My words reverberated in the big empty building. Bing's entire face turned fire engine red for once, not just his cherry nose. I thought I might have given him a heart attack. He grabbed the receiver from me and slammed it down. We had started to draw a crowd so now everybody knew I was in a rare mood.

It wasn't just Bing. "You won't make it" was a running theme from Wade, Stretch, and Conrad, God rest his slimy soul. Since I'd started at the AutoMall when I felt sorry for myself, and it got to me, I repeated my mantra on the way home. "I scare them. I threaten them. And, that's why they are so damn mean." Somehow, I could always ride that little pony of a thought on into work each morning, but by 10 a.m. that horse was usually foundering as the old nag of "what the hell am I doing this for?" stood over it in the stall.

Today's version of that was my saying to myself: "Hey, Bird dog, why would you want to be in a place with all these assholes, one of whom is probably a murderer?" But this month, I had even bested Bingham, so I was in a career now more interesting to me and my creditors than it was before. It would be the first month in all the time I'd been back in Arizona that I wouldn't be paying late charges on credit cards, car payment and repair bills.

Montello was not in his office, so I slipped in and took my usual comfy leather chair to cool down and wait. When he stormed in past me, Jeannie was right on his heels. She was bending his ear about some management info and apparently, didn't care who heard it.

"Mike, I've been reviewing the sales for the last year out of the Phoenix Auto Auction. Did you notice that two thirds of the heaps we send to the "C" line, the junker car sales arena, were all bought by the same guy?" She looked at her notes: "A Jeffrey Lacamore. The auction desk guy said he ships them all to Broadview, Montana."

"Aren't all towns in Montana broad view?" Mike said. "What do we care who's buying them?"

"I just thought it was odd. He pays for them with an AMEX card, and he only buys the junkers." I wondered how she got all that from the auction guy.

"It's probably because Montana doesn't have an emissions test for vehicles. They're worth a lot more there." Mike was absent-minded, obviously busy. I decided to ask my customer question later, but I did make one comment.

"If one guy is buying all our junkers, and we know his name, why don't we cut out the middleman and sell to him directly?"

"That's what I was thinking," said Jeannie, looking back to Montello.

"Do you think they have telephones in Broadview?" Mike said.

"He's not in Broadview—he's in Phoenix. I'm pretty sure they do have phones there."

I was impressed with her initiative even if Mike wasn't. I let them go at it and wandered over to the Auxiliary Showroom where the air conditioning worked better—a perfect hideout to kill the rest of what I mistakenly thought was going to be just another lackluster day.

CHAPTER 51

The sound of the door echoed in the mostly empty steel annex building. Wallace built the showroom when he bought the business, and it housed his elaborate office with the Louis the 14th desk and gold trimmed chair. Really, they may have actually been Louie's.

The gilt furniture was sitting on risers, no less. It could be Trump Tower if Donald Trump also had a rack of shotguns and a shelf of cowboy hats. The office alone was not the prime use of this jewel box; it was specifically engineered to house Wallace's pride and joy—A Limited Edition 2002 Collector's sports car. It featured hand-stitched Italian leather and was majestic in every way. Under the hood was housed one of the biggest engines known to a U.S. automaker, making it supremely powerful as well as spellbinding. Even though it wasn't tall, it still loomed large and lorded it over any man or machine who dared to enter the space. There was room for several more vehicles in the building, but they didn't even dare peek in. Bingham told me, "If you aren't an enthusiast where she is concerned then you have no right to be selling cars." The exquisite convertible was the color of a luscious, purple plum. Wally acquired it from a fellow who owed him "a favor," a big one. It literally had been slid into this location, so as not to turn wheels and to keep her odometer on the fourteen original factory miles. Those four mag wheels hadn't turned since the day it left Detroit. The tin soldier-like stanchions surrounding the prize protected her chastity as though she was the original sin incarnate.

"This gem is not for sale. Period. No one is to drive her, ever." Rich repeated the mantra for me as if I hadn't heard that from every other guy I'd encountered at the AutoMall. He was dusting off a headlamp with his handkerchief. Lingering just to caress her? The men were positively weird about this vehicle.

"So, just for show then?" I said. "It seems like valuable real estate to give to something that isn't for sale."

"It's a fucking priceless piece of Americana." Rich's indignation had to do with the fact that he was hiding out in this building, and I had flushed him out like the bird dog I am. I no sooner came in, than he flew off out the door.

I looked her over from stem to stern. The boys had certainly drunk the grape Kool-Aid where she was concerned; a car like this was most every man's fantasy.

I heard the back door shut and I stared unmoving as Wallace J. Winchell walked without looking up from his mail from the back of the building to his office. I glanced over both shoulders to see who might be running in after him and then I realized nobody knows he's here. If they did, they would be mobbing the place like he was a rock star, especially Montello, who always came running up to Wally like a wiggly, tail-wagging, puppy. He practically peed on his shoes. It was disgusting.

When I was noticed, he spoke. "How's it going, Miss Birdie?" Wallace's caring voice shocked me every time I encountered him. "Are those boys still trying to run you off?" *Wade, your nephew, is.* "That's what they'll do at every opportunity. Don't you listen to them." I was following him into his office but he was still looking at his mail.

"Some of it is Montello's fault. I asked him to shut that stuff down, like the keying thing. I know it makes it hard, especially for a woman, even though the women I've seen are even more competitive than the men. I will tell you this; they'll change their tune as soon as you outsell them. I understand you are ahead of most of them this month, aren't you?" I nodded. "You're smart and you will outsell them."

"I didn't come here to make friends, sir." Again, I sounded like I wasn't a team player "I mean. I'm really... I'm doing okay."

He picked up his phone. I backed out of his office. I considered genuflecting.

At the other end of the showroom, behind the sacred vehicle, were more racks of propaganda books from the manufacturers so I busied myself there even though I didn't like them much. Don't people become librarians because they love books, you might ask? Becoming a librarian because you love books is like becoming a valet parking attendant because you love cars. You both file things in and out of slots all day long without ever having time to look under the hood. But I am not a librarian, anymore, am I? And if the want ads were telling the truth, there was never going to be an opening for me to get back to a life more like the one I knew. So, what was I now? I decided to be a super sleuth and moved over to a quiet corner to research ConMan using my phone. It was rather easy to find his drug conviction and six-year sentence once I knew where to look. Why hadn't Montello ever looked? Or did he know? There were dozens of Mason Moores in the data base but only one convicted in Colorado that was originally addressed in Copper Springs, Arizona. Also six years. They were literally partners-in-crime. Angel was right to worry about Mater and Mike needed to know.

Ever the librarian, I squatted down near the floor to straighten the bottom row of catalogs before I left the room, when I peripherally caught sight of an exquisitely cut designer pant leg which I followed up to see a truly gorgeous man. He had been stealthy enough to slip in a door without me even hearing him enter the building.

I tipped so far back to look up at his face that I toppled over backwards on my fanny and threw my left hand back to brace my fall. As I went down, stacks of books left my hands then sailed like sloops across the shiny checkerboard design showroom floor, skidding out in every direction. In attempting to get up, I slipped again, this time flat on my back. The beautiful man leaned forward to try to catch me and ended up straddling me. I was staring up at the crotch of what looked like Michelangelo's David now over the top of me. Had I hit my head and died? Those trousers must be worsted wool. He offered to help, and I gave him my left hand, eliciting a wince. It hurt.

"I'm so sorry I startled you. Let me help pick these up." I tried to protest but in no time we were both upright, catalogs in hand. Thank goodness Wallace hadn't seen me.

"Did you hurt your wrist?" He saw me rubbing it.

"Oh, no, I'm okay," I said.

"I'm a surgeon, let me look." So, with feigned reluctance, I held out my left hand as if offering it for him to kiss. He did a thorough inspection with soft hands and manicured nails. I'm guessing he didn't use tweezers as Montello did. He worked each finger in a circle then maneuvered my limp hand around gracefully and said, "I think it's okay, but be sure to put some ice on it and a wrap when you get home tonight."

I nodded, said nothing, and reluctantly withdrew my hand from Prince Charming's hold. "How about we start this over? I'm Birdie Alton. I'm in sales."

He grinned. "I'm Alan Cornwall. I drove down from Phoenix to take a look at this car. Maybe you can help me, then? My wife and I are thinking of taking a trip up the Pacific Coast Highway, and I thought this would be a fun ride." I wondered if he was a good enough doctor to tell what just happened to my heart when he said the word wife.

"This vehicle? You're interested in buying this car?" I started to tell him that it was a collector's item and really not for sale, but instead, I asked if he'd ever owned one like it before. Remember always let them talk, I admonished myself. Alan launched into a list all the fantastic sports cars he'd ever owned, and I listened with rapt attention, not knowing much of what he was talking about and despite the attractiveness of the car enthusiast before me, I was wanting to get my new information about ConMan and Mater to Angel.

"What price is it?" he asked. I knew the fictitious price of $138K. "I believe it is in the neighborhood of $148,000," I said. Never talk price. What was I thinking? I added almost ten percent to the asking. Asking? No one was asking. The corollary to not talking price was 'just get them behind the wheel' but no one had ever moved past the stanchions and ribbon barrier. Is getting this doctor behind the wheel even possible? What the hell, I was all in, so I buried myself even deeper. "$148,500 to be exact." Why not? It wasn't really for sale.

"Wallace told me he might be able to negotiate a bit?"

Wallace? So that was why Wally had surreptitiously arrived. Did he already quote the lower price? And as if on cue, Wallace entered stage right and walked across the showroom floor toward us, delivering his opening line:

"She's a beauty, isn't she?"

"She is indeed," Alan said, "just like you promised." Could I just crawl under the brochure rack? Too late.

"Birdie, here," Alan turned to me. "It is Birdie?"

"Yes, it is," I squeaked.

"Birdie's informed me you're asking one forty-eight five. But we can deal, correct?"

"You bet," Wally said as he put his arm around Alan in a parental gesture, winked at me and guided him under the ribbon and toward the vehicle. The two men pored over every detail that either of them could spout off. A half hour had passed with me standing to the side as though I was a busboy with a pitcher waiting for either of them to stop drinking in the beauty and need a refill. None of my cohorts seemed to know we were there except Angel who appeared as a silhouette in the back entrance with the light shining behind her making her seem as her name implied—a heavenly messenger.

CHAPTER 52

I stole away from the two men and crept to the back of the building to meet a grim-faced Angel.

"We've got to talk," I said as I kept looking back at Wallace. "We've got a situation here. I think it involves Mater."

"I agree and I've found something. Something serious" She kept her voice low. "You need to come out back so I can show you."

"Your gun?" I said looking over my shoulder at the two men still regaling each other.

"No. Still missing. Come on, I need to show you. We have to do something."

"Angel, I'm going to sell this mega car. You couldn't get me to leave this room if my life depended on it."

"It might," she said, then, realizing what I had said, "Hey, you know he can't drive that right?" I moved aside, and she saw that Alan was talking to Wallace. She smiled briefly.

"Okay, then, just come as soon as you can," she said. "It's urgent!" Where Angel trod, drama was sure to follow.

"Do we need lawyers?"

"Someone here will. I found what I think is a bag of cocaine in the car you drove last week."

"The car ConMan dropped me out of? Geez. What next? Did you call the cops?"

"How can I do that? They'd haul me off immediately and you'd be visiting me at the State Pen. You need to come and look."

"I'm no expert on drugs. What the hell. Who else knows?" Then we were interrupted.

"Birdie, Alan would like to take her for a test drive. Wallace, the only guy who could, had approved a drive in the infamous vehicle. "Alan, you know this car has never been driven and driving it will affect her collector's value, correct?" Wallace said, giving the customer full disclosure. I glanced back. Angel had vanished.

"I do," the handsome Dr. Alan answered like a groom at the altar.

"Will it be sacrilegious to drive the vehicle after all the time she has been saved?" This sounded like two aristocratic English gentlemen negotiating for the favors of an innocent virgin. It gave me the creeps big time, but, as Bingham has told me, everything was about sex, especially sports cars.

"The key is on my desk, Birdie. Will you fill it with gas? Remember—Premium." As rattled as I was with Angel's discovery, my ego jumped to the forefront of my brain. I would be the first driver. Oh My God. It's me! It's me. When I entered the car, the luscious leather seat seemed to swallow me whole. I was wearing it instead of sitting in it. As I inched the wheels back and forth to exit the showroom, the two men held the doors open. I made the most extravagant scene possible pulling the Purple love machine up to the main building right in front of Wade's window. He rose up out of his office chair—a phoenix out of a fire. He clutched his chest. I could see his handlebar twitching. The rest of the staff were slowly tumbling to the magnitude of my egregious error. I smiled and turned my head back and forth as though I was an ingénue sitting on the General Motors float in the Rose Parade.

NewKid grinned. Clay exploded through the two front glass doors like a rocket off the pad at Cape Kennedy.

"You can't drive that! You aren't allowed to take it from the showroom. Where did you get the keys? You're going to be fired."

I ignored him. He didn't know that I had already made a solid attempt to throw the stupid job away the day before. I waltzed by him and floated the rest of the way on an imaginary red carpet. All, including the Parts guys, were now gawking first at the car and then back at me as if to say: Dead salesgirl walking. I hesitated in the entry to Montello's office and drank in the luxurious elixir of golden "lot cred" in its purest form. The boss who worked for the big boss who unbeknownst to all had agreed to sell his Plum Passion, stood speechless. It dawned on me as I stood there, that with all the uproar in his business, poor old Wallace needed the money.

"Do you mind if I take this out for a little drive to Bisbee this weekend?" I asked Mike. "You said we should test drive all our vehicles." His face showed no color, just a murderous glare. I looked around. Is somebody filming this? How I wished I could drag this out to torture him the way he tortured the rest of us.

"Wally's in the other building. A surgeon named Cornwall from Phoenix has come to buy the car. He has already negotiated the deal with Wally, and we are test driving. Wally gave me the keys to fill it up."

"Oh, my lord," Mike dropped into his chair like a deflated holiday snowman on Wally's front lawn. "You scared the shit out of me. I didn't know Wally was here. Why would he let this guy drive it when no one else has been able to?"

"Do you want to go over to the other building and second-guess him?" I asked.

"No." Mike signed the gas voucher.

"I guess this technically means I popped the cherry since I am the first to drive it." I reveled in using the street vernacular the boys had perfected.

"Don't keep the customer waiting," he growled.

As I pulled out of the lot, the salesmen and mechanics who were gathered behind the beast somehow got pelted with gravel when I took off. I didn't mean to, but you know these race car transmissions and Indy 500 tires can be hard to control.

"Birdie, would you mind if I went on the test drive with Alan?" Wallace said when I returned. Was Wallace asking my permission in front of the crowd of gawkers? Could this get any better?

"Hey," he yelled over his shoulder from the passenger seat, "If we're not back in two hours have them look for us in California."

As they pulled away, I rushed back to find Angel in the few moments I had until Wally and the good doctor returned.

"I have five minutes. Did you tell Mike yet?" She looked both ways as she dragged me out the side door to the very car Conrad pulled me from. She yanked back the inner liner of the trunk and revealed two bulging plastic bags?

"My God! NCIS Copper Springs. So, Conrad was a drug runner? Is that what you are saying? If you don't call the cops, you have got to show Mike." My heart was racing. "Do it now before someone else sees you or me." For the moment, we were the only two not out front. When I heard the sports car engine return, I headed back to meet Wally and the Doc. I looked back over my shoulder and told Angel, "Do it! Now. Conrad may be gone but this is far from over."

My surgeon was not in as much of a hurry as are most big money cash clients, but I was like a miserable cat stuck endlessly on a hot Arizona roof. I kept looking toward the back of the other building expecting to see the black and whites that Montello should have summoned by now. Finally, Wallace and I watched as the exquisite piece of 'Americana" swept out of the lot, seemingly pulling our oxygen with her to Phoenix. The crowd disbursed and Wallace and I went back to the annex building.

"Birdie," Wallace said, "You're an asset here." I blushed. It was all I could do not to cry. I'm becoming girly. He reached in his pocket for his wallet, extracted two crisp $500 bills which he handed to me.

"I made some nice money today. Go on, take it. This won't be on your W-2 and don't mention it to Montello either if you don't mind."

"Oh, my goodness, thank you. Do you want me to get someone to help me put some vehicles back in the showroom?" I asked.

"No, not yet; let's enjoy the space where she sat for a day or two." We both looked on a vast open space. The black and white checkered floor could be a "Dancing with the Stars" ballroom where the prettiest girl in the frilliest dress had just left the building. This job was not half bad, I thought. Then I remembered Angel.

CHAPTER 53

The cops were in the conference room questioning Angel. I was relieved she had called them. Clay stepped up to fill me in.

"We assume this is about Conrad. Did you know they released Juanita?"

"Angel needs a lawyer," I said. I looked down at my cell phone and saw Dana's number listed four times in a row- one text.

MEET ME AT THE NORTH SIDE OF THE DEALERSHIP

Dana was sitting in her car there waiting for me. I walked to her open window.

"I know Angel is your buddy," Dana said as she offered me an open sack of Fritos. I was so hungry that I took a generous salty handful and munched like a squirrel. "I hope this isn't your dinner," I said, "or mine either." I took another handful then moved around to get in the front seat with her. The new developments tumbled out.

"They haven't found a gun yet. They know Conrad fired Angel the night he died. And by the way, I wish you would have told me that if you knew." I didn't answer. "This gives her a motive to kill Conrad." Hell, it made it look like she was a partner in the drug ring if she tries to turn them in now.

"She didn't do it," I said. Dana knew I thought Angel's guilt was preposterous. I wanted to tell her about the drugs, but I thought I should talk to Angel first. What if it was cornstarch?

"As I told you before, they don't care if she did it. They just want someone locked up so the public doesn't think there's a murderer still at large. That's the reality here. Does she have a gun?"

"She had one but someone took it, last week." I was attempting to keep my head in the conversation.

"Did she report it stolen?"

"She reported it to me," I said as if that would impress a jury. Me, the girl with the fingerprints on the murder weapon. I'm her witness? Why were they still looking for a gun when he was hit in the head with the steel wrench in the hallway by Professor Plum? "They arrested Angel then, right?"

"I think so," Dana said. "People reported several yelling matches between them. One even told them that Angel said the place would be better off if Conrad just dropped dead.

"Oh, come on, saying drop dead is nothing like murder. We all hated that snake."

"Apparently you and Angel had the most problems with him."

"Me?" Here we went again. My beautiful day was being run through a wringer. My $1,000 bonus wouldn't begin to erase this anger and anxiety in my gut. Why did I move to Copper Springs?

"What about Mater?" I asked. "What are they doing about him?"

"What about him?" Dana said. While, we were talking, Mater pulled his beat-up tow truck up near the junk vehicles. I shivered. This was the day he was finally hauling the three heaps away. Did they all have coke in them? Someone's got to prevent Mater from leaving with them. I needed to talk to Angel and tell Montello.

"What do you know about the tow guy?"

"Dana, I gotta go," I said abruptly. "I have a lot to tell you. I'll call you in about an hour." I left the car and moved down the side of the building onto the showroom. I felt relieved that Angel was with the cops—she should be safer there.

"So, they arrested Angel?" I said to the only guy left in the building, Montello. He was getting ready to leave; it was late and crankiness had set in.

"No, just questioned her again. She had been in trouble before, you know." Why is he telling me this now?

"What about the drugs, then?" I asked.

"Drugs?" Oh, you mean her arrest a couple of years ago? I think she actually got off of that charge." Jesus Lord, has she not told him but me about her find? The phone rang and Mike got busy with a call. I decided I'd track down Angel and we'd both tell him.

CHAPTER 54

The sheriffs' cars had all left. Angel, where are you? I checked the wash bays and Detail area, with no success. She was gone. I'd get out of here too if I were her. I'd be gone already if it hadn't been for my late sale to Dr. Dreamboat. I scampered like a gecko across the showroom floor and out the other side to my car while trying to call her. Angel answer, damn it! A text came through; it was Cuervo. Was he smart enough to call his own number the other day when he had my phone? Must have been, so he had my number.

CALL ME WHEN YOU GET HOME

I HAVE BEEMER NEWS the text read.

Why was he torturing me with a damn vehicle that I didn't give a poop about? Tomorrow, Cuervo would waltz in here and hand the keys to Montello and he'd be a big hero. Meanwhile, a few kilos of coke would be on their way to Montana if I didn't find Angel.

The Mini didn't start; she didn't even try. No, not tonight. Come on, Tweety. I tried the starter again. For all her tribulations, Tweety rarely had no life at all.

I felt like I was heading back into a burning building. I tried the side door. It opened, but no one was around. Even Montello was gone. I slinked through the dark mechanics' bays to Detail to get the jumper box that we all used when a car battery was dead. My mind was whirring again, thinking up scenarios of how this drug find would play out tomorrow. Did Angel think if she told the cops when they were already interrogating her that they would haul her away for sure? Was she halfway to Barstow; a wanted woman? No.

She'd never leave those kids. I could see through the little windows high on the garage doors that Mater was parked right beside the building and was loading the first of the three coke-filled cars onto his truck. I had to get word to someone or the evidence would be on the road north within the hour.

The empty work bay was an echo chamber, and I was so mad I yelled into it: "Angel, damn it. Why didn't you tell them?" There was fear and panic in my voice as it reverberated and I didn't care. A faint tapping sound on metal answered my rant.

From the far locker on Angel's wall, the tapping came again. Angel's cupboard had a mouse. "What next?" I said aloud and turned to leave but the tapping continued. Now, the entire locker was shaking as if it might come loose from the wall. *Some mouse.* I reached out to the vertical lock on the louvered metal locker and lifted the latch. Angel, taped and no doubt terrorized, tumbled out toward me. I laid her down on the cement of her work stall. I was shaken to the core, but she looked even worse. It was hard to find the end of the tape that was across her mouth, and she was making garbled noises the entire time. I yanked a corner of it loose, but the glue was all stuck to her hair. I nearly scalped her on one side as I yanked it across her face.

"Who did this?" I screamed.

A manic Angel screamed back. "Get my knife on my bench there and cut my hands and feet free. We've got to hurry."

"Who?" I yelled again. With a telling glance toward the overhead door, she let me know who.

"Mater?" I yanked the silver tape off her limbs and struggled to get it out of her hair.

"We've got to get help here. My Mini won't start."

"Mater was out there messing with Tweety while you were finishing the sale," she said. "He's disabled it, then. He was just waiting until everyone else left." The fear that paralyzed me, fully mobilized Angel. She hopped up on a stool and looked out the high garage door window. Mater was under the first of three jalopies cinching it to the trailer. My heart was beating like I was sprinting around the middle school track.

"Hey, snap out of it," Angel said. "We've got to get out of here." Suddenly the rest of the picture came into focus. If he disabled my car, he was planning to take both of us. I checked the door to the dealership that led back to the offices—locked.

"Birdie, if he gets away with those cars, the evidence and our bodies go with him." Angel's hair was pulled back on the side of her head with a bit of the sticky tape, not a good look.

"Where are the keys to the jalopies?" I asked. She didn't answer. Then I remembered that whatever keys they still had were waiting like obedient pooches right there on the front seats.

"Will your favorite little junker run long enough to get us out of here?" she asked.

"It got me to Bonnie's house, didn't it? It has some gas."

We waited for Mater to get under the second junker to attach it to the long trailer behind his truck. He was a big man, but he could get his entire body underneath a car to hook it to the transport. When all we could see were his two work-boot covered feet, Angel started running toward the little piece of shit that I drove the day Conrad roughed me up. And I finally understood why he was so mad. The drugs were already in it then.

All we had was action, no plan. Angel, the contortionist, grabbed the top of the passenger door imitating an action figure. She pulled herself up, then threw her two feet inside and plunked her tiny ass down on the driver's seat. I stopped to look at the passenger door. The window hole seemed smaller, impossibly small. How did I get out of this window the day Conrad dropped me? Angel started the engine. Now we had Mater's undivided attention.

I stood idly outside as though I was a car hop about to attach a tray full of milkshakes. Mater was wasting no time shimmying out from under the car on the trailer.

"Get your ass in here!" Angel screamed as she made eye contact with the man we desperately needed to lose. I entered the only way I could see how to do it from this side. I dove in head first. She jammed the gear shift in low and we flew out of the back lot with my legs sticking straight out the window and Mater running and grunting alongside.

"I told you to get your ass in, not dive in." My head was all the way to the floor jammed against the tall gear shift. It was right at that moment, with most of my body high above my head that I realized the Thelma and Louise of it all. We were going to die and for whatever reason, this suddenly struck me as hilarious. I was upside down laughing and choking, and Angel was trying to pull me right-side up and still drive. When I finally got my head above the seat, I looked out the back to see if he had somehow followed us.

"He couldn't get that car off the trailer fast enough and he sure couldn't catch us with his tow truck," Angel said. We were both on adrenaline rushes and like a couple of high schoolers—not making any good decisions.

"He'll come after us. We need to get to the police station where we can get help."

"The chief thinks we might be murderers! How's that going to work?" She didn't need to know that I had been crossed off the list, but when we showed up with a car full of cocaine they'd be making a new list with only the two names on it.

"Let's head out east and take a moment to think." Burke's ranch could be the safe haven we needed. "I'll call Dana; she'll know what to do." It was already getting dark and we were flying along at breakneck speed. At this rate the Highway Patrol would find us. We wouldn't even have to look for them. My eyes were on my phone. I should have been paying better attention.

CHAPTER 55

The landscape didn't look one bit familiar and no landmarks I recognized popped up in our view. I frantically texted Dana—my text came back "Failed." I knew we had gone too far to not have arrived at Burke's, but I had no earthly idea where we were.

"We need a plan," Angel said. "What do we know for sure?

"I think the drug thing might involve a place called Broadview, Montana."

"Where's that?"

"That's what everyone will be asking if we get to the bottom of this. It's somewhere in eastern Montana."

"Why do you think the drugs are going to Montana?"

"I heard Jeannie tell Montello that the same guy was buying most of the junk cars off the "C" line at auction and then shipping them north to Montana. Jeannie and I both thought Mike should cut out the middleman, but I didn't think it was Mater. It's a brilliant plan. If the cars are intercepted, the perps can have deniability. It would look like the auction house was moving the narcotics. And guess what, we are now the middlemen, and I am pretty sure if Mater has his way, we will be the ones that are cut out." As I spoke, I texted nearly every number in my address book. "Failed. "Twenty times "Failed."

I had no service, and Angel's phone had been left behind. We bounced along on adrenaline and whatever was left in the tank, and it wasn't much. Within minutes, the blue car with the three cylinders chugged to a stop.

"Out of gas," Angel said. "Do you even know where we are?"

"Not where I wanted to be," I said. "We turned on Old Abrego Road a while back and then left. Wasn't the schoolhouse there? That wasn't too far back." I tried my phone again. Nothing.

"How long do you think this has been going on?" I said. "Mike doesn't know, does he? He's not in on it, is he?" Angel shook her head.

"I hope to hell not," she said. "I knew ConMan was bad but if Mike is in on it, then I'll have lost all faith in the human race. I wouldn't be surprised if Wade and Stretch are, though," she added. "Mater has been running those junkers to Phoenix ever since he and Conrad arrived. No wonder he doesn't have any other clients. He has a thriving drug business right under our noses."

We were once again inside a vehicle with no door handles. "Let's see you climb out that window. I tried it once and it didn't go well," I said. Angel turned and in one gesture pulled off the interior lining of the driver's door, found a cable and opened the door with it. She was definitely the one human I'd want to be stranded with on a desert island. We scrambled out and stood by the back of the car. Eventually, we migrated to the front and tried to sit on the hood without sliding off. The adrenaline was wearing off, and my brain was no longer racing, but when Dana rang us back, I became hysterical.

"Dana, Dana, thank God you answered." The connection was sketchy and she was having trouble understanding me. "We're in trouble. Just listen, okay? We're out on Old Abrego Road, we've passed the Buchanan place, but I don't know how far. We're out of gas and we need you to send a deputy to get us. It's urgent. We need you to send someone now."

"I think they're already looking for us," I said to Angel.

"We turned left at the abandoned school house and we are a ways beyond that." I heard her repeating my directions and I began to feel an ounce of relief. "We should've driven straight toward the sheriff's office," I said out loud but to myself. "Dana? Send a deputy."

"Dana? Dana?" I turned to Angel holding up the phone and shaking my head. "I'm not even sure what she heard."

The phone rang and we both jumped and then I slid off the hood to a standing position. The lousy connection lasted long enough for Dana to give me information but not long enough for her to hear me screaming back in desperation. I threw down the phone and vomited on the side of the road.

"What?" Angel said. "What did she say?"

I mouthed some words but little came out. My mouth felt like the desert dust looked. "Mater, she said she's sending Mater." Angel hung her head as though the string holding it up had been clipped. "He was there at the station reporting a stolen vehicle. 'He has a tow truck'", Dana said.

We didn't speak for several minutes.

Unlike Nebraska, where there was a broken down shed every few hundred feet, there were none in the Arizona boonies to hide in or behind, just endless miles of mesquite, palo verde trees and cactus. We were completely exposed. It was just us, the rattlers, the javelina, and the sharp-toothed, meat-eating, marauding packs of wild coyotes.

"At least we'll hear the tow truck from miles away. We can try to run," Angel said. I looked out at the endless black desert night.

"Yeah, at least we can try running."

CHAPTER 56

Thirty horrific minutes felt like an endless thirty-day month. We were huddled behind a grove of mesquite like a clutch of pheasants in a blind with a hunting party and hounds on the way. It felt as though I was at least doing something positive when I attempted to make calls and texts over and over until my thumb was sore. There was no service and my battery was draining. If only a rancher or a vigilante or a merciful human Coyote would come by.

Random memories began filling in the places of my mind that weren't already occupied by abject fear. I remembered the day Burke brought me his keys.

"Angel. Mater was there," I said. "He was listening. He was near the desk and he heard me say that coconut donuts are my favorite."

"Everybody knows about you and the donuts," she said, unimpressed. A lone road runner hustled along the roadway paying us no attention. As if we were already relegated to history.

"He heard me tell Burke the night Conrad was killed. Mater brought me a donut from Bernadette's a few days later."

"Golly Gee, wasn't that sweet of him? Let's call him Mason, though, shall we? I don't feel like continuing to call a murderer by a Disney name."

"He knew they were the only keys that weren't in the lockbox that night, I said between chattering teeth. "I don't get it. How can a guy be that bad and still be one who takes in rescue dogs?"

"What? You mean Juicebox?" Angel said.

"Look at that dog. He's obviously rescued him," I said.

"God, you are so stupid for a smart broad. Juicebox wasn't rescued by Mater. He got that pooch when he was an eight-week-old pup. Juicebox needs to be rescued." We both sat quietly wrapped in our anxiety, knowing just how Juicebox must feel. It seemed an eternity before we heard the sound of a vehicle coming along the road.

"That's not the tow truck." Angel's trained ear gave us a measure of hope. "That's a car—a diesel." My heart's normal rate doubled. Angel, despite being slim and fit, was huffing like a three pack a day smoker.

"It is! It's a car!" she shrieked.

"Maybe a cop car?" I said with the hope of a condemned man who hears the voice of the governor. We made our way from our hiding spot toward the road to try to get the driver's attention.

"Cops don't drive Beemers. That's Wally's BMW. The stolen one. I can hear the tick in the engine, "Angel said.

"Oh, my God, It's Cuervo!" I howled with delight. "He's found it." We both jumped up and ran toward the oncoming car, flailing our arms about to get the driver's attention powered by pure joy. Cuervo was going to get that kiss after all!

"It's all good now," I assured Angel. My relief energized me to leap as I ran headlong toward the black BMW. Angel caught up to me. The car stopped when we got near it. Cuervo didn't get out immediately. He opened the door slowly allowing a miniature black and white pooch to escape to the ground. An imaginary wall stopped me. Angel hit it too.

"Juicebox," she said. "Birdie, it's Juicebox," The doggie with half a tail and a broken ear was excitedly jumping at our feet. Mater already had his pistol in hand. He cocked it. Neither of us moved one fearful muscle.

"I hear you ladies are looking for a ride." I was surprised how quickly my Roomba brain figured it out. Cuervo hadn't collected the Beemer after all, probably didn't even know where it was. This was all making sense, not very good news now, but it was making sense.

"I'm going to need you to drive," Mater said motioning us to the front seat with a wave of the pistol. "Who wants the honors?" He seemed light-hearted like a coach who had just won a big game. We stood stiff and said nothing. Thelma and Louise we weren't but like them we were certain to meet a rapid end. Mater fished out the cocaine from the trunk of the jalopy and threw it in the back seat of the BMW.

"Angel, get behind the wheel. Kansas, you get in on the other side."

"I am not from Kansas," I whispered under my breath as I walked around to the passenger side. Juicebox was in the front seat with us. I held his warm little body and ran through every imaginable scenario. I had never been held at gunpoint before. The pistol looked small from the end of the barrel, a scant handful. *How do they do so much damage?* Mater sat behind Angel, with the gun not quite touching her head. The handgun looked bigger from that angle.

"Drive," he commanded. Juicebox licked at my fingers and nestled his head on my lap.

Our captor instructed Angel to go south toward Mexico and told us to keep quiet but he talked incessantly, he couldn't help himself. He had a captive audience. He babbled about the road he was taking us to and how clever he had been to keep the Beemer for this purpose. He bragged about how he'd made it look like Angel had stolen the car and was running drugs with it. "You're just collateral, Kansas," he said. "Too bad you don't know how to mind your own business."

"I remembered today that you saw Burke give me the keys to his truck the night you murdered Conrad," I said. "And that you were at the dealership all day, the day this Beemer disappeared." Angel scowled at me. "Shut up," she mouthed. I glanced at her then down at the phone beside me.

"What the hell," I said. "He's dying to tell us, so aren't we dying to hear it? He started it. Plus, he's the one with the loaded gun." The recorder on my phone wouldn't save us, but if I could hide it on my body perhaps the deputy or coroner might find it and at least clear our names.

"That's my gun," Angel said. "It's my gun." She was driving exceptionally slowly.

"Ladies. Ladies. I will tell you, but then I'll have to kill you." He belly-laughed at the sophomoric joke. "Come on, that's kind of funny, isn't it? Because I do have to kill you, so I'll tell you what happened. We have time to kill." This time his laugh was more like a deep sinister howl. The cloying scent of his Old Spice Cologne finally wafted to the front seat. I opened the door of the slow-moving vehicle then puked on the running board of Wallace's Beemer.

"Come on, Kansas; now look what you've done. You have messed up my car."

"Where did you get my gun?" Angel demanded. This was the one question she needed to have answered, but Mater didn't want to start there.

"Conrad was going to run off with that Twinkie in the front office and leave his wife and our thriving business. You know, that just wasn't going to work for me.

"Where did you get my gun?"

"He got the gun from your locker in Detail. He said he found it looking around for tape to hold the bags of coke in the trunk. He said he wasn't, but clearly, he was threatening me with the gun I mean. So, I took a wrench from the pickup, you know, because he had the gun." The ass was giving a full confession. With at least ten Moore kids in his family he was probably Catholic and for them, confession was hardwired in.

"He didn't see me take the wrench from the truck. I held it down by the tailgate as I moved around. He wasn't going to shoot me, he said—just wanted to make me listen. So, I did. I told him there were people that weren't going to like it when he called it quits. He knew. He said he had the name of another guy who we could bring in. For Christ's sake, he was telling people about our operation. I couldn't let him do that."

"I knew it," Angel said to me.

Mater was still babbling. "So, I let him have it over the head when he reached for the keys. I didn't kill him, though. He fell in the mechanic's hole, but he wasn't dead. I watched him wiggle around, pick up that gun he had dropped and try to shoot me, right there from the bottom of the hole. All I had to do was step back. He lifted it up like this and instead of shooting at me, he hit the metal lift and the bullet bounced right back at him. What a stupid bastard. He shot himself. I could tell he was dead, but I went down in the pit just to check, that's when I got the idea to bring you into this, Angel. I decided to keep the gun and stage a little scene out here in Coyote country. I thought you'd gotten away from me for an hour or two, but we are all set now, aren't we?" *Yes, almost got away, but then we didn't.*

"Hey, see that road out there? That's exit zero—our exit."

He was motioning to what looked like two ruts for truck wheels. Exit Zero, he called it. Did it stand for zero chance that we would be left alive? Angel obeyed, and we bumped along at least a half-mile into the dark and empty desert where the hope of help intervening diminished more with each rotation of the wheels. Options. Zero.

After instructing Angel to stop the car, Mater ordered us to get out. "There will be some Coyotes coming by soon. They're not happy about their drugs no longer going north."

"You prick, are you just going to leave us out here?" Angel growled.

"Tape her mouth and hands, Kansas," he said to me and shoved Angel in my direction.

When she turned around I saw the tears in her eyes. We both knew he wouldn't just drive away. She looked down at her hands and held them out to me. She opened one closed palm. It held her precious Mother's ring, the one she vowed never to remove. She was sending a message to her kids that with her last breath she had thought only of them. Then, she held both hands together, and I carefully taped the ring inside. I was next, but I had no ring or no great love to signal with a beautiful gesture. Within moments, it was not a lovely gesture that took me by surprise.

Angel erupted from my grip like a prizefighter coming out of her corner. She yanked her hands away then leapt toward the overall-wearing Goliath using her bound hands as though she were wielding a stone. Mater instinctively ducked. She hit him across the chest, but the cold-blooded devil was unfazed as he pushed her back up against the car. It became horribly obvious he was going to dispense with her by using just one shot.

He raised Angel's pistol from his hip like an Old West gun-slinger. His own pistol was still strapped under his arm where he always wore it.

I couldn't let this monster do away with Angel as if she weren't important. She was incredibly important, not just to those kids but to all of us. I couldn't let him end her life like that.

"Watch this, Kansas."

I snapped. Instantly overflowing with energy, my legs propelled me forward at a phenomenal speed. It was as if my feet were not touching the ground. I had taken flight.

"I'm from Nebraska, you fucking idiot! Nebraska!" I pushed Angel to the side with my missile like landing using one arm to knock her out of the way. Unable to break her fall, I heard her topple to the ground landing hard on her back behind me as I aimed directly at Mater's knees, remembering that his gait had been wobbly earlier. I grabbed him around the legs and dug my nails into the soft space behind one of them.

He bellowed and staggered backward as I kept hold of his leg with one arm and attempted to grab his gun with the other. He caught my body with his left knee using amazing strength that hurled me back against the BMW literally standing me up again. I was looking toward Angel when I heard a crack that seemed like the sound of a dry stick breaking and then my left shoulder yanked away from my body, pulling me with it. I folded down on top of

Angel as if we were locked in a perverse a game of Twister. As I landed, my left arm had no strength to break the fall so I rolled and we ended up eye to eye, just two tomboys, down in the dirt. The arm I would normally right myself with wasn't working. It was a mess. Deep crimson blood streamed down my left arm, but I felt no pain. Mater was still standing. I had missed my calculation completely.

"Fuck both of you. Let's get this over," he said as he raised the gun and this time it pointed directly at me. I closed my eyes and thought who would I like to signal that I was thinking of them? It was Grams, but it was too damn late.

When the second shot came, the odor of the smoke wafted our direction. Juicebox barked from a perch on the dash. Did he know his master had just killed two people? My eyes were shut but, again, I didn't feel a thing—no pain, nothing but the ringing sound in my ears. *My ears? You still hear and smell even after you're dead?* My brain pondered the improbability of that when a dusty thud occurred at our feet. I lifted my head slightly and opened one eye to see Mater face first in the dirt before us. Twenty feet away and closing fast came Cuervo.

"I told you I was going to get that car today." He was already on his cell punching in 911.

"No service here," I said.

"Mine's satellite," he said. "You might want to get one of these—next time." I heard him giving directions. Next time? Angel began to sob uncontrollably. She'd survived a near-death experience but the danger had taken its toll even on a woman as tough as her. A bare-chested Cuervo pressed his shirt on my open wound. He looked just like Eric Estrada from that old, old TV show CHiPs. That was the last thing I remembered.

CHAPTER 57

Consciousness was slow coming. I was vaguely aware of men and women in colorful scrubs twirling about me like the dance of the Sugar Plum Fairys and was told I was on the Orthopedic floor of University Hospital in Tucson. A rigid cast on my left arm all the way to the middle of my back made my skin itch as I awakened. There was a gauze wrap around my upper body. I had no idea how long I had been out, but long enough for all the florists in Pima County to fill every horizontal surface in my private room with a multi-colored jungle. I'm not that popular, some of these must be in the wrong room, I decided.

I couldn't see the floral cards from the bed but the gift sitting on the table to my right was a glowing golden bottle of 18-year-old Glenmorangie single malt with a big red bow. Mike, I didn't know you cared.

It took my groggy brain a few moments for details to seep back in. Angel? Was Mater actually dead? Or—God forbid—was he down the hall somewhere?

"Well, you're finally awake," said a nurse. "The whole town of Copper Springs has been milling around here waiting on you. I'm going to get your vitals, and then I'll see if anyone is in the waiting room who might want to drop in and say hello. Okay with you?" I nodded.

A minute later, my dear Grams popped in the room followed right behind by Cuervo, who had driven her. My savior, I wouldn't be here if not for him, either of them really. Grams held my hand and began to cry. It was heart-wrenching to watch.

"I hope you weren't listening to all this on your scanner," I said.

"No. Dana called me. She drove me here the first night."

"How many days have I been here?"

"A few," Cuervo said in what seemed like the voice of the Tin Man at the end of The Wizard of Oz then he winked at Grams. "Two surgeries. We were beginning to worry that you weren't as tough as you let on."

"It turns out that you, however, are actually a sort of tough guy. I guess you really can handle a gun," I told him. "I'll have to take back what I said."

"And I'd make you do just that if you weren't lying here with a bullet wound. I'll need to be a little faster on the draw next time."

"Next time?" I tried to lift my shoulder in an attempt to say, "No next time." But I couldn't get it off the pillow.

"I just talked to the doc out there," Cuervo said. "And I asked him if you'd be able to golf when you got healed up and he said 'you bet' so I told him, that's odd because you couldn't do it before." He was never going to let up. "But I doubt you have to worry about that 4th of July tourney this year."

"Finally, some good news," I said and looked up to see Clay and his wife peek their heads in.

"Looks like you'll do almost anything to get out of keying," he said. "Sell the studliest sports car on the lot and then you take off and don't even write."

"Don't worry, I'll be back. If I don't show up Montello will keep my commissions for this month, and I kicked your asses."

"I'll give you that. Hey, I've got news, Montello hired a new salesperson. You'll love it—her name is Kathleen!"

"Her?" I know he thought I'd be elated but I felt a bit sad. "Do we like her?"

"Not yet," he said. "But you know it takes time to get used to having a woman on the team. We'll have to pitch some shit on her and see how she takes it before we decide." He grinned.

The nurse came back to shoo them out. Grams said Angel and Dana had both been in several times and Wally and Montello wanted to come. I asked her to thank everyone for the beautiful flowers. Grams was the last to leave.

"I love your stuffins, sweetheart," she said and kissed my forehead.

"I love you too Grams," I said, and I never meant it more.

The Percocet nudged my thoughts and they began to muddle. Well, Dad, you made the car business look so glamorous and inviting. Look at me now. How the hell did it come to this? As I slipped down into deep healing slumber, I thought I saw the silhouette of a tall handsome cowboy in the doorway. Were those forgiveness roses in his arms?

THE END

GROUP DISCUSSION QUESTIONS

1. What qualities attracted Birdie to Angel's friendship even though they were so different? What important elements of a good friendship did these two possess?

2. Have you ever purchased a vehicle? Who did you take along? Were you scared or intimidated when you began negotiating the price? Were you happy with the purchase?

3. Have you ever experienced a workplace where you were the only one of your gender on staff? Was political incorrectness a problem? How might it have changed your experience to have had more gender balance?

4. What emotions go through you when you have an aging relative that you dearly love? How did you react when you had the realization that they wouldn't live forever?

5. What was the true reason Birdie could not attend the funeral of Burke's uncle Kenny? Have you ever said you would attend an event knowing full well you wouldn't? Why?

6. Have you ever exhibited amazing courage in the face of danger? What caused you to behave the way you did? Looking back, would you do the courageous act again?

ACKNOWLEDGEMENTS

To my Mom who was a writer and reporter when she met my Dad in a rural town in Montana and to my Dad, a car salesman and storyteller from Nebraska. They had more wisdom then I realized. You will find some of it here.

There are two people who stand out above all others. The first is my partner, my best friend and my world's favorite person—my husband Chris, who supported this idea (and many crazier ones) even when completion looked impossible. The second is my lifelong friend Linda, who generously shared her vast writing knowledge and encouraged me every step of the way to join her in this joyous and frustrating pursuit of storytelling. Thank you both.

And so many others: Thanks Bro, for taking me seriously when I told you I was thinking of pursuing a job in car sales —we will see how that turns out. Thanks, Gentle Beta readers— Jon, Bonnie, Gayle, Carol, Jim, Lexy, Holly, Susan, my first fan Suzanne and others for being my guinea pigs and pointing Birdie in better directions. Thank you to Lou K. for being my twenty-year writing partner—oh, how you made me laugh. Thank you to Pete Fromm, for showing me that to be a good writer you have to write a lot of good stories—not saying this is good writing Pete but better for your teachings. Thank you to my kids, grandkids, sisters, dear friends and buddies who said, "of course you will", when I said I would like to write a novel and never doubted that it would get done—though the years did pass. I named some characters after you.

Thank you to Authors of the Flathead (especially Betty and Tom) for encouraging members to seek publication not just a hobby. Thank you GV writers for listening and sharing your work with me. Special thanks to Duke, our wonderful and generous leader and to Sharon and Mary, my writing partners for this book.

Kathy M.—Thank you for your important edits and many corrections. I appreciate you.

Lance B.—I enjoyed our collaboration on cover and book set up. You're a talented guy. I hope we get to work together again.

Thank you, readers—your comments, critiques and notes are wonderful encouragement.